Shattered Peacock

A Story of Life and Revolution in Iran

LISA DI VITA

From the library of Historia Vitae Books, Los Angeles.

This book is a work of fiction. Any resemblance to actual events, locales, or persons, living or dead, is entirely coincidental. With the exception of certain public personages who are noted at the back of the book, as well as certain historical incidents and quotations, all other characters, incidents and dialogue are drawn from the writer's imagination or are used fictitiously.

Shattered Peacock/historical fiction/Lisa Di Vita
Includes bibliography and historical biographies

Book cover design by RockingBookCovers.com

Lisadivita.com

For Chuck, my favorite creative genius.

CONTENTS

Foreward

The process of researching and writing this book has created a season of exciting growth for me. Nothing we encounter in life leaves us where it found us, and writing "Shattered Peacock" is no exception. Stepping out of my own life day after day, in order to cohabitate the world of these characters, their culture and the events they faced, has sewn new elastic into my life's perspective.

Persians seem to me to be a poetic, mystical and passionate people who fiercely embrace their remarkable, tumultuous, and ancient culture.

The violent 1979 overthrow of the "last Shah of Iran," Reza Mohammad Pahlavi, signalled a cataclysmic end to ancient royal rule of the Persian Empire by a succession of dynasties dating back to 538 B.C. with Cyrus the Great, who is mentioned more than twenty-three times in the Bible.

I remember the chaotic events of 1979: The deposing of the Shah, the return of Ayatollah Khomeini and the plight of the American Embassy hostages. Perhaps that's why I've kept the plotline historically accurate, and also explains the inclusion of some real life political figures. Biographies of these personages are found at the back of the book. I heartily encourage readers to utilize the resource, for as they say, truth is stranger than fiction.

After Shah Pahlavi's exile, many Iranians were forced to flee. For example: Those associated with the Shah or his military, those with Western leanings or educations, and the many employees of American and British oil companies. This frantic emigration of educated citizens during 1978 and 1979 left behind a massive brain drain in Iran.

"Shattered Peacock" depicts the experiences of some of those who fled. We must remember that while history is written with 20/20 hindsight, historical events occur in real time to people, and who thus are bereft of historic insight. And so it behooves us to remember that our "today" will be history tomorrow, dissected and repackaged as well.

"Shattered Peacock" has been a communal effort. I'm grateful for the generous support of family and friends.

Firstly, much love to my spectacularly talented and accomplished friend, Nancy Parker, who orchestrated and inspired this journey. Without her, there would be no book.

Secondly, an eternal "thank you" to Nina J. Trasoff, my chosen sister and dearest friend of 40 years, who fed me emotional sustenance as well as consistantly productive suggestions throughout the process.

Then there's the divine editor Anita Garner, nymph of California's redwood trees, who critiqued the initial version of this book and always encouraged me. She infallibly knew when I needed a pat on the back. And thus, many thanks to Don Barrett - historian, author and Los Angeles radio guru, for recommending Anita to me.

I am most grateful to all the Persian expatriates with whom I spoke, both for their candor and for their willingness to share stories, most especially to dear Homa and Alireza, who opened wide their home and hearts to me.

Gratitude and love to son Stephen, who listens to my ideas, and when I least expect it, drops bombs of wisdom into my head. His circular thought process guides my linear mind around an assortment of mental roadblocks.

Most importantly, my love and admiration to my soul mate and loving husband, Chuck, who, for some reason, believes I can do anything. He's been telling me to write for years. Thank you for being my rock, for loving me, for supporting me and for always making me laugh.

Chapter 1

Country of Sand

Registan Desert, Afghanistan, December 9, 1979

SORAYA SULTAN wrestled with Despair, determined to keep him at bay by shoving the monster to the outermost edges of her mind. Still, she wondered, what had they done to deserve this kind of misery? Obviously, Despair deemed the exhaustion, rain, hunger, and freezing temperatures to be insufficient punishment, because now the desert demigods were unleashing these flogging winds. Tentacles of blowing sand entangled them like serpents from the abyss, waiting to swallow them whole.

She wrapped her body around her son like a sock, shielding him against the sand storm. The chador pulled across her face proved a flimsy defense against the stinging darts. She held her breath until her lungs screamed for air.

Squinting through the opaque darkness, she spotted faint silhouettes of the others, huddling together in small clumps, coughing from the whipping sand. Even the men with semi-automatics who kept guard over them were struggling to breathe. Were it not for eight-year-old Darius,

Soraya would have wilted, but for his sake she dug her fingers deeper into the clay of maternal strength.

This nightmare was a mistake. It had to be. They didn't belong inside of it. She estimated they'd been traveling for about a week, and during that time her attitude toward life had turned from rosy to surreal, and then to bitter. The dissonance between what she'd imagined and their reality was deafening. Obviously, she'd been betrayed. Two weeks ago, she'd have poured out her anger, but clearly, self-righteous indignation was not going to affect these men who covered their faces and who never put down their weapons. Still, she resented the commanding power they wielded over her life.

When the winds began to dwindle, the tallest man strode over to them. His bottomless coal black eyes were all they could see of his face. He handed them cheese and bread before snarling at them.

"You will not get up and walk around. You will not dare wander away, because we will not look for you and you will die out here, alone, and we won't care anymore than the desert does. Do you understand?"

She nodded. Soraya couldn't fathom his hostility but she accepted his indifference. He moved on toward the next cluster of humanity. Soraya was down to the last spoonful of composure. She sat with her legs pulled close to her delicate body, willing her thoughts to meander, lest panic organize them into overwhelming terror.

The freezing cold had slithered in-between the layers of Darius' wet clothes, turning them to sheets of ice. He shivered violently. Both yearned for the dawn to come pry off night's frigid fingers.

The winds sagged further, spent from punishing them. Soraya felt grit in her mouth. Not knowing what else to do, she spat, watching the bubbles glitter briefly on the sand before sinking beneath it. She couldn't recall ever having done anything so coarse as spitting before, but it felt liberating, even appropriate, given their circumstances. Proper etiquette here was as useful as wearing a party gown for coal mining. Her mouth twisted into a bitter smile. How she longed for the designer dresses she'd left behind at their mansion. Perhaps Mehdi was right: Maybe her upbringing had been too sheltered. Well, I'm not sheltered any longer, she thought, and experienced at least a gnat-sized sense of accomplishment. She swept her tongue over her teeth, and spat again at her deflowered naïveté.

"Mama, did you just spit?"

"No, darling. I'm quite sure you imagined it. Think. Have you ever seen Mama spit? No, of course not."

Darius was skeptical, but he didn't argue. His teeth were chattering so hard he could barely talk. Threads of regret knotted Soraya's mind. They might have been better off staying in Tehran. Why hadn't she waited it out? Soraya cradled her son. She was grateful he was sleeping, but she never imagined that he was recalling the mansion's Cire Trudon candles and the way their fragrance mingled with the creamy white tuberose stalks in the ballroom's floral arrangements. Darius was studying the party guests through the hazy lens of cigarette smoke. A group of the Shah's "Immortals" nonchalantly piled appetizers on their plates. These Imperial Guards, who served the king, were tall and handsome, and their broad shoulders were draped with gold braids. Their bright uniforms with rows of shiny medals stood in sharp contrast to the subtle gray shades of the Savile Row bespoke suits worn by the foreign ambassadors and international businessmen. Darius listened carefully, discerningly. A cacophony of Persian, English, French, Arabic, and German mingled into an exotic Babel-tongue he pretended he understood.

Darius singled out the conversation of a government official discussing oil production and prices with a circle of British and American businessmen.

But something was going horribly wrong. Jarring voices spiked above the gaiety. A group of guests was yelling, confusing Darius.

Without warning, he was yanked from the railing.

"Nanny, what are you doing?" She was pulling him away from the scene. "Wait a minute, Nanny, I want to see what's happening!"

Darius' feet dragged on the carpet as he flailed to find his balance. "No, Nanny, I don't want to go yet!"

He opened his eyes and the scene vanished. They were in the desert and the masked men were yelling at them. His mother was dragging him through the hot sand, toward the trucks.

Darius was shocked to see it was late afternoon. What had happened to the dawn for which they'd been longing? He realized his clothes were dry. Had he really slept through an entire day? He forced his feet to cooperate, running alongside his mother, but even in his groggy state he noted an irony: Usually, nightmares disappeared when he woke up, but this one disappeared only when he slept.

They were on the move again.

Chapter 2

Darius

Tehran, March 1978

DARIUS PEEKED at the classroom clock, willing it to tick faster, yet careful not to let Mrs. Lashgari catch him looking again. He'd already gotten into trouble for his clock-watching. But as usual, it seemed the school day would never end.

Mrs. Lashgari, a veteran teacher in her early 40s, was a competent and dedicated educator. Despite having no children of her own, she'd amassed an impressive set of child management skills. She figured she'd encountered every flavor of child during her fifteen years of teaching. Little shook her sense of control. If she had an Achilles' heel, it was a lack of patience, which erupted daily around 2:00 p.m. That was when her sugar levels began to drop.

It was now 2:30 and her mind was foggy. She regretted finishing off the Butter Rum Lifesavers she kept hidden in the bottom desk drawer. She'd mastered the art of rifling aimlessly through the drawer, blocking her face from the children, and slyly slipping a candy into her mouth.

Now she wished she'd stashed an emergency roll somewhere for a bit of energy.

But with only forty-five minutes of class remaining, she forged ahead. Afternoon's wan light was eking through the classroom's windows. She stood in its pale spotlight, reading portions from "Shahnameh, The Book of Kings," the masterful poem by Persia's 10th century writer, Hakim Ferdowsi. Its 50,000 couplets read like a graphic novel, featuring kings, super-heroes, ruthless villains, war and mayhem, as well as morals. Year after year, she captivated her students with this tale of ancient Persia. She fervently wanted her students to understand that the bloodied hands of their forefathers had written Persian history, and that in a few years, they would hold its future in their own hands.

Mrs. Lashgari was gratified too, that Mohammad Reza Shah Pahlavi recently had encouraged teachers to introduce the text. The class sat spellbound - except for Darius, who tapped his pencil on the desk even as Ferdowsi's ancient pen drew the scene of a gruesome battle against the Arabs, whose ultimate victory had brought Islam to Iran.

Mrs. Lashgari tried to ignore Darius, ever the class clown, until her patience snapped.

"Darius! Perhaps you actually did your homework last night and memorized the final passage? Surely your recitation is better than mine? Why don't you come up here and finish the story for us?"

The class dissolved into giggles. Any way you sliced it, this was going to be rich. Darius lowered his chin to hide the grin spreading between his ears. Didn't his teacher remember he had a poetry tutor twice a week? Most of the wealthy children did. Mrs. Lashgari winced. She rued making the same mistake ... again. How did this imp routinely get the better of her?

Darius looked up and responded with an overly-polite, "Yes, teacher." Slipping the pencil in his front pocket, he sauntered leisurely to the front of the room, instinctively stepping into the pool of sunlight.

Here we go, Lashgari mentally moaned. Once again, I've exited into the wings and left the center stage open for this child to steal the show.

Darius struck a dramatic pose. Although he was on the short side and not particularly athletic, he was smart and funny, with a smile that could charm a cobra from a basket even without a *pungi's* melody. The class twittered again. Their anticipation was palpable and teetering on the verge of mayhem. Darius was the maestro and the class, his orchestra. They waited, poised to follow his downbeat into hilarity. Mrs. Lashgari sank weakly into her chair.

Darius leaped into action. Picking up where his teacher had left off, he recited a line, and then drew the pencil from his pocket like a sword from a scabbard. He tossed the poem's words into the air and skewered them with the tip of his pencil. The lines he forgot, he made up or pantomimed. He twirled in the throes of battle, fighting off opponents right and left, falling on the floor to re-enact a gory death by banging his fists in tragic defeat. After feigning his demise twice, he finally laid still, blank eyes staring at the ceiling and tongue lolling out to the side of his mouth. The class held its breath for the grand finale.

Darius stood up, stretched out his arms, dramatically enunciated the final line, and bowed low. The children went wild. They stood. They cheered. They clapped.

"Class, please," Mrs. Lashgari begged, her voice wilting inside the noise. Darius was both her pride and a thorn in her side.

She mused over whether today's note to Mrs. Sultan would focus on his irrepressible behavior or his impressive intelligence. With Darius, it was usually a mixture of both.

Outside, 26-year-old Nanny Fatima leaned against the limousine, waiting for the school bell to release Darius. His nanny since birth, her long dark hair framed a kind, heart-shaped face. She had a lazy right eye that made her face look vaguely asymmetrical; people meeting her for the first time couldn't put their finger on why her face seemed "off."

But to Darius she was perfectly beautiful. Their mutual devotion flowed like honey.

He knew exactly where Mr. Nassiri would park the Daimler DS420 Jaguar. The limousine looked like polished hematite in the afternoon sun, drawing jealous stares from passers-by and the other limo drivers.

The bell rang. Thirty seconds later Darius bolted out the school doors, glancing toward Fatima to confirm she was watching before taking a running leap down the last four steps. Fatima feigned a heart attack, something she did each time her young charge jumped, which was every day. He giggled and ran into her arms.

"I've brought a note from Mrs. Lashgari, Nanny," he announced. "She's impressed with the way I recited the 'Shahnameh,' and she's sent home a hand-written note!"

Fatima's eyebrows rose.

"Hmmm. Let me see it. I'll give it to your mother."

She opened the envelope to read the message, swallowing a smile before slipping it into her purse. Darius threw his backpack onto the back seat and tumbled in after it. Fatima slid in next to him.

"Mr. Nassiri, will you be so kind as to take us to the Bazaar before we go home? We have some things to buy."

Darius nearly burst with excitement. The Grand Bazaar! Nassiri drove through Tehran, through the choking smog and honking drivers, adroitly maneuvering between cars, darting down back alleys and side streets to circumvent the city's unruly traffic. He believed a vehicle as fine as the Daimler demanded deference, and he wouldn't allow it to become snarled amongst the common cars.

The closer they got to the Bazaar, the more old alleyways they passed. To drive here was to go back in time. Darius pressed his nose against the window, waving at the people who stared at the limo, until they pulled into the parking lot at the Bazaar's *Sabze meydoon* entrance.

"Darius," Fatima said, "did you know that sections of the Bazaar used to be camel stables for travelers along the Silk Road?"

Fatima took every opportunity to teach.

Darius replied, "I hope they've cleaned up the camel poop since then. Be careful where you step, Nanny!"

Fatima laughed. "Mr. Nassiri," she said, "we'll meet you back here in front of the fountain in an hour."

The Daimler was always easy to spot, as it was the only one in all of Tehran. The Sultans owned four other cars, but this was the crown jewel of the fleet. His papa had purchased the car in England and had it flown home. Its dove gray finish glowed with the aura of wealth.

The chauffeur scanned the lot for a parking space far away from other vehicles. He planned on sauntering past a few of the 20,000 vendors, himself.

Fatima grabbed Darius by the hand as Nassiri opened the door for them.

"Do it! You have to do it," she said.

"I'm too old," protested Darius, but his chortling betrayed his feigned reluctance.

"If I'm not too old, you're not too old. One. Two. Three. Okay, go!"

Holding hands, they skipped from the sunlit winter afternoon into the dimness of Tehran's Grand Bazaar. If the city streets were choked with cars, there was human gridlock inside the Bazaar. Overhead skylights dropped a dusty light onto the market's sights. Buyers inched shoulder-to-shoulder past the booths and down the long corridors. The air inside felt warm and humid.

Sound percussed off the old walls: The shrill laughter of gossiping teens, the crisp baritones of bankers discussing the economy, and the trebly grace notes of women who bargained with merchants for the best deal. Deliverymen pushing their handcarts repeated endlessly, *"Bebakshid,"* or "Permission to pass," in a melodic counterpoint. The Grand Bazaar made Darius giddy to the point of being lightheaded. Everything that could be sold was sold right here - millions of items packed tightly together throughout the Bazaar's six-mile length. It was easy to get lost in its maze of corridors, but Fatima navigated it expertly. Darius peered down a long corridor on his right that sold only Persian rugs. Piles of folded carpets were out on display.

"Nanny, look," said Darius. "See the way the carpets are folded? They look like kneeling camels. Maybe this is where the camel stables were."

She laughed. "Oh goodness, Darius, leave it to you to come up with that. I'll never look at those carpets in the same way again."

Darius knew that nomads probably had woven many of the rugs. He was intrigued by the notion of families constantly moving, living in tents instead of a big house like his, and he wondered how the children moved all their toys from place to place. He'd have to find out some day.

To his left was an endless row of jewellery stores. Gold necklaces and large diamonds glittered brightly under lights. Another corridor offered leather goods: Purses, belts, camel saddles, shoes, and wallets. He inhaled the leather's earthy scent. It made him slightly dizzy.

Fatima nudged him around a corner.

"Come, we'll pick up the spices first." She drew a list from her purse. "Let's see ... we need *zaafaran* (saffron), cumin, turmeric and ginger." This was a magical corridor, jammed with *bazaaris* offering nuts, dried fruits as well as the pungent spices rising in peaks above the rims of large, gleaming copper pots: Golden-red cinnamon, poppy-orange saffron, and crow-black pepper. A spice shop at the bazaar was an edible painter's palette, luring shoppers with mounds of color and savory aromas that awakened one's hunger. Darius' stomach loudly grumbled something about wanting food.

Bashu Banai's spice shop was half way down the aisle. He carried only the highest quality spices from the area's most select farms. If he charged his clients more, they didn't care, and Banai was smart enough to treat them well. He always set aside some of his finest Persian saffron for the Sultans. It wasn't often that a merchant could call a family as prominent as they were, his exclusive customers. *Bazaari* blood ran through Banai's veins and bragging about their patronage raised his prestige among the other merchants.

Forty-five-year-old Banai was a third generation spice merchant. Already crusty by nature, he had also recently endured a bitter divorce. These days he felt emotion only occasionally, and only when it caught him off-guard. Yet despite his petrified heart, and against all probability, Bashu Banai, the spice merchant, was sweet on Fatima.

As she approached, his blood pressure jumped. He quickly combed his fingers through his beard to free it of lunch's crumbs possibly entrapped by its straggly hairs. The sight of her always released a flood of hormones. He desperately yearned to woo Fatima. Alas, flirting never was his forte. He stole a quick glance at her before sending his eyes back to the floor.

"Good afternoon. You are looking most ..." he paused, flailing for an appropriate word, " ... most healthy this afternoon."

"Thank you, Mr. Banai. You do not look ill, either."

Banai sighed. He was terrible with women. Fingering his apron and clearing his throat, he started over. "I mean you look well, quite nice, perhaps, well, like you're ready for more spices. Are you ready to buy?"

No, no, no, he thought. He hurled one last frantic compliment her way.

"I meant to say that your face looks as happy as *zaafaron*." He paused before spitting out his greatest wish. "And I would be honored if you finally began calling me Bashu." A horrified, hot flush crawled from his toes to the top of his balding head. He felt it, so he knew it showed.

Fatima smiled and started to rescue him, but his discomfort was so sweet to watch that she allowed him to stumble a little while longer.

"Oh my goodness, Mr. Banai, right now the color of your face matches the pot of cinnamon behind you."

Balls of sweat dotted Bashu's forehead. His ineptitude at mating was humiliating. Fatima felt sorry for him and tossed him a lifeline.

"You are most kind, sir, and it is a pleasure to see you again. We are here to stock up on spices for *Nowruz*. Like everyone else, we're making ready."

Nowruz, the Persian New Year, was coming up on the spring equinox, and preparations already were well underway at the Sultan's house. The staff was performing a ceiling-to-floor scrubbing of the mansion, a ritual designed to push out the old year, making way for the new one. People everywhere were shopping for new outfits, because no one wanted to drag the old year into a brand new one.

Soraya had prepared a detailed menu for Chef Alaleh, who as usual, would ignore it, creating her own menu and then after its success, would beg Mrs. Sultan's forgiveness for the transgressions. Alaleh's entire kitchen staff would prep and cook virtually nonstop for the three days prior to *Nowruz*, utilizing the spices Fatima was buying today.

Bashu filled Fatima's order with great deliberateness, hoping to avoid further blunders. He puttered and muttered, filled and packaged while Fatima waited patiently.

A bored Darius wandered among the spices. When neither adult was looking, he licked his index finger and plunged it into the Ceylon Cinnamon, pulling it out to lick off the sweetness. Cinnamon granules stuck under his fingernail, and he quickly sucked out all the incriminating evidence. He was eager to taste this on top of the Persian Saffron Rice Pudding he knew Alaleh would make.

"What do I owe you, Mr. Banai?" asked Fatima.

"Oh no, Miss Fatima," he answered, as she expected he would, "I cannot charge you."

They were commencing Persian hospitality, or *tarof*. It was a pleasant enough *pas de deux* and both knew how to dance the steps well.

"But Mr. Banai, such a gift is too much and would be unfair to you."

"You are from the Sultan household, my best clients. The spices are a *Nowruz* gift. You must take them."

Fatima insisted. "And you must make a living, Mr. Banai."

He looked genuinely pained. The next words sprang directly from his heart.

"Please, please call me Bashu. No more 'Mr. Banai' after all these years. And I cannot charge such a lovely lady as you."

Fatima was genuinely touched. "Then if you truly care for me, please let me pay you, Bashu."

His knees went weak to hear Fatima utter his given name. Fatima noticed and her heart melted. She resolved to give this awkward man a sporting chance next time. As was called for by *tarof*, Bashu handed her the bill, which she paid. The tango was over; the deal was done.

"Thank you for your business, Fatima. Which merchant will you grace with your presence next?" Banai was stalling. He desperately wanted her to linger.

"Well, first I thought I'd buy Darius some kebobs."

The boy's head swivelled around at the mention of food.

"Then I've some linens to buy, a gift to select for a friend, and then we'll stop by the supermarket."

Bashu's smile plummeted from his face and splattered all over the floor.

"The supermarket." He spat with precision between pots. "We have the Shah to thank for this *Gharbzadegi*, this 'Westoxication.' We are no longer Iranians. We are 'Western-stricken,' fake Americans, and Pahlavi dances like a puppet while they pull his strings every which way. For what purpose do Iranians need supermarkets?"

Fatima rued having mentioned the modern convenience. She tried placating him.

"Now, now, dear Bashu," she said. "Nothing will ever replace the Grand Bazaar for the important items."

Bashu Banai would have none of it. His hormones had gone cold and his day had soured.

Chapter 3

Soraya

The Sultan compound

A GOSSAMER-THIN frown line traversed the soft space between Soraya's eyebrows. Her mind was rifling through a litany of details faster than she could write. She leaned against the parlor's Steinway grand piano and tapped a notepad with her Montblanc Ballpoint pen, making a sound like rain pattering on the roof.

Even with a furrowed brow, Soraya was lovely, as soft and exotic as a peacock's feather. Beauty and she were conjoined, difficult to view separately. She was small-boned, with creamy skin the shade of almond meat, and her sable-colored eyes were flecked with gold.

She was surprisingly unconscious of her beauty, not out of humility, but because she'd never known a day without it, just as she'd never known a day without social status; therefore, she unapologetically accepted the entitlements with which life had indulged her. She was rich, well educated and lovely. She was also pampered, fawned over, sheltered and possessor of a quick, pouty temper, but her elegance gave the appearance of substance, a reasonable substitute for actual personal depth.

Soraya had been educated at Tehran's Lycée Jeanne d'Arc; she'd then learned etiquette at the finishing school Château Mont-Choisi, in Lausanne, Switzerland. Social grace enabled her to glide through most situations. So too, did her ability to stay organized, a trait she'd inherited from her grandpapa, General Zhuban Cyrus, a World War I hero. His manner, so commanding and stern, and his mouth that never smiled, deeply affected Soraya.

One day, as a little girl, she'd asked Grandmama why Grandpapa was always gloomy. Before her grandmother answered, she'd steeped a pot of jasmine tea and set out a plate of cookies. Then she sat young Soraya down at the kitchen table. Soraya could still remember crunching into a sesame cookie while Grandmama poured the tea with a flourish into flowery cups.

"My pretty Soraya," she had explained, "Your grandpapa relives The Great War every night in his dreams. He sees the dead bodies of Armenian Christians - thousands of them, some naked, some shot, others crucified – do you know what it means to be crucified?"

Soraya shook her head, no.

"Never mind, it's only important to understand that they were killed by the Ottomans and left strewn like rag dolls along the road to Syria. Would you like another cookie?"

"No, thank you, Grandmama." She was no longer hungry.

"Well, then, drink more tea. Difficult news is easier to swallow with some tea. Your grandpapa saw the Armenian genocide with his very own eyes," she'd explained, stroking Soraya's hair, "and thinking about those poor souls haunts him."

"But it wasn't his fault."

"I know, but he thinks he failed because he couldn't save them, and the pain has torn the smile off his face. So, we must do everything we can to make him feel better."

Soraya resolved in that moment that she would give him back his smile, eating two more cookies to seal her vow.

Ardeshir Cyrus, Zhuban's son and Soraya's father, rode the coattails of his father's wartime fame into politics. Reza Shah Pahlavi, father of the current Mohammad Reza Shah, had liked Ardeshir, granting him powerful government appointments during the 1940s, which brought him wealth and privilege, things Ardeshir unabashedly craved.

Soraya was a hybrid of both men. While she ran the household as tightly as a military operation, her leadership focused on lavish social gatherings. She enjoyed being the center of attention of groups of people more than one-on-one friendships, which was why she knew by name virtually every important person in Tehran. She freely gave out air kisses, but rarely spent time with women who were not on her paid staff.

Today she was composing instructions for the upcoming New Year's celebration. Lists were her *modus operandi*, so pens and pads were placed in every room just for her. She wrote furiously.

Soraya's elbow jostled a photo atop the grand piano. The instrument's lid held a forest of photographs set in sterling silver frames. The staff hated clearing them off the piano to dust the lid, but Soraya wanted the photos there, and so there they stayed. The images, their gradations of gray fixed on shiny paper and imprisoned by glass and cardboard, were reminders of the impressive Cyrus and Sultan family trees. There was her Grandpapa Cyrus, seated, wearing his military uniform with sword, and looking dashing but for the dour look on his face. She squinted at him for a moment before covering his face with her thumb.

And here was Mehdi's family, including his great-grandfather, grandfather, and his father, Feroze, all of them high-ranking politicians. They had slipped in and out of favor over the years, but they'd amassed power and riches along the way, in no small measure because Mehdi's grandfather was a distant cousin to Reza Shah.

Mehdi had contemplated a political career, but shrewdly

chosen instead to start up an Italian marble import business. The Shah's government had just shaken Iran loose from Great Britain's grip on its oil production. Nationalized Iranian oil production kept more cash inside the country, so the Shah was modernizing its infrastructure and expanding educational outreach. The optimism early on in his "White Revolution" caused the affluent to spend money beautifying their business buildings and mansions with marble. Mehdi's profits soared.

Soraya studied a photo of their wedding day. She'd worn an *haute couture* gown from Dior. She still loved its pearl-seeded bodice. Mehdi wore a hand-stitched Brioni tuxedo tailored with precision to his body. She'd seen Hollywood actor Sean Connery wear Brioni suits in those James Bond films, but always maintained that Mehdi wore them better. This photo had been taken at their second wedding, a do-over especially for her beloved Uncle Mahmud, who quite unfortunately, had missed the first wedding as a convicted political prisoner and sat in a lonely SAVAK jail cell during the event.

Soraya couldn't recall of which political crime the secret Iranian Security and Intelligence Service had accused him, but he'd insisted the first wedding proceed without him; however, once he was back in the Shah's good graces, they'd happily done it again for him. Mahmud had cried and laughed and had a ball, making it worth the effort and added expense. Besides, Soraya actually preferred this wedding dress to the first one.

Footsteps came clicking down the hallway.

"Poolak, look." Soraya summoned her assistant. Poolak stuck her head into the room. Soraya held up the photo.

Poolak grinned.

"You were at both wedding receptions," said Soraya. "Do you remember the drama about the lamb?"

Poolak laughed, causing her dress to flutter across her amply rounded belly.

"Oh my, of course. You screamed bloody murder as you stepped out of the limo, because you heard the lamb being slaughtered."

Soraya shuddered. "I'll never forget the poor thing bleating its heart out and the horrid silence right after they slit its throat."

"I also remember Mr. Sultan putting his arm around you to turn you away from the sight. Whatever did he say to calm you down? Do you remember?"

"Every word. He said, 'Now, now, Soraya, you knew there would be a sacrifice. We just timed our arrival badly. The lamb isn't scared anymore, and his meat will feed the poor.' Then he instructed me to greet the guests. Can't you just hear him ordering me about and comforting me at the same time?"

"I'll bet you didn't see him motion behind your back for a waiter to bring a glass of that amazing Château d'Yquem Ygrec," said Poolak.

"He did? I never knew that. All I know is someone put a glass in my hand and I drank it without taking a breath. I didn't even notice the taste, but the alcohol helped. I wish they'd given some to the lamb."

Poolak rested her clipboard on her stomach and brushed back the strands of gray hair escaping from her bun.

"It was a glorious night. You certainly had an impressive turnout of politicians and foreign businessmen, although I was sorry the Shah and Shahbanu didn't come."

"They were out of the country, in Belgium, as I recall. But there were a lot of the king's relatives in attendance. Most I'd never met before."

"It was the wedding of the season. I remember getting personal calls from socialites who begged to be invited."

Soraya sighed. "We really only wanted the top tier to attend. Once you drop down into the "B" list, the "A" list isn't as interested in coming."

"Naturally. Mrs. Sultan, do you have any new instructions for me? I'm half way down the current list."

"I'll have more within an hour or so. So much to do. Make sure you don't wander too far away," Soraya said.

"I'll be within earshot," Poolak promised, sticking the pencil through her bun.

Soraya ran her finger along the wedding photo's frame. She hadn't looked at this photo for ages. How odd that eventually one stopped noticing pictures. Perhaps being squeezed between glass and cardboard drained the emotion from photos until they desiccated inside their silver coffins.

But today this she could hear Uncle Mahmud's voice: "Soraya! Mehdi! You beautiful children, look up so I can take your picture!"

Little did he know that he'd interrupted a whispered exchange of sexual fantasies. Soraya could see the arousal captured in her eyes and the smoldering fire in Mehdi's. Thank goodness, only the two of them knew how erotic the photo really was. They'd put their libidos on ice as the reception roared into the night. Hundreds of large lanterns hung in the trees, draped with gardenia-studded moss. The wedding dinner included Soraya's favorite, Saffron *Tachin* Rice, mounds of it, baked until the bottom was crusty and golden, then carefully flipped over, revealing a crunchy top and gaily festooned with lime green pistachios, slivered almonds and ruby red barberries.

She and Mehdi had toasted the 200-plus guests with 1975 Louis Roederer Brut Cristal, thanking them for the bags of gold and jewelry lying in piles on the gift tables.

The night concluded with a fireworks display.

Tehran's top society columnist had proclaimed the affair as spectacular as the Shah's marriage to his wife, Shahbanu Farah Diba, and no one had disputed the comparison, Soraya remembered with deep satisfaction.

"Mrs. Sultan?"

Ebi, the head gardener, stuck his head into the parlor. His sinewy arm hoisted a bucket of flowers snipped from the conservatory. Their joyous fragrance filled the air.

"Lovely, Ebi. Tell Mohsen to make three arrangements for the dinner table and one large one for the foyer."

She placed the wedding photo back in its proper spot. One unpleasant element of their marriage was Mehdi's frequent business trips and the resulting friction. Each time he came home he lectured her about being too soft on Darius. She always bristled. The last time, they'd had a heated argument.

"My son needs to be raised like a prince who can lead, not like a princess who whiles away the hours," Mehdi had shouted.

She'd snapped back.

"Well, while the king goes off to slay dragons, someone else at the castle has to make the hard decisions. Maybe the king should stay home more."

Eventually they'd spent nearly an hour "forgiving" each

other in the shower. Shoehorning him back into family dynamics always took effort, but she was glad he'd be home from Washington, D.C., the day after tomorrow.

At that moment, Darius lay asleep in the back seat of the limo, draped like a scarf across Nanny's lap. Nassiri was passing Sultan Street 1, the home of Darius' paternal grandmother. At the next intersection he turned right onto Sultan Street 2, where the Cyrus side of the family lived. When Nassiri swung left towards the north gates on Sultan Street 3, Fatima gently shook the boy.

"*Naz Nazy*, Cutie Pie. Time to wake up. We're home."

Darius wiped saliva from the corner of his mouth and yawned loudly.

"Cover your mouth, please, you silly boy."

They drove through the compound's ornate gates. The first dwelling on the right housed Nassiri, his wife, Leyla, and nine-year-old Nema.

In all, twenty-eight staff members with their families lived on the premises, contributing some ready-made playmates for Darius. Nema was his best friend, but there was also Ebi's wife and baby girl; Poolak's 10-year-old twin grandchildren and their widowed mother; Mohsen, the butler, his wife and four teenagers; Alaleh, the head chef, her husband and their 15-year-old girl; and three younger children belonging to the two *sous chefs*. Yousef, the 20-

year-old assistant gardener, was a bachelor. There were others who lived outside of the compound, including six other gardeners and three more *sous chefs*.

Darius saw Nema playing in the driveway, bouncing a ball off the garage door. He waved.

"Come back and play with me!"

Darius smiled charmingly at Fatima. She shot him a you-know-better-than-that look and kissed his cheek. Dinnertime was approaching. She needed to supervise his homework and make certain he bathed before dinner.

Darius sighed. He would have to wait until the weekend to play ball with his friend.

The limo skated gracefully around the circular drive, rolling to a smooth stop at the front door. Darius leaped out, ran up the steps and burst into the foyer.

"Mama, we're home! We went all over town, to the Bazaar and the Supermarket."

Soraya emerged from the parlor, heading down the long hall to the kitchen.

"You've had a busy day, my son! Come have some pistachios to distract your stomach until dinner."

Fatima lagged behind him, waving the envelope. Soraya recognized Mrs. Lashgari's handwriting. Oh dear, what had he done now?

"A busy day, indeed," she said, handing him the

porcelain bowl of jade-colored nutmeats.

Dinner was formally served two hours later. Fatima ate in the kitchen, with Alaleh. Soraya and Darius sat primly at one end of the large dining room table looking dwarfed; rather like ants nibbling food in one corner of a picnic blanket. Mohsen had tried to mitigate the emptiness with artfully placed floral arrangements. Soraya sat at the head of the table in Mehdi's absence with Darius on her left. There was silence except for the dainty percussive sounds of their utensils touching the china, accented by the ice glancing against the sides of crystal water goblets.

For now, Darius' shampooed hair lay neatly tamed, but copious curls would spring from his head as soon as it began to dry. Having already finished his homework, Darius ate with a light heart. He had Mohsen spoon a third helping of cilantro chicken on his plate.

Soraya decided it was time.

"How was school today, my son?" she asked, trying to sound interested without tipping her hand.

"Great," mumbled Darius, his mouth full of chicken.

"Please chew and swallow your food before speaking."

He gulped down the chicken and wiped his chin.

"School went great."

"That's wonderful, my son, that's very good, except that, well ..." Soraya studied the hand-beaded design on the tablecloth, fingering the beads like a rosary for inspiration. "As you know, Mrs. Lashgari sent home a little note this afternoon."

"Aha!" Darius exclaimed. "My 'Shahnameh.' The class loved it!"

Soraya took a deep breath, considering her response. She didn't want to break her son's spirit, but if he was going to succeed at school he had to learn discipline.

"Well, there's good news and there's bad news."

I'm equivocating, she thought. That sentence alone would have earned her a lecture from Mehdi about how indulging him risked creating a mama's boy. With her husband's words ringing in her ear, she forged ahead.

"Mrs. Lashgari was very pleased that you knew your homework, but ..."

"But what ...?" Darius stopped mid-chew and blinked. Soraya chose not to remind him about swallowing first.

"She said that your, well, your energetic re-enactment disrupted the class. We've talked about this, Darius. You need top grades and good character recommendations from your teachers to get into the *Institut Le Rosey* when you're fourteen. That's very important. You'll want to go to school in Switzerland like the Shah and his son, like my grandfather and my father, and even your father and your uncle. Won't that be a new and exciting adventure for you?"

He sulked.

"No. It doesn't sound so great to me. I like living here."

He stabbed his fork into another piece of chicken. The tine slipped, scraping loudly against the china.

"Darius! Be careful!" She gave cajoling another try. "But Darius, you'll learn to speak English and French and you'd be in Switzerland. During summer, the school offers sailing and scuba lessons. They'll even teach you to fly a plane there at *Le Rosey*!"

He simply had to go there. *Institut Le Rosey*, by most accounts the world's most expensive prep school, taught students to be world leaders on their two breath-taking campuses: The summer campus on the lush shores of Lake Geneva and a winter campus in the Swiss resort village of Gstaad. She knew that their mission was to develop what they called a spectrum of "multiple intelligences." Whatever those were, she wanted her son to have them.

Furthermore, children of the world's royal and most wealthy families had walked those halls since 1880. Darius needed to be one of them. Graduates were automatically considered worthy of international attention, which was why competition for admission was brutal.

"Would Nanny be coming? She loves Switzerland."

Darius brightened at the possibility.

Soraya sat up and immediately quashed the idea.

"No, *Aziz Jaan*. That's the reason we're not sending you there until you're a little older. We want to keep you close for a few extra years."

"But I want to stay close to Nanny forever."

Soraya frowned, her pride stung. Fatima certainly had a way with him. Soraya wanted to be number one in his life; she just didn't know how to achieve that ranking.

His face brightened again and he said, "Is Nema going?"

Soraya sighed.

"No, I'm certain he won't be attending *Le Rosey*. I realize he's your best friend, but our family is a little better, well, better known than his. But you'll be ready when it's time. She could hear Mehdi in her ear, insisting that she had to let Darius know who was in charge. Tonight it obviously wasn't she. She sighed again. Too bad that finishing school hadn't offered parenting courses.

Mohsen entered the dining room. He removed and stacked their plates on the cart without making a sound.

Soraya pursed her lips and folded her linen napkin. She creased the fabric's edge with her fingernail, smoothing it resolutely and hoping Darius would view it as an act of maternal dominance. But while the napkin lay firmly creased and chastised, Darius remained unimpressed. A desperate Soraya threw diplomacy out the window.

"All right, my son. The point is this that your classroom

behavior has to improve." An idea came to her. "Do you want me to discipline you or would you prefer your father?"

The boy's eyes widened.

"Papa's coming home? When?

"He returns home from the United States the day after tomorrow."

There was no need for deliberation. Darius knew his mother's worst punishment would be gentler than any discipline his father would mete out. He slid from his chair and threw his arms around her.

"You, Mama, you punish me."

His warm little body snipped away her shreds of resolve.

"All right then, well, let's see. You will write an 'I'm so very sorry' note to your teacher and you must promise me you'll be exceptionally well behaved the rest of the year so Mrs. Lashgari will see that you are worthy of attending *Le Rosey* and give you a glowing recommendation. Promise?"

"I'll quiet as a little lamb. Really. She'll think I'm absent, I'll be so invisible."

"Just be well-behaved enough so that no more notes are sent home this year and I'll be happy. And write Mrs. Lashgari that apology before bed."

It wasn't much of a punishment, but it was the best she could come up with. Soraya rang the bell for Mohsen to bring in dessert. Darius was already practicing being quiet.

"Don't fret, you'll be ready to go to boarding school and make new friends by the time you're fourteen."

"No, I won't. I'm staying with Nanny and Nema," he said flatly.

Soraya sighed. Her son had hijacked the conversation, turning it into a failed sales pitch for a school that most children would sell their souls to attend. She could hear Mehdi now, but she'd worry about that tomorrow.

"Mohsen, please tell Nanny Fatima that Darius must write an apology to his teacher before bed."

"Yes, Ma'am."

After a dessert of *Sohan Asali* made with cashews and honey, Darius sat at his desk, biting his lip, writing the apology. Fatima stood behind him. He was her little angel.

"Your handwriting is so pretty, Darius. Good boy. However," she continued, "you've written 'so' five times and 'very' eight times. Let's go ahead and write the word 'sorry." I think Mrs. Lashgari will sense your remorse."

"Then am I all done being punished?"

Fatima laughed. "Oh, the torture. Yes, you're done."

"Mama's punishment isn't so bad, you know. Papa would have been meaner."

"Go brush your teeth. Your father isn't mean. He loves you and misses you. Doesn't he always bring you something wonderful when he comes home? What will it be?"

That's right! Another present from America! In his excitement, Darius squeezed the toothpaste tube too hard. Blue goo dripped off the edges of his toothbrush before it plopped onto the white porcelain. Fatima didn't say anything. She'd clean the sink later.

Darius chattered on. "Yes! I wonder what he'll bring me from New York this time. I hope he brings music cassettes. I need more American rock music."

He waved the toothbrush across his front teeth.

Fatima said, "Don't forget the back teeth. I need to see blue foam falling from your sweet mouth."

Darius took a half-hearted swipe at each side, rinsed off the brush, and picked up the sterling silver cup with his name engraved on it, running the tap until the water got cold before taking a big gulp. Aiming at the glob of toothpaste, he spat as hard as he could. It didn't budge.

"Good enough, Nanny?"

"Good enough. Did you kiss your mother goodnight?"

He nodded.

"Then let's tuck you in."

Darius bounced onto the mattress.

"Tell me a story?"

Fatima fluffed his pillow before he lay down.

"Hmm. I'll recite you a poem, since you like them so much. Let's play our game. See if you can guess who wrote this poem:

> *Human beings are members of a whole,*
> *In creation, of one essence and soul,*
> *If one member is afflicted with pain,*
> *Other members uneasy will remain.*
> *If you've no sympathy for human pain,*
> *The name of human you cannot retain!*

Darius wrinkled his nose.

"I need a hint."

"The poet is famous and the poem was written a long time ago, " Fatima said.

"All your poets are famous and wrote a long time ago," he whimpered. "I need a real hint!"

"All right. This poet lived about 800 years ago; he had a hard life and wandered from place to place for thirty years and he was a Sufi," she said. "That's all you get."

"I know who it is, I know!" Darius frog leaped in a circle around his mattress. "It's Sa'di! What do I win?"

She kissed him on the forehead.

"My undying love." She pulled the covers up under his chin before turning to her own bed, positioned just a few feet from Darius'.

"When are you coming to bed? I'll stay awake."

"No you won't, even if you try. You've had a big day and you need rest. Please, I want you to go to sleep.

I'm going to see if your mother needs me, then I'll read the newspaper and after that I'll come to bed. Tell you what, if you're still awake, I'll let you guess another poet."

She started to leave.

"Wait, Nanny," Darius said. "I have a poem for you to guess! You'll never get it."

Fatima rested her hand on the light switch.

"All right. See if you can stump me."

Darius sang exuberantly in accented English:

Whether you're a brother or whether you're a mother,

You're stayin' alive, stayin' alive.

Feel the city breakin' and everybody shakin',

And we're stayin' alive, stayin' alive.

Ah, ha, ha, ha, stayin' alive, stayin' alive.

Ah, ha, ha, ha, stayin' alive.

They heard Soraya laughing down the hall.

"Time to rest, my son," she said.

"Almost, Mama, " Darius promised. "Well, Nanny, who wrote it? I'll bet you don't know."

"That's way too modern for me, and the poet certainly wasn't Persian. Is it a song by those Gee Wee Brothers you like so much?"

Darius convulsed with laughter. "Gee Wee Brothers? Nanny, they're the Bee Gees! I stumped you! I win, I win!"

"I guess you do. You know I don't speak much English, so I'm not sure what the song's about, but I quite like it. Yes, you stumped me."

She snapped off the light.

Normally, Fatima didn't care for American music, but this particular melody was infectious.

"Ah, ha, ha, ha ..."

She boogied her way down the hallway.

Chapter 4

Mehdi

MEHDI SULTAN gazed out the window of the limo carrying him to JFK Airport, happy to leave behind the United States as well as the inherent pressures of doing business abroad. These two months had been productive, but intense. He sagged into the buttery leather backseat and sipped Chivas Regal from Baccarat crystal. *Nowruz* was mere days away and the prospect of sharing it with his family over plates of Persian food sang like a siren in his head.

It wasn't that Mehdi disliked America or Americans. The United States was impressive. He found its citizens friendly and straightforward. What utterly confounded him was their consistent aversion toward learning about other cultures, especially one as vital to the balance of world power as was his own. Americans appeared to him to be oblivious to its importance in the region, as the lone remaining nation buffering the West against Soviet aggression. Didn't they understand that Iran was their staunchest friend in the whole of the Middle East? Yet all that Mehdi saw on the American news programs were those unruly student demonstrations on American college campuses. These students demanded the Shah's removal over human rights violations, which they claimed were perpetrated by SAVAK, Shah Pahlavi's secret police. Mehdi had his own suspicions about SAVAK, but he also firmly believed the American government was blind to the greater evils potentially arising from the ashes of a burned Peacock Throne. It was a recipe for disaster.

Mehdi sighed. Myopic Yanks.

JFK Airport loomed just ahead. His driver pointed.

"There she is, Mr. Sultan."

"Impossible to miss, isn't she?" said Mehdi.

"She" was Pan Am's Worldspot Terminal 3 and its massive "flying saucer" roof, glinting in the afternoon sun like an interstellar space vehicle left behind by little green men. Was he booked to Tehran or to Mars?

Mehdi patted his inside pocket to double-check for his passport and ticket. Tehran would be only about twenty hours away once Flight #78 was in the air. He'd checked the weather forecast this morning, and it bode well for a smooth ride.

Boarding the 747 Jumbo Jet, a weary Mehdi eased into first class' luxury. He'd stay awake for the next eight hours before allowing himself to sleep. Hopefully, he'd be well-enough rested when they landed in Tehran.

"Good afternoon, Mr. Sultan. My name is Becky. May I offer you today's New York Times, or a magazine?"

Mehdi looked up. The stewardess was predictably lovely, with Caribbean-blue eyes and beach-colored hair. She stirred Mehdi's interest, but after sizing her up, he saw she was much taller than he. Mehdi imagined the two of them, horizontal and under the sheets. No, he felt too short, and he required dominance in sexual encounters. Power was his aphrodisiac. Still, he admired the way her body was outlined by the navy blue uniform. Mehdi couldn't find an inch of the tailored fabric that she didn't fill out.

"Just the New York Times. Thank you, Becky."

She flashed a smile of straight, white teeth. Mehdi nodded a thank you. Nobody smiled more than Americans. Maybe it was because they spent so much on their teeth that they wanted to get their money's worth. Then there were the Brits. He had enjoyed many beautiful British women, but even they often had crooked, yellowish teeth. Overall, American women were more attractive, and Italian women even more sensuous than the Americans.

He needed to rein in his fantasies. Reaching for his wallet, he slid out his wife's photo. She looked gorgeous and alluring. He worshipped Persian women above all others: Their love of makeup, jewelry and perfume, everything worn with exuberance, and which made him yearn to bury his face between their breasts. Persian femininity would always rank as his first choice. While he allowed himself to mentally scrapbook his fantasies of women from all over the world, he rarely acted on his impulses, and when he did, he made discretion the top priority.

He'd married Tehran's most beautiful woman, and he chose not to ... how did the Americans put it? Oh yes, he chose not to "shoot himself in the foot."

Shifting focus, he perused the front section of the Times. The captain's voice blared over the speaker.

"We're pleased to welcome you aboard today. Our in-flight film will begin once we've served dinner. Tonight's movie is 'Superman,' starring Christopher Reeve."

"Superman" sounded ideal. Mehdi hadn't seen any movies over the last several months and some mindless entertainment sounded perfect. He'd sleep afterwards.

All too quickly, he was startled awake by the captain's announcement that the plane was descending into Tehran Mehrabad International. Mehdi slid open the window shade and peered down at his native city. The top of the King's Memorial poked through the layer of heavy brown pollution, a beacon of beauty rising above the muck. The seven-year-old marble tower looked to him like a cross between the Eiffel Tower and that hamburger chain's golden arch, only with the addition of flying buttresses.

Becky walked the aisles a final time. "Any trash I can take off your hands, Mr. Sultan?"

He handed her the newspaper. "Thank you, Becky."

No question, she had piqued his interest. If their paths crossed again, who knew? But for now she was flying on to another city, and he was arriving home.

Nassiri stood waiting at the gate.

"Welcome home, sir," he said, relieving his employer of the grey Chanel overcoat and Hermes carry-on bag.

"It's great to be back, Ali," Mehdi said, "but I noticed during the descent that our smog problem hasn't improved. Tehran's air is the same shade of filth."

"I'm afraid it will only get worse this summer, sir."

They strolled toward baggage claim. Mehdi enjoyed being on home soil again. Persians surrounded him, the airport's food court smelled of Persian cooking, and the cadence of Farsi, the Persian language, played like music to his ears. Conversing in his native tongue was like wearing his favorite slippers. The words rolled comfortably inside his mouth before tumbling out. The subject, though, was deadly serious.

"I've been following the student demonstrations in the States, but I don't trust American networks. Their news seems skewed for political reasons. But still, you should see the number of protestors. Their numbers are growing and their voices are getting louder. What's most astonishing to me is that many of the demonstrators are Persian."

Nassiri was surprised. "No kidding."

"Yes. Many of them are Iranian college students who are attending the American universities courtesy of the Shah's government, the ingrates. What can you tell me about the demonstrations here?"

"Their numbers are on the rise. The clerics are actively stirring up people's anger. Obviously, the Ayatollah Khomeini is communicating just fine from his hole in Iraq."

"Except I heard this week that Saddam Hussein has 'invited' the Ayatollah to leave Iraq and that France most likely will take him in."

"I hadn't heard that, yet, but I did hear that the clerics are joining forces with the Communists against Mohammad Reza Shah," said Ali.

"Strange bedfellows. It's difficult to imagine the atheistic Tudeh Party joining with the fanatic religious groups. I guess a common enemy unites such people. That's bad news for Shah Pahlavi, though. It doubles the strength of insurgents. I'm afraid the ugliness will get worse this summer, like the smog."

Mehdi was too engrossed in their exchange to notice the attention he garnered from women in the terminal. But then, he was used to it. Despite being on the short side, Mehdi cut a striking figure. An impeccably dressed man, he was well proportioned and muscular, with a gait that exuded panache. He wore affluence as effortlessly as he did his grey flannel Brioni suit, with the jacket nipped in subtly at the waist and the trousers neatly brushing the tops of his Hermes shoes. The women might have completely swooned had they glimpsed his blue and yellow argyle socks.

Nassiri pulled luggage off the carousel while Mehdi took stock of his energy level. He already knew he was too tired for the grand "Welcome Home" dinner his party-centric wife was throwing tonight. He pined for an authentic Persian dinner, a glass of fine cognac, then a goodnight chat with Darius and finally, torrid sex with his wife before sleeping in until noon.

But Soraya's reputation as the city's finest hostess needed to be upheld and expanded, and she always relished the opportunity to entertain Tehran's elite. Tonight's party would make the social columns. Her parties always did.

"All right, he said. "Let's do our part to add to Tehran's pollution by driving home in our gas-guzzling limo."

Seeing the familiar neighborhoods was gratifying.

"I'm going to have to drink just to fortify my pretense of charm at tonight's party. You know how important it is to Soraya that I perform a convincing 'smile and nod' act."

"You perform it well, sir."

"I just want to stay at home for awhile."

"I understand. It won't be long now, sir. Darius was very excited when I left for the airport."

Actually, Darius had been so excited that morning that by now he'd wearied from the hours of anticipation. He still peered out his bedroom window for a glimpse of the Daimler, but as the afternoon lumbered by, he checked his toy closet for distraction. He sighed. There were too many toys in there and he couldn't focus enough to choose one.

Meanwhile, Nema was watching for his father, too. He sat perched on the back of the couch and stared down the street. From here he would be the first one to spot the limo as it turned into the compound and pointed its hood ornament toward the main house. Catching a glimpse of the car, he sprinted out the front door and up the main driveway. Nassiri saw his son running, slowing down so he could beat the limousine to the front door.

"Darius! They're home! Hurry up, they're here!"

Darius bolted downstairs yelling, "Mama, hurry, he's here! Nanny, he's home! Let's start the party!"

"One minute, Darius," said Soraya.

Etiquette required that her husband receive a proper welcome home. She scrutinized her reflection in the foyer mirror. There was no lipstick on her teeth, but her long bangs needed smoothing. Once she was satisfied with her appearance, Soraya stepped outside, and casually but regally, posed like a Greek goddess between two marble columns.

Mehdi caught his breath at the sight of her, shaking his head at his good fortune. Soraya was a Cecil Beaton fashion photo shoot come to life. But no magazine photo could capture her unexpected earthiness. Those deep-set eyes, so innocent at first glance, hid flashes of passion he was certain only he could inspire.

She was already dressed for the evening's party. Her new gown, created for her by a designer to the Empress Farah Pahlavi, was a dusky rose color with lines flowing from an empire waistline to the floor in a subtle A-line. Three inches of French opaque pink paillette sequins were hand sewn along the hem's edge, creating just enough weight to make the dress swing gently as she walked.

Nassiri opened the passenger door and Soraya glided down the steps to greet her husband with a genteel but promising kiss. She'd had her hair and makeup done early today for Mehdi's benefit. It never hurt to remind him of why he'd married her.

"It's good to be home," he whispered in her ear. Then he turned to Darius, who like a grasshopper, was jumping at his side, and smiled. "Darius, my son." Darius threw his arms around his father. "Ah, yes. You definitely have grown. Come, shake my hand, son, for I can see that you are becoming a man."

Darius stretched himself an inch taller. Nassiri bearhugged Nema and together they began unloading the suitcases.

Up in the master bathroom a little later, Mehdi splashed cold water on his skin, running his fingers across his chin to feel its shaven smoothness. He stared at his haggard image. The bed's reflection in the mirror beckoned to him, but guests would be arriving shortly and he knew if he lay down, Mohsen would feel loath to wake him. Besides, a party was more than just a party. A soirée cemented political and business relationships.

Soraya had lain out a fresh suit and shirt for him.

He changed and headed down the staircase. Business trips let him see their palatial home with fresh eyes. He was struck by the tasteful extravagance of his mansion. We should featured in Architectural Digest Magazine, Mehdi thought with great pleasure. It had taken six years after the home's architectural design to the completion of its 13,000-square-foot magnificence. Mehdi had utilized his formidable business contacts to snag one of Tehran's finest architects. But he'd let Soraya choose the interior designers.

Perhaps his wife didn't understand politics or religion, but she did have exquisite taste. Even the designers deferred to her unique personal style. The result was this spectacular showcase, and every inch of it sparkled for tonight's party. Baccarat crystal vases were filled with blooms; long, linen-covered tables were laden with gleaming silver platters and ornate serving utensils; and the downstairs red marble floors Mehdi had imported from Italy shone like mirrors.

He admired the original artwork hanging on the walls of flocked wallpaper, each work specifically lit. If the overall effect was ornate, that was strictly intentional.

The doorbell rang. Soraya moved gracefully, but with the swiftness of a thoroughbred breaking from the gate. Most socialites would have let the butler answer the door, but Soraya liked to personally welcome each guest. She glided toward the front door, three lengths ahead of Mohsen.

Blowing a kiss to Mehdi on the way, she said, "Darling, you look marvelous."

"Not nearly as marvelous as you, *Soraya-joon*. Here we go," he said, toasting the air with his scotch on the rocks.

Soraya was in her element. Her melodic voice charmed and welcomed.

"Ambassador Diaz, so wonderful to see you again. But shame on you! You neglected to tell me how beautiful your wife is! Mrs. Diaz, what a pleasure to meet you. I hear you've recently returned from visiting your native Chile. Please come in. No, you are not too early. Now that you're here, the party is underway. And aren't you the lucky ones! For a brief while you'll have the complete attention of all the servers!"

Mohsen took Mrs. Diaz' fur stole as a waiter quickly appeared, offering them champagne in crystal flutes. As the couple stepped inside, they were stopped in their tracks by its beauty. Rising from the sea of red marble flooring were two gracefully curving staircases with intricate, balusters of sea serpents molded in black wrought iron and highlighted in gold gilt. Overhead, the massive, rock crystal chandelier glittered amid the multitude of bulbs that lighted the ceiling and cast a glowing ambience across the walls.

Beneath the chandelier was a 1952 Lalique Amber Cactus table, its crystalline, succulent-leaf base curving upwards to hold a thick glass tabletop. Mrs. Diaz was entranced. On the tabletop stood a tall floral arrangement featuring Juliet Peach Roses, Black Dahlias, long, tapering stalks of fragrant Tuberose, patterned Costa Rica tropical orchids, as well as some unrestrained Ming Fern, artfully placed inside a white Carrara marble vase.

"Magnificent, just magnificent," oozed Mrs. Diaz. "And, oh my goodness, these bronzes: Wherever did you find them?" she asked, touching the arm of a diaphanously clothed nymph, one of the two gracing the entryway.

"I saw them at a Paris auction," said Soraya. "They're

late eighteenth century. How could I resist?"

Mrs. Diaz was beginning to feel like a country bumpkin, but the ambassador was very pleased to be seen here tonight. This was a boost to his fledgling diplomatic career. He slipped his arm around his wife's waist and guided her toward the ballroom, where members from the Tehran Symphony were playing Hayden's String Quartet Number Five in D Major. Soraya, whose greatest talent lay in party giving, had chosen to showcase "The Lark's" filigreed passages. She'd mastered the art of tantalizing her guests. But still, producing such an event was complex. A guest list of almost one hundred required seamless planning from Soraya and precise execution from her house staff.

The mansion shortly teemed with guests. Waiters circled the room offering Grenadine-laden cocktails, Perrier-Jouet Grand Brut, and Kobrand wine. Alcohol in hand and noses in the air, guests reached for hot hors d'oeuvres from off the passing trays.

The table of cold hors d'oeuvres featured a three-foot-high ice sculpture of the Taj Mahal. Limpid ivy tendrils tucked beneath its base led the eye toward the mounds of caviar from the Caspian Sea. The Sultans could have afforded the more expensive Beluga sturgeon caviar, but Soraya chose Sevruga sturgeon's caviar, not to cut costs, but because it was more delicious. Her guests appreciated the culinary statement.

Darius plopped down on the staircase's landing to watch the show. He threw back his head and sniffed like a coyote. Delicious scents were billowing into the ballroom. The entrée was nearly ready, and it was Darius' favorite: Entrecôte Café de Paris. A few hours earlier, he'd been there when Alaleh and her staff prepped the delicate sauce made of blanched chicken livers, pans of cream with white Dijon mustard and an infusion of thyme flowers, gently simmered.

Darius had stuck his finger into a pan of the warm creamy mixture and licked it, causing Alaleh to scold him. Fatima stepped in to arbitrate.

"Darius! Don't be rude to Alaleh. Are your hands clean?" But he knew she wasn't really angry because she winked even while shaking her finger at him.

"It's alright, Fatima," Alaleh said grudgingly, grumpy over the hygienic infraction. "I'll talk you through the recipe, Darius," she continued. "Now, you can see the *sous chefs* mincing the chicken livers. Next they'll press them through a strainer into the warmed cream you like so well, Darius, and then they'll add butter, salt and pepper until it tastes right."

Before she could continue, Darius jumped in.

"I know what happens next! They stir it all together until

it makes an ugly, brown foam that no one wants to eat."

Fatima laughed. Not Alaleh. She pursed her lips and looked away.

"Well, he's not wrong, Alaleh," said Fatima. "It always does look like someone has made a terrible mistake."

Alaleh shrugged. "Certainly, but then the magic happens: That ugly brown froth becomes a creamy green sauce that everyone loves. The staff grills the steaks to medium rare as fast as they can while the waiters gather the plates. As soon as Mohsen announces dinner is ready, we place the steaks on top of the sauce, drizzle more sauce over the meat for color, and serve the plates as quickly as possible."

Just thinking about the recipe made him drool. Darius could hardly wait for the feast he and Nanny would share together upstairs.

Down below he saw his father leaning into a conversation with several British Petroleum executives. They accented their talking points by swirling the ice cubes in their drinks.

Darius could no longer hear the string quartet above the din, but since their bows were still moving up and down, he assumed they were still playing.

His mother glanced up from cocktail-speak with the wife of an Imperial Guard and smiled. Darius waved. Soraya wore her glittering diamond and emerald necklace around her neck. It sparkled gaily.

"Darius," she'd once explained as his father helped put on the necklace, "this Cartier is my greatest treasure, my favorite heirloom, because my great-great-grandfather gave it to my great-great-grandmother on their wedding day. One day you'll give to your bride. This is a treasure, not just because it's valuable, but because it connects us to our family roots."

"Mama, you say that about all our old stuff."

Her laugh was musical. "Well," she said, "it's true. These beautiful things were touched and worn and cared for by family members. When I wear this necklace, I wear it for all the women in the Cyrus bloodline. You'll understand one day, my darling."

His father had grinned and said, "Son, your mother is very attached to wearing old neck confetti."

"Oh, stop it, Mehdi," she retorted. "This is important for him to understand."

His father had walked away, whistling innocently.

It was true that Soraya felt commissioned to ensure that Darius matured into an aristocratic man, one knowing how to conduct himself as a gentleman in all circumstances, and possessing discriminating taste. It was the reason she talked to him about family heirlooms, why she dressed him expensively and saw to it that he understood gourmet food.

And that was why, despite Mehdi's disapproval, she had Darius inspect and approve all of her gowns. Soraya insisted that her son develop an appreciation for well-designed, hand-sewn clothing and fine fabrics. Mehdi vehemently disagreed, but Soraya had won the war, *de facto*, because she did it anyway.

Thus, two months before any event, Soraya would show Darius the original sketches of her new gown. Next she had him see, feel and evaluate the material.

After the gown was partly assembled, he observed a fitting. When the finished garment was delivered to the mansion, she asked him to check the quality of the work. The day of the event she asked Darius for final approval.

Earlier today, while Darius had wriggled impatiently outside his mother's dressing room while the seamstress sewed Soraya into tonight's gown.

"Mama, are you done yet?" He knocked on the door for good measure.

"Almost ready. Please have patience, my son. Rome was not built in a day, and being sewn into a gown is much more complicated!"

Just when he thought he'd explode, the door swept open and his mother emerged, like a glorious butterfly from its cocoon.

"Well?" she said. "First of all, does it fit properly?"

Darius scrutinized the garment, trying to appear professional and exacting.

"Turn around slowly so I can see."

"All right. Tell me how the dress flows."

She twirled slowly.

The eight-year-old couldn't control his exuberance.

"I hear the paillettes when you move! They sound like tiny crickets!"

"How do they change the way the dress hangs?"

"They make the hem heavier, so it swings more."

"Exactly. Do you approve?"

"Yes, Mama! This is a well-made dress and you look as beautiful as the Empress."

She kissed him on the forehead.

"Good. All I need now is the necklace."

"That old neck confetti?" said Darius.

"Honestly, you and your father. Men!"

Darius was thrilled that she'd called him a man. Now, as he waved at her, he was convinced his mother was the most beautiful woman in a ballroom full of stunning women.

Mohsen appeared. Before he could announce dinner, Darius sang out to Nanny, "It's time to eat!"

Mohsen glowered and formally announced dinner.

Fatima headed to the kitchen to get their plates as Darius skipped down the hall, his mouth already watering.

Chapter 5

A Life Lesson

Tehran, evening, March 15, 1978

SMALL FIRES CRACKLED mirthfully along the dimming streets of Tehran. Firewood, placed inside foil pans, lighted up personal courtyards, downtown's city streets, and up the back alleys, anywhere and everywhere. Laughter rose with the smoky air. Tonight was *Chaharshanbe Suri*, the last Wednesday of the old year. It was a night to joyfully anticipate the coming New Year.

Darius and Nema were playing outside the gates of the compound in the approaching dusk. They looked down the street and began jumping up and down.

"Here they come!" Darius shouted.

Jingling bells, faint but fast approaching, heralded the firelighters, comedic characters sporting high hats and painted faces. The boys giggled over the clowns' harlequin outfits and their buffoonery.

"Look!" said Darius. Following behind the firelighters came an acrobat doing a series of backflips down the street's hard pavement. Trailing after him was a parade of dancers and singers. The streets were lined with relatives and friends congregating to watch, talk and snack. At some point tonight, everyone would leap over one of these fires chanting, "My pallor to you, your ruddiness to me," to burn away any bad luck from last year.

So far, Darius hadn't done any jumping. He slid behind Fatima, squeezing her hand hard. He saw other kids his age leaping confidently over the flames, but because he wasn't athletic, he worried that a spark would set him on fire.

The Sultan and Cyrus clans milled in front of the main gates of Mehdi and Soraya's house. The children's voices were at shriek-level decibels, especially those children who roamed door-to-door, banging spoons on pots and pans, only stopping long enough to collect treats from the neighbors.

Most of the adults stood around casually, joking and snacking on the "problem-solving nuts," *Ajil-e Moshkel-Gosha*.

Soraya tried to coax Darius into jumping. He was big enough to do it alone, but he wasn't biting.

"I've never jumped alone. Nanny's always carried me."

"You don't need anyone this year, Darius," Soraya urged. "Or maybe Nema can jump with you."

"I can't, I won't, not unless someone will carry me."

Suddenly his father appeared, a serious look on his face.

"Come, Darius." Mehdi held out his hand.

Darius shuddered. Obviously, a polite, "No, thank you, Papa," was not going to be an acceptable response. Soraya's protective instincts kicked in.

"If he's not ready, he's not. Please don't force him."

Mehdi gave her a withering look.

"There's only one way for a man to confront fear. He's eight years old. My son will be a man soon. I'll handle this."

Her blood pressure rose and she wanted to say more, but clenched her teeth together to stop the words from tumbling out. When her husband's jaw was set, silence was smarter than a retort.

Mehdi turned back to Darius. His tone was firm.

"Darius. We are the men of the family. The fire will burn away your fear. You don't have to jump alone. We'll jump together, but I won't carry you."

Darius wanted to disappear.

Mehdi spoke quietly but authoritatively.

"Hold my hand. I promise you won't catch on fire. You must trust me."

Mehdi walked Darius forward, quickening the pace as they approached the flames, until they were running. Darius verged on panic. His father's grip hurt. Just when he thought they were going to run straight into the fire, his father said, "Jump!"

They shouted together, soaring like birds to the other side, "My pallor to you; your ruddiness to me!"

Darius was amazed how easy it was. His father let go of his hand. Soraya applauded and Nanny ran up to hug him, comparing his heroics to those of King Cyrus.

Darius grinned at his father.

"That was fun."

Mehdi knelt, placing his hands on his son's shoulders. His eyes blazed with intensity, as though he longed to write on Darius' heart.

"Remember what happened here tonight," he said. "Whenever life places a fire in your way, run at it hard and fast. With courage, you can leap over obstacles, instead of going through the flames of despair. Jump high enough, and no fire can burn your soul."

Darius was too awash in elation to digest such a solemn metaphor. He quivered with adrenaline.

"Sure, Papa," he said, feeling closer to his father than he ever had. Mehdi ruffled his son's hair.

"You'll remember the lesson when you need it."

Darius was riding the wild horse of exhilaration. He threw an arm around Nema's shoulder. "Come on, Nema, let's go jumping. Don't be afraid. We'll do it together!"

Chapter 6

Nowruz

Monday, March 20, 1978

THE FIRES of *Chaharshanbe Suri* cooled quickly in the minds of the children. Now a flash flood of excitement coursed through the city in anticipation of the New Year. Persian families and their children had been celebrating *Nowruz* for more than 2500 years, dating back to the philosopher Zoroastar.

A privileged boy like Darius properly assumed that many gifts would be coming his way. Nanny had scrubbed him so thoroughly during last night's bath that he still smelled of soap this morning. He preened in his new Disco outfit, feeling like a Bee Gee in the new white bell bottomed pants that they'd paired with a burnt orange silk shirt. In fact, he'd been rocking to "You Should Be Dancing" in front of his bedroom mirror since breakfast.

Now he was searching for Nanny. He'd been instructed not to peek at the redecorated living room until the relatives arrived, but he thought he could talk Nanny into cheating, just a little. Padding down the hallway past his parents' bedroom, he heard muffled voices. He pressed his ear to the door, but their voices were too low to make out words.

He decided against interrupting their *tête-à-tête*, the term his mother used whenever she wanted to have a boring grownup discussion. He stuck his head inside Nanny's room. Nope, it was empty.

It would be a solo expedition, then. His chest tingled with the danger. Creeping toward the living room, he pretended he was an explorer landing on a windswept beach to claim an undiscovered land. But could he reach the French doors without being intercepted by a pirate, a cannibal, or worst of all, by an adult?

He was thrilled when he reached his undiscovered land, undetected. Turing the gold-plated knobs on the living room doors, he shoved them open.

Standing more perfectly still than he ever did for Nanny, Darius soaked up the splendor. From its freshly painted walls down to new inlaid wood flooring and new furniture, the room was completely different, excepting, of course, for his family's heirlooms: His great-great grandmother's tall silver candlesticks, the 18th-century gold Russian samovar and a collection of museum quality marble busts.

He ran his hand over the soft kid leather of the new couches. Matching loveseats and antique side chairs were grouped conversationally around a large, gleaming Carrara marble coffee tabletop with filigreed wrought iron legs.

A huge mirror in a gilt frame leaned artfully against the wall. Darius gazed into it, his reflection dwarfed by the room's grandeur. Pale blue drapes cascaded like fabric waterfalls into pools on the floor. Nanny had told him yesterday that the fabric was antique silk from Tokyo. The afternoon light played on the material's sheen. Darius thought it made the curtains look like real water.

He wandered through the room, smudging fingerprints on the Brazilian mahogany side tables and knocking the sofa pillows askew. The candles placed around the room entranced him. How beautifully they'd glow later on. Darius knew they were Cire Trudon candles because of the wax cameos pressed into the base of each pillar. He fingered the red candle with a black cameo of Julius Caesar, and the brown one with a green cameo of Poseidon, but the black candle with a gold wax cameo of Napoleon Bonaparte captivated him. Mama had told him the story of how in 1811 Napoleon Bonaparte had presented his newborn son with a single gift: A Trudon candle with three real gold coins bearing the Emperor's profile pressed into the wax. Darius secretly hoped that one day his parents would give him a personalized Trudon too, excepting he wanted gold coins with the likeness of Shah Pahlavi. But he liked this Napoleon Bonaparte, who gave his son such great presents.

Rosewater sweetened the air. He sniffed like a bloodhound to discover the enameled bowl filled with fragrant water, the *Golab*, symbolizing the earth's oceans and their cleansing properties.

Today would be filled with symbolism. Seven such items, very important ones, would be on the *Haft Sin* table in the dining room. He did hope, though, that the staff had forgotten to put out the bowl of vinegar, the *Serkeh*.

Even though he knew that vinegar represented patience and maturity, he possessed neither, and thought the vinegar smelled awful. Wait a minute! Darius suddenly wondered if the staff might have placed some *Sekkeh*, the traditional gold coins, around the living room? Just maybe. Now he became a pirate, searching for treasure!

"What are you doing in here, Darius?" asked his father, who was standing in the doorway.

Darius jumped. He thought he was in trouble, but his father didn't seem upset. "Uh, the *Sekkeh*," Darius said. I hope the staff doesn't forget about it."

Mehdi untied a velvet bag he held and opened it so Darius could see inside. The boy's eyes popped. There were so many gold coins inside!

"I told them I would lay out the *Sekkeh* in the dining room," Mehdi answered. "Would you like to help me?"

"Yes! Let me!" he answered, gleefully plunging both

hands into the bag. "Where's Mama?"

"She's dressing. You know how long it takes women to get ready."

"I couldn't find Nanny."

"Nanny and Poolak are in the craft room, gathering the presents they wrapped for everyone," Mehdi said.

"But isn't it almost the New Year? When is the *Tahvil*? I want to open presents now," said Darius, for whom time was moving catatonically.

"Son," he answered, "it's only about an hour away. Be patient a little while longer."

"Patience stinks like vinegar," He brightened. "But Papa, what did you bring me from New York? Please, please give me a hint?" begged Darius.

"Not even a little one. But I promise you'll like it."

Nanny Fatima appeared behind a tall pile of presents.

"Look what I have here!" she said. The box on top began to slide off. "Uh, oh."

Mehdi caught it before it hit the floor. They juggled the pile into a heap on the nearest sofa. Soraya was approaching from the far hallway, her arrival proceeded by the clicking sound of her high heels.

"Happy *Nowruz* to my favorite men!"

Her favorite men couldn't respond. They were staring at her in awe. She looked stunningly chic in a crisp, tomato red

Versace dress with tailored geometric lines. The high collar cut away to form a dramatic halter-top. Her hair was pulled back in a ponytail and topped with a mod vinyl cap, and she wore knee-high white leather go-go boots. But what drew their stares was the generous space between the top of the boots and the dress's hemline, which rose nearly six inches above her knees. Soraya only stood 5'3" but today she appeared much taller, all of it legs. Mehdi's face flushed.

"Do you like it?" she asked as she turned in a circle for the full effect, her swooping bangs framing her face with its high cheekbones, full lips and Elizabeth Taylor eyebrows. Her face was a work of art in and of itself.

"Mama, you look so mod!" Darius exclaimed, clapping his hands. "All we need now is a mirror ball!"

"You look stunning, darling," said Mehdi.

"Well, before I'm too old to wear short skirts, I'm going to enjoy them." Soraya pouted alluringly.

"We'll all enjoy your short skirts," countered Mehdi, wrapping his arms around her to nuzzle the softness of her shoulders. He had every intention of enjoying the dress right off of her later on.

But the moment had passed for Darius.

"Nanny, can we go into the dining room and see the *Haft Sin* table now? Papa said I could help set out the *Sekkeh.*"

Fatima agreed it was time to leave.

"The bag is on the sofa," said Mehdi, his voice muffled. He was busy exploring the curve of Soraya's neck. Fatima and Darius beat a hasty retreat.

"Nanny!" Darius exclaimed. "Look at our beautiful *Haft Sin* table!"

The table, covered by a thin Persian rug, or "cloth of seven dishes," held a spectacular centerpiece. Exuberant purple and white hyacinths sprang from mounds of Scottish Moss representing the plants of the earth, (*Sonbol*). Tall, white candles in Iris Lalique candleholders flanked the hyacinths.

"Look, Nanny!" said Darius, "The flowers look like they're growing in the moss!"

A small mound of delicate lentil sprouts representing rebirth (*Sabzeh*) mixed among branches of sumac laden with berries the color of sunrise.

Nanny set about placing some coins into the moss. Darius sat down at the table to study a large fishbowl resting on an oval mirror. The lazy circles made by the long-finned goldfish captivated him. Mirrors represented honesty and self-reflection, which he knew all too well, as he endured regular chidings on the subject of fibbing. The fish referenced new beginnings. He wiggled his fingertips in the water, inviting them to nibble. Darius was ticking off the seven items, the *Haft Sin* symbols, when vinegar molecules assaulted his nostrils.

He whined. "Nanny, do I have to smell the ..."

"I've already arranged for us to sit at the other end of the table, *Naz Nazy*."

"Good. Oh, Nanny, did you see the eggs?"

He'd just noticed them, gloriously hand-painted and artistically nestled among the foliage.

"Yes, and they're the prettiest I've ever seen. Which one is your favorite?"

He deliberated. He liked the ones painted ruby red and turquoise blue with lots of gold flourishes, while the eggs with geometric designs were too grown up and the flowery ones were for girls. He spotted one with a watery blue background and a single elongated goldfish swimming in endlessly dreamy circles around the ovoid. He picked it up.

"Ha!" he said. "I get it. This isn't just life within life, but life within life within life."

Darius carefully set it back on the table. He didn't want to break anything, especially anything as important as life.

"I think maybe this one is my favorite."

He poked his way down the arrangement. Then he saw it: An egg painted like a pistachio, complete with green nutmeat peeking out from a shell. The artist obviously knew how much his mother loved pistachios. What a good joke!

"This one! This is my favorite." He moved the egg to a more prominent place, where his mother would see it the moment she entered.

Fatima reminded him, "Darius, weren't you going to help put out the coins?"

He took a few and placed them around the fish bowl, dropping the last one into the water just to watch the fish dart away.

The aroma of roasted chickpea cookies wafted into the dining room from the kitchen, tickling his nose. Darius wondered if he could convince Nanny to sneak a few cookies to him right now, but his scheming was interrupted by loud voices coming from the foyer. His paternal grandparents had arrived, and next came the unmistakably exuberant voice of his Great-Uncle Mahmud booming the traditional Persian New Year greeting, *"Nowruz Mobarak!"*

Darius would soon be barraged with hugs and kisses.

Nanny smiled. "Aren't you excited? It's finally time to celebrate."

In no time, they were chanting, "Three, two, one!"

A cheer went up and the adults toasted the New Year. Off in the distance, celebratory gunshots echoed like popcorn popping. The children chanted *"Eidi, eidi!"* hoping to open their presents right away, but Mehdi stood firm.

"In this house we share food and fellowship before we open presents."

The children sat.

Mohsen gave the signal and Chef Alaleh's magnificent parade of food began, starting with traditional herbed, emerald-green rice with fried fish; thick lamb chops; Persian omelettes; chunks of tender lamb served with noodles and rice; fruits and soup. The servers walked ruts into the floor, circling from kitchen to dining room until Soraya laughingly begged them to stop, even as she agreed to another helping. The cousins teased each other and laughed loudly. Happy mayhem reigned inside the lasvish dining room, until the conversation took a sudden turn toward politics.

Feroze Sultan's voice carved a jagged hole into the festivities.

"Without a moral compass that demonstrates to the world the direction the monarchy is heading," he said, "the Shah's government is doomed. It's riddled with corruption and he's completely inconsistent. Why is it, that only one week after the American President Jimmy Carter visits our country, Pahlavi's soldiers kill 75 students and mullahs in Qom? Does the Shah think he is so beloved by America that he can get away with murder? Are his actions the result of stupidity or arrogance? He has to know that newspaper articles attacking the Ayatollah Khomeini are going to anger the dissidents and create violence. What does the man expect? I don't like Khomeini either, but the king's government is blind to its failings."

Ardeshir Cyrus responded sharply. "You know that the article was just a plant. The radicals needed an excuse to riot, and the Ayatollah stirred things up until the protest spun out of control. Feroze, you and I know that many of the 'protestors' are paid hoodlums bussed in from nearby towns. They're goons, destroying shops and restaurants until the army is provoked into action."

Soraya recklessly jumped into the fray.

"And they didn't kill 75 people. The mullahs made up those numbers to make the Shah look heartless," she said. "I read that only two people were killed and they weren't students; they were Tudeh, Communists. You can't believe what the radicals say. And Tehran is mostly quiet, except for a strike here and there."

Feroze shot Mehdi a why-can't-you-control-your-wife look, and talked past her to his son.

"Well, Soraya roars again. Mehdi, remind your lioness that she is a woman, then please inform her that Tehran is a simmering pot that will soon boil over. Work stoppages, strikes – they're only the tip of the iceberg. The Tudeh and the ulama have formed an alliance that will crumple the Pahlavi dynasty. The 'Light of the Aryans' is drawing his last few breaths as Shah."

Soraya was furious. Mehdi squeezed her hand under the table, but anyone criticizing the Shah drew her ire, and everyone in the room was well aware of that, especially her father-in-law. She continued, even though Mehdi squeezed harder.

"Can anyone truly believe the religious have aligned with the Communists? The Tudeh are completely secular. Anyway, the United States and Britain will support the Shah. He favors the West, and ..."

Feroze cut her off without directly talking to her.

"Mehdi, explain to everyone at the table that the ulama and Tudeh Party alliance is a reality. Their common enemy is the Shah. For that reason they ignore their differences. Not only does the West no longer favor the Shah, they want him gone. He should have shut down his secret police a long time ago if he wanted to salvage the illusion of an open government. SAVAK has committed too many atrocities to hide and they are in bed with America's CIA. Allegations against them are now coming from across the globe. They will become the West's excuse to destroy him."

She snapped back at him. "Then why was it that when President Carter and his wife visited Tehran they said that our countries are the closest of friends? Was the president lying? Mrs. Carter said she planned on spending the New

Year with Shah Pahlavi and the Empress Farah. It certainly was in all the newspapers," she said, "for those who care to read them."

She'd stepped over the line. That was a real insult and she knew it. She cringed.

Feroze's face turned purple.

"Carter will say whatever's expedient until it's time to cut ties. Then Carter and his *Amrika* will saw the legs off the Peacock throne and throw its splinters away."

Mehdi squeezed her hand again, painfully so, a clear signal to cease speaking and be invisible. She acquiesced, fuming. She was no good at being the modest and submissive Persian woman her father-in-law expected. Did he think she'd been raised in a harem? Ardeshir smiled calmly at his daughter, but didn't defend her. Soraya was gratified when her brother Arash took up her cause.

"With the greatest respect, *Ghorban*, Excellency, it is a fact that Shah Pahlavi has done an heroic job of keeping oil money here in Iran, of modernizing our infrastructure and educating our people, and he did return land that his father had taken from small land owners. The majority of Iranians acknowledge the good he has done. Don't you think the troublemakers will be squelched?"

"First of all, the Shah gave the people plots of land too

small to work and tractors that have rusted because the farmers have no means of repairing them."

Mehdi had heard enough. He would now take back control of his house.

"Excuse me, Father. My dear family," he said, "let's take a breath. We stride into the New Year with confidence and optimism. Our country will survive this dissension. So please, while you digest the entrées so exquisitely prepared by Chef Alaleh and her staff, I will share a poem by Persia's beloved Divan of Hafiz."

Arash took the cue, rising with a glass of wine and toasting, "*Salam ati Nush*! Enjoy! And here's to family, our country and the New Year!"

The family echoed, "To Iran and the New Year!"

Deep down, everyone wanted to forget about politics on this festive day.

Mehdi stood and taking Soraya by the hand, he recited:

> *My lady that did change this house of mine*
> *Into a heaven when that she dwelt therein,*
> *From head to foot an angel's grace divine*
> *Enwrapped her; pure she was, spotless of sin;*
> *Fair as the moon her countenance, and wise;*
> *Lords of the kind and tender glance, her eyes*
> *With an abounding loveliness did shine ...*

Soraya fanned herself coquettishly with her napkin.

Mehdi had salved her wounded ego. Once again, she was bathed in approval, back where she belonged. The family cheered. Even Feroze was feeling the spirit of the day again.

Washing down his final bite of food with some Dom Pérignon, Ardeshir cleared his throat, declaring, "I, too, have poetry to share. I will now recite from the ... oh, never mind, the 'Shahnameh' needs no introduction."

Ardeshir was a master storyteller in the finest Persian tradition. His deep voice gift-wrapped words, and its melodic cadence mesmerized listeners. Today he included Darius in the storytelling. Whenever he reached a line he suspected his favorite grandchild would know, he pointed at Darius to complete it.

Darius had grown up hearing the book. He knew many of the famous lines and the ones he didn't, he made up or acted out. The discrepancy between Ardeshir's sonorous bass and Darius' high-pitched contributions provided much hilarity and shouts of encouragement.

With gaiety restored, Mohsen announced that dessert would be served. Astonishingly, a roomful of those with already loosened belts found more space for the train of confections chugging out of the kitchen: Saffron Rich pudding; *Noghi* (sugarcoated almonds); Persian nougat; *Toot* (Persian marzipan); sweet and flaky baghlava; three flavors of homemade sherbet; and the chickpea cookies.

Darius stuffed a cookie in his mouth. "Let's eat fast," he urged a cousin, "so we can get to the presents."

Before long, the children were ripping open their *eidi*. Foil wrapping paper flew through the air like shiny paper airplanes. After all the gifts were opened, Darius sat contentedly on the floor with Nanny next to him and his spoils all around him. He counted again the money he'd received from his grandparents and mused over what new toys he would buy with it.

Nanny's present to him was a new soccer ball. His mother's gift was a Tiffany's bedside clock, so he could "learn to get himself up." But it was his father's gift that had made him ecstatic. He'd let out a whoop when he unrolled the Bee Gees' poster and saw that Andy Gibb had signed it: "To my friend, Darius, in Tehran. Hello from Los Angeles. Come see me sometime, Andy Gibb."

"How did you get this, Papa? Did Andy Gibb really sign it for real? Did you meet him? Is he nice?" Darius motor-mouthed with excitement. "When can I go meet him? Is he your friend now? Where did you meet him?"

"Well," his father said, "Let's just say I know people who know him. But yes, he really signed it. And one day you'll meet him." Darius knew exactly where the poster would hang: At the head of his bed.

"This is going to be the best year of our whole lives!"

Chapter 7

Cracks in the Peacock Throne

September 7, 1978

TEARS ran down Darius' cheeks. "It's not fair!"

Nassiri, Nanny, Darius and Nema were clustered in the kitchen, where Darius was pleading his case.

"You promised that Nema and I could go see 'Grease' when it came to Tehran. You promised!"

Nanny Fatima wiped away his tears, holding the handkerchief up to his nose.

"Blow, *Naz Nazy*. Good boy. You're right. It's not fair you can't go to the cinema, and it's not fair that the strikes and the demonstrations are making our lives difficult. But Mr. Nassiri and I can't make them go away. Right now even the Shah can't make them go away."

The boys had been waiting for months for the American-made movie musical to come to Tehran. Now they wouldn't be allowed to see it.

A radio clicked on in the family room. Apparently Mehdi was checking the news. They could hear a male news anchor questioning a female field reporter. Their dialogue sounded solemn, and the news must have been bad because the volume was quickly turned down.

Nassiri folded his arms and leaned against the refrigerator. He was not mincing words.

"I talked to Manu just this morning. He says it's not safe to drive anywhere in the city right now and I'm certainly not going to have protestors see a limo dropping off two young boys to see an American film. And who knows if the cinema's even open? It's probably been closed as a 'business of corruption.'"

"You see, Darius," said Nanny. "Mr. Nassiri's brother would know. He's a captain in the army."

Darius rolled his eyes.

"Manu said the violence is getting worse," Ali said, "and that the insurgents are bolder, capable of anything."

"That's enough, Mr. Nassiri, we understand."

She knew, she knew. Did he think she could forget that a few weeks ago protestors had locked the exit doors of the Cinema Rex in Abadan, and then set it on fire; that 377 moviegoers, fellow citizens, had been burned alive, innocent people who simply went to see a popular Persian film? But she would not allow Nassiri to frighten the boys. She'd fiercely protect Darius from the fallout of Iran's imploding society because he deserved a childhood. While keeping his life normal might become impossible, she wouldn't give up trying until she had no choice.

"I know what," she said brightly, "let's get your new soccer ball, round up friends and have a soccer match."

Within the hour Darius and his buddies were kicking his *Nowruz* ball around the pitch. Nanny sat on the sidelines in her blue lawn chair, reading the newspaper. She glanced up occasionally to cheer.

"Go, Darius! Watch that first touch. Stay onside. Yes, mark him - he's fast. Great defense, Nema!"

Reading the newspaper was difficult these days. She'd been trying to comprehend the reasons for the escalating violence. It was perplexing. She wondered whether or not the Shah's government would react and what sort of reaction could push back the swelling tide. Lately it seemed the Shah couldn't decide whether to be heavy-handed or overly lenient with the protestors. No matter, neither method was working. She found an editorial chronicling Iran's unrest and tracing how the protests had begun in Iran's smaller towns, growing larger and louder at universities and gathering momentum until they spilled onto the streets. Now mobs were burning and looting. Had an undertow of discontent become a tsunami capable of toppling the government?

She prayed it wouldn't happen. The Pahlavi crown had benefitted not only the upper class, but also the lives of the lower classes. The Shah's White Revolution had created programs like the Health Corps care for rural areas, free food for needy mothers, suffrage for women, and childhood education provided by the Literacy Corps for those without access to schools. It was obvious to her things were improving, even if the clergy and the landlords disliked having their influence compromised.

Further down the page was the assertion that the United States and Great Britain desperately needed Iran to maintain the balance of power in the Middle East. It was in their best national interests, the editor wrote, to keep Mohammad Reza Shah Pahlavi in power.

Yet, the Shah continued losing control. Normally, these holy days of Ramadan would be a time of prayer and fasting. But this year, the ayatollahs were whipping the faithful into screaming mobs. Religious extremists were unleashing their vitriol toward the Shah's largely secular government. Nothing was safe from destruction; not banks, hotels, liquor stores or government buildings. Maybe, Fatima worried, not even the Sultan compound.

Urgent, loud voices were coming from the house. Mehdi bolted out the front door, striding towards the pitch. Soraya followed half a step behind him, looking distressed. She clapped her hands.

"Boys, enough soccer for now. I'm glad you got to play.

Come inside. Alaleh is making you snacks."

The boys groaned. It was a good match.

"Now!" said Mehdi.

There was that non-negotiable tone of his. Nema tossed the ball to Darius and the boys headed toward the mansion.

As Nanny gathered her things, Mehdi called to her. She stopped. Soraya was obviously upset. Mehdi spoke so softly that both women had to lean in to hear.

"Martial law has been imposed. It was just on the radio. While the boys are eating, call their parents and let's get them home as quickly as possible."

Soraya choked out a question. "How bad are things?"

Mehdi hesitated before giving a measured response to his wife. He hated upsetting her because she didn't handle bad news well.

"It depends on whether martial law holds and people stay off the streets. The government's calling in anyone with a uniform: Military, policemen, probably even dogcatchers."

Soraya needed to hear some mitigating news.

"But the Shah's forces are loyal and strong enough to keep things quiet, don't you think?"

Fatima added, "And so far he still has support from the West, yes?"

Mehdi's answer ripped away their hopes.

"Let's remember, the Brits helped put Reza Mohammad

on the throne in 1925 and then used him to squeeze a lot of oil money out of Iran," he said. "Since our oil has been nationalized and most of the profits kept here, unhappily for the Brits and the Yanks, I don't think they feel the same concern for the Imperial government. I heard that the American government came out with a report suggesting the Shah's power remains strong enough to hold the throne independently, but either they're fooling themselves or it's a political ruse and a setup to ensure his failure. If they don't whole heartedly support his throne I fear it will shatter before our eyes."

Soraya was horrified.

"They won't let that happen. They can't."

"Are you asking whether the United States and Britain would desert a sinking ship or not? You know what they say about rats. I guess we'll find out what type of animals our Western friends are soon enough."

That night, as the Sevres mantle clock displayed 12:00 a.m., Soraya sat at her vanity table wearing her favorite Chinese silk robe with the hand-embroidered lavender chrysanthemums and green leaves. She wore it nightly while she combed ginger lily oil into her hair. Her shining black locks already fell softly around her shoulders. Each time she lifted the comb to make another languorous stroke, her robe gaped open above the waist, exposing a breast. Mehdi lay stretched out on the gold satin bedspread in his boxer shorts, hands clasped behind his head, staring intently. He found her ritual highly erotic.

The crisply ironed sheets on the king-sized bed already were turned down. Mehdi wanted to pick Soraya up, throw her on the bed and ravish her, but out of respect, he would clean up first. The shower was running. He was waiting for the water to get hot and for the bathroom to get steamy.

Soraya swiveled around to face him.

"You have to go," she said.

"I said no." He couldn't believe she'd broken the mood. It annoyed him. This wasn't the first time she'd brought up difficult subjects before having sex.

"But you're in real danger if they find out."

"I have a business trip scheduled to Paris next month. I can stay longer if I need to. But they won't find out."

He knew he sounded curt, but he didn't care. Mehdi sighed. Now he'd have to fantasize in the shower to get back into the mood.

She pressed the issue, making him more irritated.

"But what if next month is a month too late, a week too late, or even a day too late? Can't you set up a business trip to somewhere?"

"And leave you two in Tehran to face ... whatever? No."

Soraya still couldn't let it go.

"We have a full staff living here. Besides, those crazies wouldn't dare do anything to a woman and a child. And my brother is next door if I need protecting. Please head to Villefranche-sur-Mer. We'll join you as soon as we can. I'll call the staff tomorrow. They'll prepare for your arrival."

"Stop it. You don't know what you're talking about."

Mehdi sat up and swung his legs to the floor. He stared at the wall for a moment, thinking. Steam seeped out from beneath the bathroom door.

"I'm taking a shower. There will be no more serious discussions tonight."

He emerged fifteen minutes later wearing only a towel knotted at his waist. Taking the comb from her hand, he slid his hands inside her robe, slowly running them down her breasts. He admired her body in the mirror for a minute and then gently pulled the robe off of her shoulders. Untying his towel, he let it fall and climbed naked into bed.

"Now, *Soraya-joon.*"

She moved to the side of the bed with the top of her robe draped over its belt. Mehdi untied the knot, keeping the belt as the robe slid down her legs and onto the carpet. He took her by the hips, guiding her onto the mattress.

Mehdi wasn't in a hurry. He would build his wife's anticipation until she begged him to take her. Rolling on top of her, he supported his body above hers. As though on cue, her body tensed. He'd come to expect this momentary hesitation. He didn't know what it was or why it was, nor did he care. He liked the personal challenge. Once she relaxed, he could do anything and she would pleasure him.

He kissed a trail across her forehead. Inhaling her hair's fragrance, he nuzzled his face into her neck and began stroking her breasts with his fingertips, barely touching her skin until goose bumps arose. Moving down her body, he lingered on her stomach, making small circles. She was close to the precious moment of surrender. When he heard a small catch in her breath he knew he'd won. Soraya's body relaxed. She opened her eyes.

"Please, Mehdi," she begged, pulling him close.

He stretched her arms above her head, softly tying her wrists together with the belt. Her submission was deeply intoxicating. It reconfirmed his power over her and the tinge of sadism heightened his arousal. Mehdi was in full control, confident in his prowess. Her heavy breathing turned to moans, so he took her, marking her as his own.

Chapter 8

Black Friday: Zhaleh Square

September 8, 1978

BASHU BANAI had never felt so invigorated. He stood shoulder to shoulder with the men assembled in front of the Melli Bank, shading his eyes against autumn's sunlight to assess the sea of protestors below. Thousands had gathered over the last few days in defiance of the Shah. There were workers, ulama, Marxists, Communists, *bazaaris* and university students, all united in one cause: The overthrow of the monarchy and the establishment of a democratic Islamic Republic.

History was being made, and Banai was exhilarated to be part of it. Everywhere he looked, humanity had crammed into the downtown. Without an open patch of sidewalk it was disorienting and difficult to find familiar landmarks, now swallowed up by the masses.

But Banai was confident that this display of power would prove that the citizens of Iran were taking back their country. He and his fellow merchants had consulted with the local mullahs for more than a year, debating various strategies. Together, they carefully disseminated all the information to their customers and organized strikes.

Like many, Banai believed the Shah wanted to crush the *bazaari* class because it wasn't required to pay taxes, but not even the arrests and brutal torture inflicted on them by SAVAK had quieted the dissension. They were the people of Allah, The Giver of Honor. Banai's heart swelled over the bravery of God's people.

A sit-down protest was planned today in South Tehran's Zhaleh Square, located a few blocks away from where he now was watching banners being unfurled, some written in English for the benefit of the BBC and American network crews, and reading:

"Death to the Shah and the Imperialists."

"God is great!"

"Khomeini is our leader."

"Bring back Ayatollah Khomeini!"

Let the Americans sit up and take note, Banai thought. Iranians are not your puppets. He longed to march in the very front line to Zhaleh Square. Let the whole world see him to be a righteous man.

A group of fellow merchants huddled below him were organizing just such a line. Banai shoved his way down the steps and through the bodies to join his compatriots. Tightly linking arms, they walked, united as warriors, like an ancient Sumerian phalanx, taking boldness for shields. Falling in behind them came the rest, between five and twenty thousand of them, according to varying accounts, but each of them gripped by a fervor manifesting in violence. An agitated group of young men set a trash bin on fire. Cars were overturned and torched. Bats and clubs materialized from thin air and the sound of breaking glass played counterpoint to shouts of "Death to the Shah," "Death to Israel," and "Death to America." Gasoline spilled onto the streets. Automatic rifles, pistols, homemade bombs and tear gas canisters appeared. Shots were fired into the air. Any sense of peaceful dissension evaporated.

The mob's fury was fueled by its very size. The hair on the back of Banai's neck stood on end with its electricity. A monstrous amount of power was surging from behind. He could feel heat leaping closer row-by-row, creating an ever-growing feeling of invincibility among the marchers, as though their safety was secured by virtue of their numbers. The palpable force hit Banai and his fellow *bazaari* like flames licking at the back of their shirts, propelling them forward until they, too caught fire. Banai had never experienced this level of adrenaline. It made him euphoric.

Captain Manu Nassiri, dressed in full riot gear, was waiting for the leading edge of the insurgents to turn the corner towards Zhaleh Square. After fifteen years in the army, he was as experienced at handling protests and crowd control as he was at formal war. He was uncertain how many protestors there were today, but he was sickened by the hunch that the number was astronomical.

He and the other soldiers had heard shouts of "Death to the Shah" coming closer for more than twenty minutes now. How many people were there, to create such noise? It even drowned out the thwapping blades of the helicopters that hovered overhead.

The shouts of "Death to Imperialism!" were becoming deafening and the ground shook. Manu fought off a rare attack of nerves. These people were fanatical. It would be impossible to contain them. So then what?

When the front line of protestors turned the corner to Zhaleh Square they discovered that between them and their goal stood hundreds of the Shah's troops, poised in formation, weapons at the ready. A momentary wave of uncertainty fell over the mob, and the front line hesitated mid-step, but it was too late to change their minds, because the thousands who followed behind forced them forward, ever closer to inevitable disaster.

The Imperial Guard's intelligence unit had informed the

army that the mob was riddled with professional agitators, trained and planted into the crowd by Yassar Arafat's Palestine Liberation Organization. If true, it profoundly altered the psychological makeup of this confrontation. Manu was concerned.

He studied the army troops standing directly in the path of the oncoming dissidents. Oh man, he thought glumly, some of these guys are really young. They fidgeted nervously with their weapons. He realized these sacrificial lambs were raw recruits and his heart sank. Of all days, these were the soldiers assigned to defuse a volatile, game-changing situation.

Captain Nassiri wondered if half of the protestors even knew about last night's declaration of martial law. Probably not. Many of them had been hanging out on the streets for the last several days.

Specifically included in the Shah's edict were orders for the army to disperse illegal crowds via nonlethal means. Manu hoped to hell these baby soldiers had brought their balls with them. He'd faced down many a mob and knew the nerves of steel it took to stay cool.

"Although," he muttered to himself, "it looks like we might as well just hit ourselves with bricks and save these protestors the effort of throwing them."

He adjusted his helmet, rechecked his weapon, and

quickly assessed the approaching mob, trying to spot armed agitators, and hoping to anticipate some of the trouble.

A general from the Shah's Imperial Guard, one of the Immortals, stood up on the seat of a military Jeep. Lifting a bullhorn, he addressed the angry crowd.

"By order of the government, you will disperse! Martial law has been put into effect. It is unlawful to congregate!"

He was drowned out by the cries of "Death to the Shah!" The protestors began to inch forward again, cautiously, but steadily.

The truck moved into the middle of the thoroughfare to block their path. From this new vantage point, the general tried again.

"Go back home! This gathering is unlawful. Martial law is in effect."

The mass of humanity continued to advance.

An officer barked an order and the front row of soldiers knelt down in the street, aiming their guns directly into the mob. Less than thirty feet separated the opposing sides.

The protestors, who now were looking down the barrels of automatic weapons, momentarily paused. Some raised their hands above their heads to show they were unarmed. The general saw a glimmer of hope. He lowered his tone in one final attempt.

"You will respect the requirements of martial law and

disperse immediately."

In the silence that followed, Manu heard an ominous sound in his head. They'd stepped on an invisible landmine. He'd heard an inaudible click. The next moment was armed. Any movement and history would change. Oh man, Manu thought. Flinch and the world as we know it will blow up.

Bashu Banai was staring at the rows of weapons pointed in his direction, his jaw slack with shock. Helicopters whirred overhead like circling buzzards. He was trapped. The army in front of him threatened and a tightly packed mob trailing for more than a mile behind him pushed him forward. Escape was impossible. The exhilaration that had buoyed him vanished, replaced by the dread of violence.

In the distance came a low, rumbling sound. It came closer, growing louder. Finally, an army tank lumbered into view, a soulless killing machine that symbolized the Shah's ruthlessness. The sight of it enraged the crowd.

Bashu Banai could hear the Ayatollah Khomeini's exhortations of martyrdom's glory playing in his head. Resolute fury rose in his chest. He knew that his fellow demonstrators felt it too. Their hearts beat as one, their minds thought as one and their voices roared together in one defiant voice: "Death to the Shah!"

A bottle bomb flew through the air toward the soldiers, but landed on a patch of soft grass and failed to ignite.

A shot rang out. Captain Nassiri thought it came from inside the mob, but he couldn't tell and it didn't matter. His military instincts kicked in. He ascertained the apex of the lunging crowd and began firing. Some of the demonstrators were firing back. A soldier to his left fell into him. Manu pushed the body out of the way. The sound of whizzing bullets was buried inside the relentless screams of the terrified, the injured and the dying. A horrific scene was playing out in front of him. Manu just wanted it to be over.

Overhead, helicopters chased fleeing protestors like hunters chasing prey. Banai spun around in a panic, looking to run away and not caring in which direction. He wanted to live. A *bazaari* next to him dropped silently to the ground. People on all sides of him were being hit as volleys spun from out the soldiers' weapons.

Their fallen bodies suddenly appeared to him like stepping-stones, a convenient but grisly escape route for Banai. He leaped from body to body without any guilt, struggling to stay above the blood that was now flowing onto the street. He'd be trampled to death if he fell. People were pushing and shoving to get away. He pushed and shoved harder. Let them be the ones to fall, he thought.

A hot poker slammed into his leg. Banai stumbled, but his momentum and adrenaline kept him moving until for some unknown reason, the leg simply stopped working. He stopped in his tracks, puzzled. Time blurred and he was confused. His mind was dissolving into a shapeless cloud.

He looked down at his left leg. A large chunk of flesh was missing just above the knee to halfway up his thigh and his foot dangled at an odd angle. He examined the wound with utter detachment. A grotesquely splintered bone jutted outward from his knee. It looked like a clothes-hook, strong enough to hang his heavy jacket on, he mused, intently watching the blood pour down his shin, then circle around his calf and slide into the widening pool at his feet. How curious, he thought numbly. An encompassing wave of fog obscured his vision. The street twisted violently. He was losing consciousness, yet he remained eerily focused. Banai's resolve stayed intact. He craved martyrdom, glorious martyrdom. He'd die in the name of Allah for his country and furthermore, he would die bravely, facing his enemy, not running away, like an infidel. Banai struggled to stand up on his one good leg. Wiping the sweat from his eyes so he could see, he turned to face the troops. He threw open his arms, welcoming the death he now desired more than life.

Bashu Banai lifted his face to the sky.

"Allahu akbar!" he shouted jubilantly. "God is great!"

Chapter 9

Exposed

SORAYA refolded the cream-colored linen shirt and laid it carefully on top of the other clothes in Mehdi's suitcase. She noticed that she'd folded it poorly yet again. Annoyed, she yanked it out for a third attempt. If her hands would just stop trembling, she could do an expert job of packing for her husband, something she preferred to do herself because no one on the staff could perform it as well as she. However, she no longer felt the calm she'd had when she urged him to leave town a few nights ago; not after the horrific massacre at Zhaleh Square on Black Friday, certainly not after hundreds, maybe thousands lay dead, depending on who you believed.

In reality, an accurate body count was irrelevant, because the violence had already imprinted indelible images on the world stage of the Shah's forces gunning down his citizens. No one cared a whit about his insistence that he hadn't ordered the violence. The world was aghast.

Calls for Reza Mohammad Shah Pahlavi to step down were echoing from the halls of Congress in Washington to London's House of Parliament. The Pahlavi Dynasty was collapsing like a house built of toothpicks. The Shah's fortunes had turned down a dead end street.

Mehdi had to leave Iran right now, of that Soraya was certain. To begin with, it had become too dangerous for any member of the Bahá'í faith to stay. Should Mehdi's secret be discovered in this current political climate, it would be a death sentence. The two of them had kept kept his religion a secret for years, just in case, which was why none of the Sultan's employees knew. It'd been a smart thing to do.

To a devout Muslim, Mehdi was a heretic and a political subversive because he followed a prophet born after Mohammad. Báb and Bahá'u'lláh just had to come along, thought Soraya. They just had to proclaim themselves God's messengers, and Mehdi's grandfather just had to introduce the religion to him. Even Soraya, who was only nominally Muslim, found her husband's religion strange, especially the way it left interpretation of scriptures up to each individual. That created a religious free-for-all, to her way of thinking.

At the same time, the idea of living in these frightening times without Mehdi made her weepy. She had never lived without the support of a man. Mehdi was convinced their phone lines already were tapped, so if he left now, how would they discuss important matters? The Sultan and the Cyrus families were too wealthy to escape attention from the revolutionaries. Without Mehdi, who would help her make crucial decisions? What if the city burned down around them? Nothing in her background had prepared her for this. This was not the way her life was supposed to be, and frankly, she resented the turn of events.

Luckily, feeling the resentment steadied her hands and she deftly creased the shirt into obeisance. It would barely wrinkle in the suitcase now. She placed it on top of a pair of slacks and admired her orderly packing.

If only she could pack her life as beautifully as she packed suitcases, perhaps her life wouldn't wrinkle too badly either, no matter where the journey led. And maybe at the end of this turmoil, her life could be unpacked again.

Mehdi's arms slipped around her waist. He pressed his body into hers, and whispered in her ear.

"It won't be a long separation. Either the situation here will calm down so I can come home or I'll fly you and Darius out to stay with me like it's a vacation. I hope you understand that if we all leave together, it will be obvious that we're fleeing the country and the militants will wonder what anti-revolutionary actions we have to hide."

She nodded.

"That's my sweet girl. In the meantime, I'll have people checking on your safety. You might not notice they're there, but they will keep me informed."

Soraya turned and buried her face in his chest. Her anxiety poured out in tears.

"What if the revolutionaries come to burn down the compound? What am I supposed to do?"

"Don't worry. I've talked to each member of the staff without tipping my hand. They will take good care of you, I promise. Now, you can't let them see you cry because they could suspect something is different about this trip. And if you fall apart, you'll lose authority in their eyes. Pretend you're Empress Farah, trained to stay calm in any situation."

He removed one of his monogrammed handkerchiefs from the suitcase and dabbed at her wet streaks of mascara.

"Go touch up your makeup. I'm almost finished packing my valise. When you're ready, we'll go down to the car together, like this is just another business trip."

Soraya set her jaw and sat down at the vanity to repair her face. She swiped fresh mascara over her wet lashes and covered her red nose with foundation.

Mehdi pulled out a weathered, leather-bound and untitled book from the nightstand drawer. "My 'Qur'an'," he said. "If necessary, I can flash it around a bit at the airport and look like a good Muslim."

"Darling, what are you doing? Have you lost your mind? That's dangerous. If someone notices that inside the cover are Bahá'í scriptures, they'll arrest you. Let me borrow a real Qur'an from Fatima."

"No," said Mehdi. "I don't want the Qur'an. This copy of 'Prayers and Meditations' belonged to my grandfather and it stays with me in case I can't come back. Plus I won't endanger you by leaving it behind. It's safer to take it."

He tucked the book in a side pocket of his carry-on.

"You're pigheaded. What if an authority should decide to examine your bags?"

"If they do, I'll remove the book from my valise and hold it reverently while they search the bag. They've no reason to open up the book to check it."

Soraya was upset enough to attack.

"I truly don't understand why you cling to your odd little religion," she said.

While she tolerated this side of her husband, his devotion to it confounded her.

"I'm devoted because I admired my grandfather and because my faith in God gives me strength."

"These days it would be safer to find strength in Allah," Soraya retorted.

"*Soraya-Joon*, Bahá'u'lláh teaches respect of all religions.

If only you Muslims would accept us, we could all work together toward universal peace."

Soraya shot him "the look."

"Me, a Muslim? I'm not even convinced there is an Allah. I'm not like you, Mehdi."

"Perhaps growing up in a secular Muslim household has framed your obstinacy. Be a Muslim if you wish, or a Christian, a Zoroastrian, or a Jew. I don't care which one you choose if it makes you happy and you find peace."

"I'll find a modicum of peace when you're safely out of the country."

Darius bounded into the room.

"Papa, I hope you're already thinking about what to buy for me on this trip, but it'll be hard to come up with a present better than my Bee Gees poster."

Mehdi picked up his son and tossed him on the bed.

"Don't tell anyone how badly we've spoiled you."

Darius was giggling too hard to put up much of a defense. Mehdi gave him a warm hug and let him up.

"It's time to go."

Nassiri held the passenger door of the limo. Mehdi gave Soraya a long, remember-me kind of kiss. Then he picked up Darius for a peck on the cheek and climbed into the car. Rolling down the window he beckoned to his son.

"Darius, you're old enough for me to make you the man

of the house while I'm away. Nanny will take good care of you, and you have to take good care of your mother. I'll see you soon."

Darius proudly accepted his new responsibility. "I will, Papa, I promise. Don't you worry about anything."

Nassiri closed the trunk and sat behind the wheel.

"Are you ready, sir?"

Mehdi rolled up the window. "No, not really, Ali, but let's head to the airport anyway. Do you think I should just rent a room there? It seems we're always coming from or going to that infernal place."

He fell quiet as the limo pulled away from the house. Once they were on the road he spoke.

"Now that we're alone, tell me, what does Manu say about the massacre at Zhaleh Square?"

Nassiri sighed. "He hasn't talked about it much yet. Of course, what can you say? It's an ugly situation. The masses are even more mobilized against the Shah, if that's possible, and they're drunker and angrier than ever. Guns are going off across the city."

"I heard on the news there may be more than six million protestors out on the streets today. What dreadful thing comes next, does Manu think?"

"Something nasty, for sure," replied Nassiri. "He says there are rooms full of dead bodies from Black Friday's massacre, row after row of them wrapped and neatly laid out, waiting for family members to identify them. He also says that a number of soldiers and police were also killed, even though the news isn't reporting it."

"What started it all?" asked Mehdi.

"Manu couldn't say for sure how the shooting started, but he said all hell broke loose and he's never seen anything like it. He's shaken up, which is very unlike him. Manu's always been the tough guy, but this time it's different. I'll sit down with him over a good meal so we can talk things through. I think he's upset that he was forced to shoot his own countrymen."

"Remind him he didn't have a choice. It was a lose-lose situation. There won't be any negotiating with the insurgents now. There are too many martyrs and the Shah's influence is waning too quickly. The Yanks and the Brits will likely pull away for good, I think. The very knots of our Persian rug are unraveling, Ali."

"I fear you're right. How long do you expect to be gone, sir? Is this another major business trip?"

"I hope not, but possibly. I'm concerned about leaving Soraya alone right now. You will stay aware of her security as we discussed?" asked Mehdi. "If the worst happens while I'm gone, I'm not sure she can handle it. She's never had to take care of herself, you know. She doesn't know how."

"Of course, sir."

Ali swore under his breath as they pulled into the airport. "Look, Mr. Sultan."

The airport was awash with frantic travelers, many of them foreign nationals who were terrified of waking up tomorrow on the wrong side of a revolution. It seemed half of Tehran was trying to flee. Diplomats, businessmen, journalists, and anyone with ties to the West realized this was an excellent time to leave.

Nassiri deftly wove through cars to park curbside. Horns blared as he cut off vehicles to secure a prime spot in front of the terminal.

"I think this is the best I can do, sir," he said. "Are you sure I can't park and see you to the gate?"

"Right here is fine, Ali. I can only imagine what it's like inside. I'm eternally glad I only fly first class."

"As you wish. I'll place your luggage on the curb for the porter. I'd suggest you stay in the car while I pull out the bags. There's pushing and shoving going on near the terminal entrance. Tempers are short. Too many people are trying to leave the country at once."

Mehdi surveyed the crowd from the back seat, stroking his moustache and thinking.

Nassiri circled around to the trunk. He'd noticed that today's luggage was heavier than normal, which was why he'd surmised this would be a long business trip. He yanked hard on the heaviest bag so it cleared the trunk's lip, and in the process, inadvertently knocked over Mehdi's valise, springing open its latch. Mehdi's personal items tumbled out into the trunk. Chagrined at his clumsiness, Ali quickly replaced the thick notebook, a pen case and some toiletries. Lastly, he picked up a worn Qur'an, intending to set it carefully on top. Its leather was soft and beautifully smooth from use. This had to be a family heirloom. Curious, Ali opened the book to find the publishing date, except that the inside of the book looked nothing like a Qur'an. Startled, Ali flipped through some pages. It became clear that these were not the words of Mohammad. He struggled to understand what he was reading.

When he saw the name "Bahá'u'lláh," he knew. This was not a Qur'an at all, and obviously Mehdi was not a Muslim. The book was a ruse. He was a Bahá'í, a member of a most disgusting faith. Ali realized that his employer was an infidel, a heretic who worshipped a false prophet. Better for him if he were a Christian.

Nassiri's eyes widened as all the pieces came together. Of course Mehdi was going on a "business trip." If the Shah fell and hardline mullahs took over the government, Mehdi's family, his property, and his life were in danger. Mehdi wouldn't be returning to Iran any time soon. Now he understood the depth of Mehdi's concern over his wife and son. The man didn't know when or if he could return to Iran. Well, thought Nassiri, if he wants to live, he won't try.

He tried to sympathize with Mehdi's situation, but couldn't, nor could he understand the man's arrogance, gambling with his family's safety by carrying this book. Somehow, his otherwise bright employer didn't grasp the scope and implications of his apostasy.

Ali jumped. The limo door was opening. He snapped shut the latch after burying the book so it wouldn't fall out again. As much as the Bahá'í cult offended Allah, he didn't care to personally get Mehdi in trouble.

"Is everything okay?" asked Mehdi.

"Yes, sir," he answered. "You are ready to go."

Mehdi waited on the curb while Nassiri neatly lined up the suitcases on the sidewalk, calling over a porter and handing Mehdi the valise. Mehdi smiled, reaching out to shake his hand.

"Thank you as always, Ali," he said.

Ali hesitated ever so slightly before clasping his palm. Mehdi caught the tentativeness and noted the averted eyes.

"Is everything all right? You seem preoccupied."

Nassiri recovered his professional posture. After all, he reminded himself, this was a stable job and Mehdi had always been fair to him and his family.

"Yes sir, everything is fine. I promise that the staff and I will take good care of your household while you're gone. Safe travels to France and don't worry. And please say hello to the Riviera for me. The French know how to eat – and even better, how to sunbathe."

"Thank you. I promise to return home soon."

Mehdi followed behind the porter into the terminal, letting the luggage cart wedge a path through the hordes of people clamoring to buy tickets.

There was an unusual sense of urgency blowing through the concourse. Mehdi had never witnessed such chaos at the airport. A man desperate to catch his flight nearly knocked him over as he went running by.

If the Shah does fall from power, Mehdi thought, getting out of Iran would become a hellish nightmare.

He looked around for a pay phone. He wanted to tell Soraya he loved her one more time.

Chapter 10

Manu

November 4, 1978

TEENAGERS flooded the street leading up to the University of Tehran. High school girls coquetted their way down the wide avenue, arms linked in carefree camaraderie, their shrill giggles drawing the scrutiny of the boys who walked closely behind them, joking and meticulously evaluating each girl's assets.

Ahead of teens loomed the main entrance to the University, impressive even from two blocks away. The teens were delirious with power. Only an hour ago they'd forced their high school to close early, freeing them to join today's demonstration on the college campus. The air around them snapped with electricity, showering sparks of enthusiasm on the approaching novices.

The university was a petri dish for revolutionary dissent. Most of the college professors teaching there adhered either to Communism or radical Islam, and their students were too unsophisticated to discern any discrepancies in the political alloy. Idealism held its universally potent appeal to this age group. The appeal rolled smoothly from professor to the graduate student; to the undergraduate and finally, to the high school student, gathering momentum as it flowed downstream.

Already, the campus was bulging with thousands of assembled students waving large posters of Ayatollah Khomeini, while others unfurled banners condemning Shah Pahlavi, the white fabric billowing and heaving above the crowd like sails in the wind.

Demonstrating nearly constituted an occupation in Tehran these days, but then, there wasn't much else to do. Except for the foreigners who still went daily to their jobs, the ancient city lay moribund from strikes.

Dissidents had devised a quick and efficient way to disseminate information. Upcoming demonstrations were announced on Tehran radio. Local mosques then passed along the information to the faithful, who further pumped the word throughout the capillaries of their particular neighborhood. It had taken less than twelve hours to organize these students for today's protest.

Hardcore, experienced revolutionaries in the crowd wore cloth bags on their heads with raggedy, snipped holes for their eyes. They patrolled campus perimeters with semi-automatic weapons. One stopped to pull a Sharpie from his pocket. He wrote on a wall: "Kings are the disgrace of history. You are the most disgraceful king. Death to Imperialism."

In the center of the university's quad, a pretty coed slipped a cassette into a boom box. Its power cable snaked up and around a gnarled tree trunk, winding upwards as high as a ladder could take it, where it was connected to a speaker hanging from a tree limb.

A professor plugged the other end of the cord into the boom box, causing an ear-splitting pop. It hushed the masses, if only for a moment.

Then the low, gravelly, recorded voice of the Ayatollah Ruholla Khomeini rumbled end over end across the quad. His flat intonations clung low to the ground, weaving his message between and around the rapt listeners. He exhorted his acolytes to unite against the secular, satanic values of Imperialistic America. He repeatedly condemned Shah Pahlavi as America's lap dog, urging Iranians to sacrifice their blood in overthrowing his government. Then, he promised, he would bring an Islamic Republic back to Iran and purge the country of its insidious Western evils.

Since being forced out of Iraq, the ayatollah had resided in a flat near Paris, a place that served him like a new mistress. The City of Lights fawned over him. He deftly pulled the strings of the insurgency from France, sending his recorded speeches to Iran on Air France flights.

Shah Pahlavi most likely regretted exiling the Ayatollah fourteen years earlier, on this very day. The exile had only further glorified the ayatollah to his followers, and today they swayed rhythmically to the cadence of their leader's words. Fervor squeezed against their hearts until they released its unbearable tension by chanting the endless mantras of "Death to the Shah!" "Death to Israel!" and "Death to America!" while churning the air with their fists.

Just outside the university's entrance, the high school students who were within earshot of the commotion slowed their pace, overwhelmed by the righteous fury they heard roiling inside. Still, it called to them, luring them into an intoxicating vortex, even though its power was frightening.

An intoxicating current washed over them. They hurried inside, drunk with the spirit of revolution.

"Captain Nassiri, sir?"

The First Lieutenant saluted his superior.

Manu looked up, annoyed, from behind his desk in the *ad hoc* field headquarters set up in what once had been a Bank of Tehran.

"Yes, what is it, soldier?"

"The men are restless. Have we received our orders?"

"Not yet, but I'll make sure you're the first to know when we do." Manu was astounded to see that his sarcasm had eluded the young officer.

"Thank you, sir." The young man looked relieved. "I appreciate that." He turned to leave.

Captain Nassiri jerked him to a stop with his voice. Apparently the soldier needed things spelled out, so he spat out the syllables.

"Lieutenant."

"Yes, sir."

"Go take a shower."

"Sir?"

"You reek of fear. I can smell it, as can your men."

"Yes, sir. Oh. Of course." Shame spread across his reddening face. "I understand. Yes, sir."

The young man wandered away, dazed with humiliation.

The captain knew that morale was low. His troops were sickened with the malaise that infects soldiers fighting for a lost cause. Their resolve was weakened. They were being stalked by an imminent revolution, and they lived under the ominous cloud that in the near future, they would probably discover they wore the wrong uniform. Still, Iran's military was mostly remaining loyal to the Pahlavi Dynasty's rule. Captain Nassiri doubted the Shah could hold onto power unless the United States and Britain lent overt support, which they appeared disinclined to do, meaning the Shah didn't have much time left. The captain avoided pondering what would happen when the monarchy fell.

Troops were staged a quarter mile south of the university. Sharpshooters positioned on rooftops around the school's perimeter were monitoring the situation. So far all the reports were unanimous: The simmering pot was about to boil over.

His desk phone rang. Captain Nassiri listened to his superior with a grim look on his face. "Yes, sir," he said and hung up. He exhaled sharply and leaned back in his chair. They'd received their orders to move.

A sniper's voice crackled over the walkie-talkie.

"Captain, the demonstrators are pulling down the statue of Shah Pahlavi with ropes and chains. The situation has deteriorated. I repeat: The situation is rapidly deteriorating. Movement toward the streets is imminent. Recommend immediate counter response."

The walkie-talkie fell silent. Captain Nassiri pictured the ropes and chains wrapped around the statue's neck, envisioning the students' hatred-fueled strength yanking the bronze image off its pedestal. Could Shah Pahlavi feel his power being yanked off of its pedestal? Was he choking inside the noose of fanatics who were bent on squeezing the last drop of life from his reign?

Shah Pahlavi's Marble Palace was crumbling around him. His subjects neither respected nor feared him. It was over. Nassiri pushed back from the desk and stood. He was a soldier. He had his orders.

The men mobilized in minutes, nerves quickening their preparations. The fleet of army trucks rolled up in front the University of Tehran's gates just as the tip of the mob bulged onto the main avenue. Orders were to contain them inside university grounds. Soldiers stood eyeball to eyeball with the demonstrators, fellow Persians looking distrustfully at one another. Captain Nassiri wasn't surprised to see some of his men break rank and desert, evaporating into the crowd. Movement stirred from within the protestors. The students were hot with anger. With their blood boiling, they hurtled towards the soldiers. A brick flew from inside the crowd toward the troops. Nassiri knew that orders were superfluous. The soldiers were shooting to kill.

Later that night, Soraya hid in the den, sitting erect and still while watching the evening news. Tears welled in her eyes. This evening's lead story featured the footage of Tehran University students lying dead in the street. She gasped at the gruesome close-up of a pretty coed. Blackened blood had pooled on her blouse. Her eyes gaped at the sky and her hijab was askew. Soraya wanted to straighten the scarf, an irrational impulse, she knew, but she couldn't bear to see this lovely young woman looking disheveled in death.

Encircling her, the young woman's friends' screamed their requiem in anguish. Soraya knew that his girl would have hated her for being wealthy and for supporting of the Shah; still, she felt a deep empathy for her, one beauty to another. Although she tried to avert her eyes, they stayed locked to the repulsively hypnotic footage. Soraya failed to notice when Fatima entered the room. The nanny had heard about the dreadful violence and knew Soraya would need some company. She'd brought a tray of sliced Persian cucumbers topped with feta cheese and walnuts. Comfort food to share.

Setting the tray on the coffee table, she drooped onto the arm of the sofa, watching the news coverage until a commercial break.

"I thought you might be hungry. Dinner isn't ready."

Soraya jumped.

"I can't eat. The soldiers look like monsters."

The women sat in shock, staring blankly at a local used car lot advertisement. Soraya walked over to the television and turned down the sound on a Coca Cola commercial.

Real life was too tragic for banality. She gathered herself and addressed the universe.

"President Carter has no choice. I'm certain he's in contact with the Shah. They're good friends. He won't allow our Shah to fall from power."

Fatima didn't answer. Instead, reality spoke for her inside the silence, but Soraya refused to hear it.

More bloody pictures flickered noiselessly on the screen. Soraya turned to Fatima. Fatima pretended to be transfixed by the cucumbers on the tray.

Soraya flailed against the obvious. "Because there's no other way. If they don't throw their weight behind him right now, the Shah's government will be overthrown."

To that, Fatima could respond. "Yes, the Shah will be overthrown without immediate outside support."

Hope broke into a thousand little pieces. Clarity had mauled its way into Soraya's mind and shoved her face-first into the muck. Snapping off the television, she went upstairs to bed. She sat propped up in bed most of the night, a distressed butterfly upon a mountain of pillows. She stared at the night-shrouded garden; wishing that Mehdi had never left. It wasn't until a bird sang the new day into existence that she could let everything go. She draped one arm over her eyes to block out the sunlight, and slept.

Chapter 11
Shah Pahlavi

Friday, January 16, 1979

IT WAS JUST PAST NOON, and trash swirled inside mini-cyclones as a cold wind blew across the tarmac at Tehran's International Airport, where passengers, pilots, stewardesses and airport workers left oily smudges on the terminal windows. They pressed their foreheads and fingers against the glass, vying for a glimpse of history.

Mohammad Reza Shah Pahlavi and his third wife, the Empress Farah Diba Pahlavi, moved slowly down the line of well-wishers, quietly thanking their staff and members of the Imperial Guard. The Empress looked strikingly regal in her midi-length, fawn-colored coat trimmed with rows of chestnut ermine pelts that curved around the neckline and met in a "V" at her waist. Her honey-colored hair was upswept and crowned by a fur-trimmed hat. Her black gloves matched her knee-high black boots.

The Shah was attired in a superbly tailored suit with a three-quarter-length heavy overcoat and striped tie. He walked a step or two ahead of his wife, looking unwell, but still meting out gentle encouragement to his supporters, and promising to return as soon as the people of Iran called him back. He was tired, he explained, and needed a vacation before resuming his reign.

An Imperial Guard, overcome with grief, fell prostrate at the Shah's feet. Kneeling down, the Shah lifted the soldier to his feet. The man kissed his king's hand. After that, the Shah fixed his gaze at the ground, shielding his emotions.

Mohammad Reza Shah Pahlavi had been certain for years that he understood his subjects better than they could ever understand themselves. He'd had several visions to which he held fast – visions from Allah telling him that he had been chosen to lead Iran. When his health improved, he promised himself, he would reign again.

The royal couple walked beneath a copy of the Holy Qu'ran. They turned back to kiss the scripture before boarding the plane with the rest of the family.

Spectators in the terminal squinted at the Boeing 707, hoping to make out Shah Pahlavi settling into the cockpit. Watching their monarch take the pilot's seat was poignant. How exceedingly rare to witness a king fly himself into exile. The Shah gave them a final, tired wave.

In his vulnerability, experiencing introspection on a new level, the Shah wondered what lay ahead in his future. The political tide had turned against him. The world was calling his regime a failure; his body was filling with cancer, and he was leaving his beloved country to a precarious fate. He had asked the Americans for help; he'd turned to the British for support, but instead, both countries were pressuring him to leave. He'd become a political orphan, a lonely man on whom the world had turned its back. Thank heaven for the welcoming arms of his friend, President Anwar El-Sadat and his wife, Jehan, awaiting them in Egypt.

Mohammed Reza adjusted the plane's instruments with his long, elegant fingers and flipped once more through the weather reports, sitting tall in his seat, gratefully engrossed in the task. An air traffic controller's voice came over his headset.

"Your Highness, you are cleared for taxiway three."

"Thank you."

The co-pilot glanced at the once mighty *Shahanshah*, the King of kings. Maybe the man was the megalomaniac his detractors claimed he was, but his goals, his aspirations for Iran had been visionary, and while over the last few years his dreams had suffered defeat, the man remained unbowed. Or perhaps he was simply blind. Perhaps he hadn't noticed the poor getting poorer. Iranians had rejected and replaced his White Revolution with a bloody one, and yet his royal hands lay serenely on the armrest. He appeared innocently confident that the Peacock Throne would rise from the ashes like a golden phoenix. Unfortunately, it was a delusional dream, since now Great Britain and the United States were sending funds to bolster Khomeini instead.

The Shah had fallen from the tree of power, like a piece of overly ripe and rotting fruit. His shoulders imperceptibly slumped. If his emotions were surging, he was keeping them tamped down. Clearing his throat, he used a well-practiced voice of authority to alert the tower.

"Ready for take off. Thank you, Tehran."

By the time nighttime fell, the entire city vibrated. Many of Tehran's citizens were in a state of euphoria, while others were nervously making plans to leave.

Every light was on at the Sultan house, blazing out the windows into the street as though a party were going on, but inside the kitchen, relatives, staff and neighbors milled about aimlessly, distress etched on their faces, even as they debated their country's future.

Soraya stood motionless in the midst of the whirl. She was fixated on the headline of the Kayhan News: SHAH RAFT, The Shah has gone.

The headline filled the entire front page in a bold font so large it nearly screamed. It made her ears and her heart hurt.

Chef Alaleh, on the other hand, was ready to scream at the guests. A young couple engaging in a deep political discussion stood directly in front of the oven. She ordered them to step aside so she could take food from the oven. This crush of people invading her territory frustrated her. Poolak caught her attention and nodded encouragingly, but the chef just rolled her eyes. She was elbowing her way in-between loud arguments, trying to piece together snacks for the visitors, because whenever the world careened out of control, good food became even more important to Persians, and Alaleh was doing her best to produce copious amounts of it. She'd already instructed her *sous chefs* to carry the dishes to the dining room in an effort to relocate people from her kitchen, but it wasn't working. Once their plates were piled with food, people circled back like homing pigeons into the kitchen's "coop."

The chef grudgingly understood their neediness, even if she didn't like it. The kitchen was always the comfort room of a house, and so she'd infused many aromas of chopped herbs, freshly brewed coffee together with a variety of hot appetizers, serving unsuspecting guests the emotional sustenance they needed. At least that was the concept, she reminded herself, even though they were making her job nearly impossible. Poolak poured three cups of steaming Arabica, handing one of them to Soraya and one to Fatima.

"Come, sit, Mrs. Sultan, and take a breath. This is crazy," Poolak said, taking in the noisy kitchen.

Fatima offered, "May I kick everyone out? Please?"

"No. We need to be together. Whatever is coming next, better to face it together. I don't want to be alone tonight."

Only seven miles away, a very different crowd gathered in downtown Tehran, where a million people dampened city streets with their joyful tears: Shah Pahlavi was no more! They had successfully run the dictator out of the country like a criminal! They shook their fists in victory. They kissed each other. They danced. They sang. The man they reviled from the depths of their souls was gone. Now free from his oppression, they were convinced that democracy would flourish and the constitution would be reinstated. They rejoiced with the kind of conviction that exists briefly, and only, during the fragile, ephemeral moments between a successful coup and the reality that follows soon after.

SHAH RAFT.

The headline thrilled them. It was only two simple words and merely eight letters - SHAH RAFT - separately signifying little, but printed within tonight's context, a political statement of historic proportions celebrating an apocalyptic shift in the world's balance of power.

Jubilation billowed up the city's wide avenues and flowed down its narrow alleys. Newspapers fluttered on the street like autumn leaves. Militants, intoxicated by victory and alcohol, cried in relief, hugging and kissing before brandishing weapons and shouting praises to Allah. Tanks festooned with flowers sat in the middle of boulevards. Cars hurtled around corners, their occupants hanging out of the windows and waving pictures of the Ayatollah while others rode on the hoods of cars, celebrating while holding on for dear life.

The masses had overthrown their sworn enemy and they would now plunder the despot's political capital. Tonight the population was calling for the spoils of revolution, most of all, the return of their leader, Ayatollah Khomeini.

Soraya heard the phone ring above the din.

"I'll take it in the bedroom. I'm sure it's Mehdi." She hurried up the stairs. "Hello?"

His baritone voice poured balm on her heart. "Darling," he said, "Are you all right? The whole world is following the Shah's deposing."

"It's hard to imagine how things can get worse, Mehdi, but we're okay. Half the neighborhood is here. For better or for worse, we seem to be the headquarters for loyalists."

"Good, there's safety in numbers. Keep people around you. I'll tell Ali you may need him as a bodyguard. Darling, let's see if Bahktiar's government can hold on until the Shah returns. As long as you're safe, it would be best if we don't abandon the house because we're liable to lose it if you're not there. Are you too frightened to stay in Tehran?"

She was, but didn't want to sound weak.

"I'm fine, Mehdi. We have lots of people around to help." There wasn't much more to say. The issues facing them were too large to squeeze through telephone lines.

"Give Darius a hug from me. And please be careful. I miss you both."

Chapter 12

History Swerves

February 1, 1979

PANDEMONIUM. Five million delirious Iranians lined the roads from the airport all the way into the heart of Tehran, more than thirty miles of jubilant humanity waiting to welcome home the Ayatollah Ruhollah Khomeini from his fourteen years in exile.

Upturned faces searched the sky for a glimpse of the Air France jet that would pass overhead. This was the day they had longed for, and they wanted, no, they *needed* to witness it so they could reverence their beloved leader.

But for those who did not revere Khomeini, the city's vibrancy quickly was beginning already to suffocate beneath the heavy hand of Islamic fundamentalism. Overnight, no woman dared to appear in public without wearing a hijab head covering, or to appear in public unless accompanied by a male relative. Banks were empty, looters swept through supermarkets, emptying them of the little that remained, and gas stations dispensed fuel only to the revolutionaries.

In theory, Shapour Bakhtiar was running the country. Mohammad Reza Shah had appointed him Prime Minister of a constitutional government in late in 1978, as part of his desperate attempt to placate the opposition. Relying on the loyalty of the military, Bakhtiar struggled to keep the country in one piece. He had implemented some of the revolutionaries' demands: The freeing of political prisoners, dismantling of despised SAVAK, and promises of a review of all foreign relationships, but it came too late and his leadership proved to be eggshell-thin, riddled with fractures and smashed by the loud clamor for Ayatollah Khomeini's return. Three days after the Shah's flight, more than a million protestors demanded Bakhtiar's resignation.

Bakhtiar's hand-me-down power slipped through his fingers like raw egg whites, and his provisional government disintegrated in thirty-six days, creating a convenient political vacuum for the ayatollah.

So, at 9:30 a.m. on the day of Khomeini's return, a sea of "beards," or clerics, nearly one thousand of them, as well as members of the Royal Air Force, cheered when the Air France 747 jumbo jet carrying Khomeini taxied to the gate at Mehrabad International Airport.

They watched personnel and press descend the tall stairs. It took seven minutes before Khomeini emerged. If clerics noticed his frailty, no one remarked. He walked down the steps of the Air France jet on the arm of the pilot.

A blaze of cameras snapped, at once, capturing his

monotonously grim expression and his black eyes, orbs vacant of even a flicker of emotion; however, as soon as he reached the bottom of the stairs, Khomeini dropped to his knees and kissed Iranian soil.

Inside the terminal, clerics jostled each other in an effort to stand near the ayatollah, who calmly sequestered himself in the shadows, listening to the endless songs of welcome and recitations of prayers.

When he finally stepped forward to speak, his remarks were brutally clear. Khomeini long ago had mastered the art of reaching the common man, an artistry that forever eluded the Shah. Khomeini's words bludgeoned the hopes of the Western world, but they thrilled his airport audience.

"This is the first step in the final defeat of fifty years of criminal rule," he said. "We must cut off the hands of the foreigners who are responsible for our ills and cast out all the roots of the old regime ... I shall slap this government in the mouth. I shall determine the government with the backing of this nation, because this nation accepts me."

And the people of Iran, along with most people around the world, did accept and believe in him. They even believed him when he'd proclaimed himself a spiritual guide only and not a political leader. After all, he'd said as much to the Associated Press in Paris, on November 7, 1978:

"Personal desire, age, and my health do not allow me to

personally have a role in running the country after the fall of the current system."

Yes, the people believed that the promised democracy would make things right, just as they believed Khomeini's holiness would lift up the country and purify it of Western corruption.

The shrewd ayatollah had emerged from the sea of chaos as pure and as seductive as Botticelli's "Birth of Venus," and yet, within weeks, he would hold a death grip on every aspect of Iranian society.

Chapter 13

The Red Spring

February 16, 1979

IRAN'S SPRING FLOWERS bloomed in the red blood of Shah Pahlavi's supporters in 1979. It was said that more people died in the month following Khomeini's return than throughout the Shah's entire reign, but keeping accurate body counts amid the confusion of a major paradigm shift is difficult, while hiding atrocities committed during the birth of a revolution is easily achieved.

Anarchy-loving gangs called *Komitehs* enforced their own justice nearly at will, sometimes without the ayatollah's knowledge, yet certainly always with his blessing. The Revolutionary Guards arrested hundreds, thousands of people, until the jails were overflowing. Executions ensued regularly without any charges filed or trials held.

Ali had heard the stories. He couldn't be sure which were true and which weren't, but he believed the worst. He picked up the phone to dial his brother, lighting a cigarette to calm his wire-taut nerves. He'd just seen film of Iranian soldiers being executed. He feared for Manu.

Taking a deep drag on his cigarette, he unconsciously

tapped his foot on the floor until his brother answered.

"Hello?"

A rush of reassurance flowed through Ali. He exhaled smoke through his nose. His brother was fine.

"Manu, tell me what's going on. The truth. I already know about the university students overrunning the American Embassy. Praise Allah that they were forced to leave. I want to know about what we don't see on TV."

Manu's voice sounded as jagged as shards of glass.

"It's bad, Ali. I'm telling you. Oh man, every day they're killing ... and yesterday they ... I don't want to ... oh well, you'll see it in tomorrow's paper anyway."

"See what?"

"The Revolutionary Tribunal arrested Generals Rahimi, Naji, Khosradad and Nassiri and put them through a snap trial ... no defense, no deliberation ... nothing."

Ali coughed out his cigarette smoke.

"All four generals at once?"

"The court labeled them, 'corruptors on earth,' and then they tortured them and dragged them out into a schoolyard for execution, just like that."

"They shot them?"

"Yeah. Then they stripped the bodies, wrapped them in sheets, laid them next to each other and took photographs, like trophies. You'll see soon enough. So many people have died, Ali, so many people. Oh man. They torture mostly for sport and then they shoot some of them, and the others ...” He hesitated. “Have you been downtown yet?”

“No,” said Ali. “It didn’t seem like a smart place to go. Are businesses even open?”

“It’s not that. It’s that they’re hanging people, mostly soldiers and politicians, but regular people, too. They hang them from crane jibs, hoisting them up, so they dangle like rags twisting in the wind, with no dignity. I’ve looked at the poor bastards through binoculars. From the looks of their bodies they must have been begging to die at the end. The Revolutionary Guards are sadistic bastards.”

“What the hell are you doing, going down there? What if they recognize you and arrest you for being in the Shah’s army? Are you crazy?”

“Well, I’m not careless, if that’s what you mean. Stop being my big brother. I know a lot of these soldiers, especially the officers. I have to go. The least I can do is give them back some respect by remembering them as the men they were. I’m safe as long as I’m careful to blend in with the Morbidity Mongers who come to gawk. And there’s no particular reason for the Guards to come after me. I wasn’t in SAVAK or anything.”

“No, you were a captain with the same last name as our second cousin General Nassiri, the man they despise for heading up SAVAK, and whom you just told me they shot in a school yard. Besides, those thugs don't need a reason. Carrying a gun and having the power to arrest is sufficient."

"I'm fine. Stop worrying."

The line went quiet. Neither brother wanted to attack the other. Manu changed the subject.

"How is the family? My nephew, is he growing like a weed? Is Nema going to be taller than both of us?"

"Definitely taller than me and probably taller than you. He idolizes you, and he's rough-and-tumble just like you were. He'll get the girls. I'll bet you don't even remember how embarrassing it was for me in school to have a better-looking brother, who ran faster, kicked the ball farther, jumped higher and was funnier."

Manu laughed.

"You've waited all this time to tell me? Embarrassing? Really? I never thought about it. All I know is that you were the smart one and the girls went out with you."

Ali snorted.

"You're crazy. Were you wearing blinders out there during football matches? You didn't notice the girls cheering you on?" He imitated their high-pitched voices. 'Go, Manu, go!' They would've dated you in a second if you'd only asked. In fact, I think most of them only went out with me, hoping you'd show up and notice them."

"So then, how come you're married to a beautiful woman and I've never been married?"

"Because you have too much female inventory to choose from. A soldier's uniform impresses the ladies a lot more than a chauffeur's. Why don't you just pick one and settle down?"

Manu laughed. "Some day. The army takes up too much time. Don't you let Nema choose a military career."

"Well, hopefully Nema has the best of us both and is smart, good-looking and athletic. Then he can get a white-collar job and have his pick of the girls. Allah help us, may he become more than a chauffeur like me. Look where being smart got me. I drive rich peoples' cars."

The drapery in the Sultan mansion's master bedroom remained drawn at 2:30 that afternoon. Soraya was still in bed. The house was quiet. The neighborhood was quiet. In fact, all of Tehran was eerily quiet, except for random gunshots fired by drunken young men roaming the streets.

The world as Soraya had known it was no more. She lay there, paralyzed by depression.

Darius knocked on her door, as soft as mouse ears. "Mama, do you feel okay? May I bring you crackers?"

"No, sweetheart. Thank you. Now be a good boy and go play at Nema's house."

Fatima was close on his heels, smiling brightly.

"*Naz Nazy*, I'll walk over with you. Run to your room and pick out some toys to take over." She spoke quietly through the door. "Mrs. Sultan, I'll be right back. I've asked Alaleh to make you *Ashe Mast* (yogurt, chickpeas, lentils, brown rice) soup. Please try to eat it. It will make you feel better."

A faint "thank you" floated out from the bedroom.

The phone rang.

"Shall I answer that for you?" Fatima asked, pressing her ear against the door.

"No thank you." Soraya said. "I'll get it."

She hoped it was Mehdi.

"Hello darling, how are you?"

She knew by the tone of his voice that already he was speaking in code. For sure, the walls had ears these days.

"Hello, my love. You know, I've been thinking, with all the upheaval you and Darius need a vacation. Why not have Poolak make reservations for you to join me here in France?"

Soraya was confused. He'd said she shouldn't leave, to retain the house, and now she couldn't imagine leaving behind their whole lives and all their beautiful belongings.

"We miss you desperately," she said. "Are you thinking the French sun would do us all some good? I mean, a short vacation sounds wonderful, but we've discussed how one of us has to be here in Tehran to run the household and keep an eye on our property."

Mehdi cringed. She'd mentioned their property over the phone. He truly hoped no government agency was eavesdropping at the moment.

"Oh sweetheart, I'm only talking about a relaxing few weeks, at most a month or so, then we'll all fly home together and throw a big party for our friends."

Soraya twisted the phone cord around her finger. She knew what Mehdi was saying, and the argument was sound. Khomeini's religious edicts were oppressive in a society that had enjoyed a Western style of freedom for decades. She attempted to think positively. Surely the revolution would implode within a month or two. Iran's citizens wouldn't tolerate a regressive government forever. Before long, the Shah would be welcomed back with fanfare and then normal life would resume. Perhaps leaving during the dreary interim wasn't a bad idea. She'd convince Mehdi to come back to Iran when things changed. Her mood lightened.

"That sounds perfect, dear. I'll have Poolak make arrangements right now. We should be there in a few days. I'll go upstairs right now and begin selecting my wardrobe.

What's the weather like? Oh, never mind, I'll bring enough for whatever the forecast is. And I do have a full closet of clothes there. This is a wonderful idea, Mehdi. You always know how to make me happy. You are my hero, you know."

She could almost hear him beam.

"That's because I love you, darling. Call me once you have your plane reservations."

He couldn't find an encoded way to explain to her how unsafe it would be for them to return to Iran anytime soon. She'd simply have to understand.

But they'd waited too long to leave. Purchasing a ticket on any commercial flight was impossible to find because very remaining foreigner and royal supporter was frantically trying to escape Tehran. All the usual means of leaving Iran were completely booked with refugees.

"I tried, Mrs. Sultan. I'm sorry," said Poolak.

"It's all right, Poolak. I'll tell Mehdi. Hopefully, he can pull the right strings," she sighed.

Chapter 14

Flight

February 18, 1979

"DARIUS, I've asked you three times to please sit down," repeated Soraya, but her chiding was useless. He was too excited because she'd allowed him to sit in the front seat of the limo on the way to the airport. Soraya gave up trying to contain him and leaned back to stare at her reflection in the window.

A chador. She couldn't believe she was wearing the long, black cloak concealing her hair and body. Thank goodness Leyla, Nassiri's wife and a devout Muslim, had loaned her one of her extras. The Revolutionary Guard was enforcing modesty codes on women and few cared to explore the consequences of noncompliance.

Mehdi had called in numerous favors from his U.S. government contacts, securing Soraya and Darius seats on one of the emergency evacuation flights from Tehran's Airport. It would take them as far as Frankfort, Germany. Pan Am, the cooperating airline, had warned passengers to pack light because they were trying to ferry the largest number of people possible to safety.

Soraya had sewn money inside the lining of her coat sleeves. She knew very well the doors that money could open if necessary. She'd also sewn the emerald and diamond necklace and her grandmother's 100-year-old pearl ring inside the neck of her cowl sweater, heirlooms too precious to leave behind.

The Pan Am 747 rested on the tarmac as they pulled into the airport, but no one in the limo noticed; they were riveted by the swarming Revolutionary Guards, bees with guns for stingers, who were pulling people aside in front of the terminal, randomly demanding to see their papers, and searching their luggage.

Nassiri cleared his throat. His place was to encourage Soraya. She and Darius were doing the smart thing by getting out. Things weren't safe anymore for people of their social stature, especially when the husband was a Bahá'í. Parking the limo curbside directly in front of the Pan Am sign, he glanced at her in the rear view mirror. Her eyes were dull with fear.

"Mrs. Sultan, I see you have your papers out and ready to go. Your things are in order and I'm sure you won't have any problems. The staff and I look forward to your return. Please enjoy your vacation."

She nodded gratefully. "Thank you, Ali. You've been

such a help getting us here. Fatima and Poolak will keep you informed of our plans."

"I'm glad to hear it, Mrs. Sultan."

He would play along with the charade, despite his conviction that she had no intention of returning. If Mehdi wouldn't take the risk, why should she?

As Nassiri let Darius out of the car, he said, "Nema is going to miss you. Shall I tell him you'll call him?"

"Yes, do! And tell him I'll write to him, too. Ask him if there's something he wants me to bring back as a present when we come home. He's my best buddy."

"I know he feels the same, Darius."

Ali searched the chaotic activity on the sidewalk for curbside porters. There were none to be seen.

"Let me park the car in the garage and I'll carry your luggage to the check-in counter."

"That won't be necessary, Ali," said Soraya. "I'm sure a porter will appear any second now. We'll wait here."

Truthfully, Soraya needed time to gather her wits before entering the fray. Nassiri drove off.

Soraya and Darius stood where Nassiri had left them, stuck in the doldrums amid a roiling ocean of humanity, waiting for a porter. Soraya finally picked up her bag, staggering under its weight. Darius grabbed his and together they braced for the cyclone inside the terminal, which immediately assaulted them. Thousands of of panic-tinged voices were ricocheting off the walls.

Soraya paused to observe the interviewing of two young, shaggy-haired Australians who waited in the endless line to check their bags. The American television crew was questioning them about leaving Iran. The young men tried to sound casual but when the reporter asked where they were headed, their composure collapsed. The taller one stammered out the truth.

"We're open to going anywhere, really."

The desperation in his voice prompted Soraya to grip Darius' hand even harder.

"Don't wander a foot from me, please, please Darius. I'll never be able to find you. Promise me."

Darius was already glued to her by choice.

"I double promise, Mama."

The lone baggage-check line coiled and stretched forever, snaking imperceptibly forward. Darius fidgeted while Soraya checked and rechecked her Patek Philippe watch, fearful they'd miss their flight. Forty-five minutes later their bags were tagged and headed to the plane.

Soraya and Daruis started toward their concourse, but turning the corner, they nearly bumped into the end of another line, a Revolutionary Guard checkpoint, where the soldiers were intimidating each nervous traveler with the interminable scrutinizing of tickets and passports.

Soraya's nerves were frazzled to the unraveling. She couldn't take much more. Maybe they'd be better off finding a pay phone and calling Ali to take them home. Take deep breaths, she told herself.

By the time it was their turn, Soraya managed to flash a disarming smile at the soldier on the stool, even as her heart raced. He was stone-faced, studying her until her knees buckled. Before she could faint, she sank to the floor, giving Darius a long hug to disguise her distress, and didn't stand again until she regained her composure.

The guard examined their passports with pursed lips.

"Mrs. Sultan, where is your husband? Why are you traveling alone? You know that's not proper. Doesn't your husband know it's not safe?"

Soraya had prepared for this line of questioning.

"Oh, yes, sir, my husband is horrified that we have to travel alone, but he was on a business trip when he had a slight stroke. That's precisely why he's sent for us. He doesn't want us to be alone while he recuperates. Thank you, sir, for your kind concern. It makes me feel much safer."

The soldier's eyes narrowed. He tugged at his thick beard, thinking. It occurred to Soraya that he could tug on that beard forever without raising his I.Q. one point. He dragged a dirty finger across their passport photos. She could see he was wrestling with vague suspicions. When he picked up the stamp, her heart leapt for joy, but he let it hover over the passports for what seemed an eternity, until Soraya wanted to scream, "Stamp them, you idiot!"

The guard finally gave a reluctant shrug and stamped the pages, waving Soraya and Darius through, but he watched them walk away. Summoning another guard, he pointed them out before turning his attention to the next passenger.

Soraya thought the worst was over until they turned onto their gate's concourse. Ahead lay another knot of passengers. She reached into her purse for their passports, before realizing they were doing body searches at this checkpoint. Oh no, what about the money in her sleeve and the jewelry in her cowl? Think, Soraya, think, she reminded herself, imagining every possible scenario and various ways to thwart their efforts.

"You, over here."

A man with a gun was motioning to her. He then pointed the weapon at Darius.

"And you, over there."

They were being separated. Darius started crying. Soraya pleaded with the man.

"Please, my son is only seven years old ..." She shot Darius a quick look to stop him from correcting her math.

He looked young for his age and it might help.

"He's too young to understand what's happening. Please let him stand next to me."

What if they took him away from her?

The man frowned.

"If there are no problems, this won't take long. You are worried. Why?"

She couldn't risk suspicion. She smiled warmly and patted Darius on the head.

"It's alright, Darius. You can still see me, yes? The men are just making sure we don't have any weapons."

A heavy-set woman in a burqua stepped forward to search Soraya. As the woman reached to pat down the sleeves, Soraya quickly pulled them up above the elbows to show there was nothing inside them, coughing a bit to hide the rustle of the bills sewn inside the lining. The woman grunted and patted her down from the waist to the floor. As she straightened up to reach for her neckline, Soraya said, "Let me help you," and turned her back to unroll the cowl.

The woman squeezed the back of the collar and taking Soraya by the shoulders, turned her back around.

She's as sharp as an eraser, Soraya thought with relief.

Very sweetly, she pulled the front of the collar down before the woman could reach for it. Grunting again, the woman shrugged and nodded to the Revolutionary Guard.

They were free to board.

At the door of the aircraft waited a lovely, tall, blond stewardess. Like the rest of the crew, she'd volunteered to serve on this evacuation flight and she flashed a bright, toothy smile.

"My name is Becky," she said in English. "Welcome to Freedom Flight Five. As soon as our 747 aircraft is 'wheels up,' you'll be on American soil. Please take any open seat you can find. Children may sit in the aisles."

A woman in the front row translated the instructions into Persian for Soraya's benefit.

"Thank you," said Soraya to Becky.

Darius tugged at her sleeve. "Mama, look."

Soraya turned toward the cabin. It was stuffed with humanity. Everyone had something on their laps, from infants to duffel bags, from a black cat to a teacup poodle, even a canary in a tiny birdcage. Personal items were crammed into every possible space. The air smelled thick with deodorant and perfume.

Soraya searched for an open seat. Inching sideways down the aisle, they stepped over people and their possessions.

"Excuse me. Oh, I'm so sorry."

They finally found a middle seat near the back. The man already on the aisle seat switched so Darius could sit on the armrest, next to his mother.

"Mama, I think we're the only Persians on the whole airplane. Everybody else is speaking English."

"That makes sense. Your papa told me that this plane was carrying a number of American government workers and business people." She slipped out of the chador and shook her hair free. "What did the stewardess call this flight, something about Freedom?"

"She said it's Freedom Flight Five and that we'll be in America as soon as we're in the air."

"Well, my hair is free already. I hate this thing."

She stuffed the chador into the seat pocket.

Darius laughed. "We're little birds flying on a big bird. We're free, free as the birds!"

Passengers who understood Persian smiled and nodded. One crossed his fingers and laughed. "Yes, now let's just get out of here. We want those wheels up!"

Becky switched on the intercom.

"Ladies and gentlemen, we'd like to welcome you on board our aircraft. We'll push back and be on our way shortly. Those who have seats, please buckle your seat belts. On behalf of the crew, let me say we are proud to serve you today on Pan Am's Freedom Flight Five to Frankfort, Germany."

Cheers swelled. But as the excitement died down, angry

voices and heavy footsteps could be heard coming down the ramp. Someone banged on the plane's door, demanding that the crew open it up. The co-pilot yelled back in Persian that the doors had already been armed. The men responded by slamming their weapons against the door, warning that bullets would come next.

The pilot signaled to Becky to disarm and open the doors. Revolutionary Guards pushed past her, brandishing their guns. The passengers screamed.

"Be quiet!" one guard shouted in English.

Noise fell like crumbs to the floor. Even the canary stopped singing, as though it had inhaled gases in a mine and died. The men strode through the aisles.

"We are looking for Mrs. Soraya Sultan and her son. This plane does not leave until she identifies herself."

Soraya gagged on fear, cowering behind the seat in front of her. The man in the middle seat pulled her chador from the magazine pocket and handed it to her.

"Here," he whispered.

He saw her hands shaking as she slipped the garment back on and he pitied her. They didn't look remotely American and would easily be recognized.

"Mama, what do we do?" Darius whispered. "Are we in trouble? Will we have to wait for the next flight?"

Soraya wanted to weep at his innocence. She put on a

brave face, and after taking some deep breaths to ensure her voice would penetrate the air calmly, she stood up.

"I'm Mrs. Sultan. How may I help you?"

All heads craned to stare at her. The heat from their curiosity scorched her heart. A Guard was at her side in three steps, towering over her and seething with anger, his finger on the trigger of his weapon.

"Why are you on this flight, Mrs. Sultan?"

She answered slowly. "I explained at the checkpoint that a month ago my husband was on a business trip when he suffered a minor stroke. We are joining him during his recuperation."

"Really? You say your husband left a month ago?" He waved some papers. "It says here that your husband left in September and now you claim that he waits not one but five months to send for you? Mrs. Sultan, you're lying."

Soraya's lungs refused to inflate. She feared she was going to throw up, which would prove her guilt then and there. She fought off the gray edges encroaching along the perimeter of her vision.

"But when I explain the details you'll understand ..."

She'd intended to keep talking but simply ran out of words. She gestured feebly into the air. She had nothing.

"Get off the plane. Your husband can 'recuperate' at home next time. What was he running from? Say goodbye to your American friends. You are Iranian. You have no reason to leave your country. It is now free."

Soraya took Darius by the hand and walked down the aisle; like a walk to the gallows, when the condemned searches for meaning in her approaching fate. Soraya knew they were in big trouble. Still she fought back an ironic realization. Once again her finishing school training had given her the wherewithal to handle a treacherous situation with poise. Take that, Mehdi.

The passengers glanced at them as they passed by, sympathetically but surreptitiously. No one even dared to speak on their behalf, fearing a similar fate if they drew attention to themselves. The cloak of anonymity was everyone else's best protection. Soraya understood their reticence, but the abandonment was still painful. Even the canary began singing again as soon as they passed by.

Becky stood waiting at the door of the aircraft. She met Soraya's eyes, mouthing, "I'm sorry," before stepping aside.

The aircraft door shut firmly behind them, like a jail door that would keep them locked up inside Tehran.

Chapter 15

Freedom

The Sultan compound

ONE LOOK at Soraya's face and the household staff knew better than to ask questions. Instead, they pretended as though Soraya and Darius had never planned to leave town; however, there were whispered conversations in the kitchen and much speculation discussed outside the back door during cigarette breaks.

Fatima was thrilled that her young charge was not leaving the country after all. She swept up Darius in a flurry of hugs, and kissed him until he protested, but even she was careful not to probe. Ali would fill her in at the right time and place.

Soraya retired to the master bedroom immediately after dinner. The world had gone mad. She needed to calm herself with some music. Joan Sutherland's "The Art of the Prima Donna" sounded perfect. Sutherland's soaring coloratura righted Soraya's world, evoking a proper world, a world of order, and a civilized world. Soraya slipped her favorite cassette into the tape deck and drowned out the day's insanity with its beauty.

At 10:00 p.m. Fatima sat at the kitchen table in her nightgown and robe, reading the newspaper. A mug of chamomile tea and some toast and jam were set in front of her. Normally this ritual let her unwind, but these days the news was so gruesome she no longer enjoyed reading the paper. Every day only brought coverage of more executions. She tossed the paper into the trash and went upstairs.

Quietly turning the door handle to Darius' bedroom she crept into the room, hanging her robe on the bedpost and climbing into her bed. As sleep began to own her, she heard an odd noise. Her eyes flew open. Darius was snuffling under the covers, trying to muffle tears.

"*Moosh*, Cutie Pie, are you awake?"

"I'm awake," he said. There was silence, then more rustling. He was wiping his nose on the sheets.

"Oh, good," she said. "I was hoping I didn't wake you up. I was just thinking how happy I am that you didn't go on your vacation today."

"Why, Nanny?" He threw back the covers.

"Well, I wanted you to see your papa, but I was going to

miss you so much since I had to stay here without you."

"Why weren't coming with us?"

"Oh, I was staying behind to help Poolak keep the others in line. Someone has to do it." She could almost hear his grin in the darkness.

"How do you keep them in line? Are you mean to them or something?"

"Only if they deserve it."

He sounded puzzled. "I've never seen you be mean. Are you sure you can be mean?"

"Oh, you've no idea what a monster I can be. Come sit on the edge of my bed and I'll show you."

He bounced over.

"Are you ready for my meanness?" she asked.

"Yep."

Fatima grabbed him and began tickling.

"Don't make any noise or I'll torture you even more."

Darius buried his face, laughing uncontrollably.

"I want to see you mean-tickle Mr. Nassiri," said Darius.

She lay back down.

"Seriously? Well, if he's a bad boy, I might have to. I'll render him so helpless he'll drive right off the road."

They lay quietly for a while. Fatima stared at the ceiling.

"Hey, *Naz Nazy*, may I ask you for a favor?"

"Sure."

"Would it be all right if you slept in my bed tonight? Then if I wake up I can reach over and touch you and everything will be okay because you're right there. Just for tonight."

Darius pretended to deliberate.

"Hmm. Yes, that'd be okay. If that helps you feel better, it's fine. Just for tonight."

"Thanks. Bring your pillow over here."

He ran to his bed and launched the pillow through the air. Fatima caught the feathered missile and plopped it next to her. Darius snuggled into its downy softness, stretching and wriggling himself comfortable. He lay still for such a long time, Fatima assumed he was asleep and rolled over.

Then came a faint whisper. "Nanny?"

"Yes?"

"I didn't like those men at the airport."

Fatima knew this was not the time to ask.

"I'm sure, *Moosh*."

"Their guns scared me."

So there had been guns.

"Guns would've scared me too."

"They were really mean to us, Nanny. But we didn't cry, not Mama, not me."

"You're very brave. It's okay to cry now, if you want."

He thought about it for moment, then shook his head.

"No thanks. I'm all done crying."

"Okay. Have a good sleep."

"Thanks, Nanny."

"I love you, Darius."

"Yeah. Me, too."

"Up and down and all around; forever and for always?"

"Up and down and all ... " He yawned. "... and all around; forever and for always."

That night, Soraya thrashed herself awake. She sat up, waiting for the stress and disappointment of the day to repossess her. Astonishingly, it didn't. The shock had worn off like a drug; her mind was clear and her depression gone. Fury had restarted her thought process and with it, life snapped back into focus. She switched on the bedside lamp and took out a notepad from the nightstand. Tonight she would write a list to organize her thoughts.

Propping herself against the quilted silk headboard, she assessed her impressions and challenges:

- Impossible to leave Tehran via airport.

- Must research other options without letting staff know.

- Communicate details of situation to Mehdi.

- Act normally.

- Instruct Darius not to share the story of the airport with his friends.

She flipped to a new page and wrote from memory the

words written by Hafiz, that would become her mantra over the coming months:

We have come into this exquisite world to experience ever and ever more deeply our divine courage, freedom and light."

Underlining "courage, freedom and light," she thought, *azadi*, freedom. Yes, especially freedom. She tore the pages from the notebook, folding them neatly and tucking them beneath the magazines in the drawer.

There. Putting things in order on paper gave her back a sense of control. She found her favorite pillow, the softest one, and fluffing it into the perfect shape, sank her head onto it, letting it puff around her face. With a sigh, she released all tension onto the feather mattress. Now she could rest.

How remarkable, she thought sleepily, that finishing school kept coming in so handy. There, she'd been taught to plan and execute events. Their escape was an event and she would plan it accordingly. She knew the analogy was suspect, but at 2:25 a.m., the connection seemed like a brilliant revelation. Unshackling her mind from further thought, she slept, her new sense of purpose rising and falling with each breath.

When morning filtered through the curtains and Soraya knew Fatima was downstairs in the kitchen having a strong cup of coffee, she tiptoed into Darius' room. It was odd to find him in Fatima's bed, but she stroked her son's cheeks until he whined a little and lifted up an eyelid.

"Good morning, darling," she said.

Darius was startled to see his mother sitting there.

"Mama! Are you okay?" He rubbed his eyes.

"Of course, my darling. Such a situation to handle we had yesterday. Did you sleep well?"

"Yes. Nanny helped me."

"She's a treasure. Did you tell her about our adventure?"

"No," lied Darius. It seemed like the right answer – the one she would want to hear.

"You know, we don't need to tell anyone about it except for Papa. We're fine now, aren't we, so why worry anyone? Especially your friends and the staff."

"Okay, Mama."

Darn. He'd wanted to tell everyone how brave he was. He wondered if there were a way to tell without "telling."

"Will you promise me that?"

"Okay, Mama, I promise."

"Besides, Mrs. Lashgari will be happy and surprised to see you this morning! You can tell her your father is recovering so quickly that he'll be home soon, so there was no need to go visit him. And it's true, Darius. He won't be gone much longer. Shah Pahlavi will come back soon and not long after that, so will Papa. We'll be together again."

"Yippee," said Darius, who just wanted everything back to normal.

"Go wash your face, get dressed and come downstairs. Won't Nanny be proud you got ready on your own!"

After breakfast, Nanny made sure he'd remembered his homework and lunch.

"I'll see you after school. I can't go with you this morning because your mama needs me, but I'll be there when school is over."

The limo idled, waiting for him in the driveway. Darius hugged his mother and Nanny goodbye and piled into the back seat. Nema was already inside and eager to hear why Darius hadn't left town.

"Tell me, tell me! I wish I could have gone on vacation and missed school. How come you didn't want to go?"

Mindful of the promise to his mother, Darius recited the agreed-upon response.

"I did, mostly. But then we found out that Papa is doing much better and so he doesn't need us to come visit. He's coming home as soon as Shah Pahlavi comes back, which will be any day now."

Nema looked out the window, dubious.

"That's not what my Uncle Manu says and he knows all about it because he's in the army."

"I know your uncle is in the army. You tell me all the

time that your uncle is in the army. 'My uncle's in the army, my uncle's in the army.' Mama says the Shah is coming back and she's met him and the Shahbanu at lots of parties. They've talked and everything. I'll bet they even called to tell her they're coming back soon. That's probably how she knows. I can't wait because when they do come back they'll punish those mean men at the airport."

The words had jumped out of his mouth before Darius could keep them restrained inside his mind. Ali began listening intently from the front seat. Nema's attention was focused on Darius.

"There were mean men? How were they mean? What did they do? What did you do?"

Darius fought a brief tug of war with his conscience while he considered his promise to Mama, but the obedient side of him let go of the rope and the words fell out as the boastful side of him won the tussle.

"Can you keep a secret?"

Nema nodded. Darius whispered, but a child's whisper cuts through the air like a knife. Ali tilted his head slightly towards the back seat, not wanting to miss a word.

"It was awful at the airport. Lots of people and there were men with guns. They made us answer all these rude questions and an ugly old lady put her hands all over Mama to see if she had something bad with her, like a gun. We got on the plane but before it took off some other men banged on the airplane with their guns and the stewardess let them on." His volume rose as the story unfolded. "They told the whole plane they were looking for Mama and me. Then they started walking up and down and aisles. So we stood up, just like that, being very brave. I didn't even cry. Neither did Mama. They made us get off the plane and said bad things about Papa. They told us we aren't allowed to leave Tehran. Before they let us go they took Mama and me into a little room and said they'd be watching us all the time, so we'd better not try to go anywhere."

Nema was thrilled by the escapade.

"Weren't you scared?"

"Nah," said Darius casually, hoping to impress his friend. A story like this one was exciting.

"Shall I have my Uncle Manu go kill those guys?"

Ali cut short the discussion.

"We're only a few blocks away, boys," he said. "Put your backpacks on."

They needn't have hurried. Traffic ground to a halt. Ali couldn't account for the congestion or why people were turning around and coming back. He craned his neck out the window, peering down the street to see the problem.

Darius reminded Nema, "You promised you wouldn't tell anyone. Do you swear?"

"I swear."

It was a well-intentioned plan, except that secrets shared between children are like puffy dandelion seeds, exploding in the slightest breeze and taking root in far-flung places. Both Darius and Nema were already thinking of other people they could swear to secrecy. Their whispers would float down the hallways today. Darius was even thinking about acting out the event for friends.

Half a block from the school, Ali discovered the cause of the gridlock. A roadblock manned by Revolutionary Guards was stopping and turning around all vehicles. Ali called out to a woman who was fighting her way back out.

"What's going on?" he asked.

"There is no more school," she said, her voice dripping with disgust. "They've shut it down for teaching the students 'Western corruption.' What's next?"

Ali shook his head as she crawled past. "Good luck to us all." He could feel his blood pressure rising.

Nema asked, "Do we get a day off, Papa?"

"You may have a lot of time off."

As the car pulled into the Sultan compound, Soraya and Nanny came flying out the front door.

"What happened? Why are you back?"

Ebi stopped pruning the rose bushes to listen. Soraya sent the boys off to play so Ali could explain the problem.

"Fatima," she said, "we've got to create some kind of stopgap home schooling curriculum for the children. Today, right now. Find Poolak. The three of us will come up with something."

Ebi spoke up, "I can teach math. I was going to become an accountant until I realized how much I hate being stuck indoors all the time."

"Wonderful," said Soraya. "If you can stand being indoors for an hour, come help us draw up the curriculum."

Ebi thought. "First I'll arrange a rose bouquet for the table – to bring the outdoors inside."

"Wonderful. We'll think better if we're enjoying nature."

As soon as Ali got home, he told Leyla the details of the Sultans being pulled off the plane and that revolutionaries had closed the school indefinitely.

Then he called Manu. "It's unbelievable. The Guards shut down the school until further notice. Mrs. Sultan has volunteered to have all the kids home schooled until things get back to normal."

"Brother, 'normal' doesn't exist anymore. First, the new regime will strip all remnants of the Shah's reign from the school, and then they'll rewrite the curriculum until it's a conglomerate mess of Islamic-Marxist-revolutionary and religious hogwash. Then they'll reopen the school."

"Let's see how many influential people are still living in

Tehran by then. Just between you and me, Manu, Mrs. Sultan and Darius tried to get out of the country but revolutionaries pulled them off the plane. I can tell she's shaken up."

"The Sultans had better be careful. Now she's on their radar and they'll target her again, especially if they find out she moved in the Shah's circles."

Ali lowered his voice so Leyla couldn't hear. "There's more. Mehdi is a practicing Bahá'í. It's why he left the country months ago."

"You're kidding. Oh man, this is a dangerous time to be Bahá'í, or even to be married to one. She's balancing on the rim of a volcano if they find out. Does anyone else on the staff know?"

"I doubt it. I only found out by accident and I haven't told anyone, not even Leyla.

"Do the family a big favor and keep it to yourself."

Chapter 16

Fatima

March 21, 1979

SORAYA was adamant. "Fatima, You must go. I know you need a break after wrangling the children today. Who knew our home would become a schoolhouse? Go, stroll around the bazaar and enjoy a little peace. I'd rather stay home any day than have to wear a chador. And yes, I'll make sure Darius completes today's homework."

"I'm sure you will. Well, I could pick up some fresh spices and vegetables there, which would make the kitchen staff happy. They haven't had any fresh ingredients to play with since the revolution."

"Excellent decision, since I've already instructed Ali to bring the car around."

Driving to the bazaar, there was none of the usual chatter between Ali and Fatima. The latter couldn't find any words to describe the devastation she saw out the window. Tehran was a crestfallen shell of its former self. Burned out and overturned cars were everywhere, piles of sandbags blocked most alleyways, and storefront after sad storefront looked grimly toward the street through shattered windows, the shelves empty, looted weeks ago.

Rough-hewn men patrolled the city, their automatic weapons slung over their shoulders or dangling casually by their sides. They laughed loudly and smoked cigarettes. The arrogance of victory shone brightly in their eyes and their swagger showed the smugness of power.

Ali drove a circuitous route to the bazaar, skirting the streets where the public executions took place. It seemed an eternity before they turned into the Bazaar's parking lot.

Ali clicked off the engine. The two of them stared at the market. Its walls slumped like an old man's shoulders, as though the bloodshed of the Iranian Revolution had wearied them. Shoppers with bags and revolutionaries with AK-47s mingled around the arches.

"Shall I accompany you?" Ali asked.

"No, thank you. I'll be fine."

Fatima walked slowly through the archway. It was business as usual inside even though the bazaar wasn't very crowded. The *bazaaris* were upbeat, empowered by their part in deposing Shah Pahlavi and quick to boast about adding their weight to the Imperial opposition.

She pulled her chador tighter around her, hoping to blend in, not wanting to look like a royal supporter. She decided she'd just quickly buy some fresh spices. That would be enough for today. The guns and paramilitaries made her uncomfortable. Bashu Banai's stall was nearby. It would be nice to see him. Maybe she'd even flirt with him just for a taste of the old days.

But the merchant wasn't standing in his usual spot in front of the rows of fragrant spices, where he normally called out to passersby.

She called out to him.

"Bashu? It's Fatima, come to visit you after too long."

"Fatima, from the Sultan household?" It was a gruff response. Banai stood up from a stool at the back of the store. She was surprised at his drawn face. His looked older than she remembered. She smiled and gave a little wave. He stared at her, his expression sliding from surprise to joy, to cold anger.

She shrank back. "How are you?"

"How am I? How am I? Here's how I am."

Banai reached for a crutch and hobbled unsteadily between the copper pots toward her. She stared in horror. Most of his left leg was missing, and his right foot twisted inwards at an odd angle.

"Bashu, what happened?"

"Your precious Shah's army tried to kill me, that's what happened. They tried to destroy us, but they failed because we were willing to pay the price for freedom. You see the price I paid. But we prevailed, didn't we? We won. Your rich employers are specks of dust now. We will sweep them into a dustpan and dump them in an alley. As for you, I no longer sell to hypocrites who sniveled at their feet. Get out of here."

Fatima froze in disbelief.

"Are you deaf? Get out, you Royalist! You're lucky I don't call over the other merchants to declare you a corruptor of the faith. They'd probably have the Guards come and arrest you, do you understand? I'm doing you a favor. But don't come to my shop again. Ever."

He turned his back to her and hobbled on the crutch back to his corner. Fatima swayed unsteadily, trying to absorb the verbal blows. Then she ran.

That evening after dinner, Soraya and Fatima sat in the new brocade wingback chairs, leaning toward one another, whispering in the sitting area of the master bedroom. The small lamp on the side table illuminated their faces in a soft, conspiratorial light.

"So would you come with us, then, once we have a new plan?" Soraya asked.

Soraya hadn't shared their intention to leave Iran with anyone, not even Fatima, but after Nanny's experience at the Grand Bazaar today, Soraya was confident the nanny understood the dangers of staying. She'd always felt maternal towards Fatima, even though only a few years separated them. As for Fatima, before today's humiliation, she wouldn't have considered fleeing the country, but now she was looking at all of her options.

"But how do I leave my mother, a widow, behind? On the other hand, I can't imagine losing Darius."

"Fatima, think of how you were treated today. Think of the merchant's threats. What's to become of you if you stay? The problem is that you're associated with Mehdi and me. The revolutionaries won't bother your mother, but you're part of our family, Fatima, and I'm terrified to leave you behind. Please let me tell Mehdi to include you. We'll pay your way."

"You've always been so good to me. If I lost my Darius I don't know what I'd do. Thank you for your kindness. Yes, I'll go with you when the time comes."

Soraya patted her hand.

"Leaving behind our lives will be difficult. But Iran is being held hostage and we risk getting caught up in the insanity if we stay. I don't know how long it will take Mehdi to put together another kind of passage, but start thinking about what you can take and what you must leave behind. And remember, it's critical that you keep quiet about it."

Chapter 17

Binoculars

Tehran, April 18, 1979

THE GLOOMY afternoon sky provided an appropriate backdrop for Manu and Ali's destination. They rumbled downtown in Manu's banged up vintage 1969 Honda that he'd affectionately dubbed the "Tehran Taxi." It had been white once, but now the paint looked as dull as the clouds. No one in town would give it a second look, unlike the Sultan's limousine. That would have screamed for attention, which was the last thing they wanted today.

"I'm not sure this is a good idea, Ali. You're not used to this ugly kind of circus," said Manu.

Jitters whittled an edge onto Ali's response.

"Don't pretend you're so callous. I've talked to you after you've been in battle situations and you're no 'stiff upper lip' Brit." He heard the bite in his voice and backed off. "I need to see it for myself. But I don't want Leyla to know we came. She can't handle hearing about it."

"Not an issue, brother. Personally I'm going to try and

forget that I brought you here because I think it's a mistake. Make sure you keep breathing no matter what you see."

Ali peered down the street. Three cranes loomed about four blocks away, their scrawny arms pointing to the gray sky overhead. Thin cables dripped from the cranes' apexes, yanked earthward by the bodies dangling high in the air.

Ali cocked his head in curiosity: Cloth dolls with the stuffing pulled out. That's what they looked like from this distance and he wished it were true, because his brain couldn't process them as human. They looked more like special effects in a movie. At the same time he felt the heavy stone of dread in his stomach, pushing his brain towards reality. All of a sudden, he wasn't sure this was such a good idea, either.

"Why don't we just keep on driving?" urged Manu. "I mean there's nothing more to see, really. They're already dead, so they're not suffering and your pity doesn't help."

"No, you were right the other day," insisted Ali, "when you said it's important to stop and remember that these were real people, citizens of our country, who've been martyred. I want to see."

Manu sighed and pulled over to the curb.

"Okay, have it your way. We'll park the Tehran Taxi here and walk the rest of the way. No need to get too close. Binoculars will bring you closer than you want to be."

He left the keys in the ignition. If someone wanted to steal the car, they could have it.

The two melted into the throng. With each step the scene grew increasingly fascinating. Ali couldn't take his eyes off the sight of the hanged bodies, just like the other gawkers loitering nearby, who formed a blanket of people staring dumbstruck, mouths gaping open, eyes unblinking, looking nearly as dead as the hanged, as though simply viewing the dead sucked life from the viewer. Some people were there to stare with morbid fascination, while others were just hoping against hope not to recognize a loved one.

Manu stopped in front of an apartment building, jogging up the short flight of steps.

"Here's my usual spot. The vantage point keeps people from blocking my splendid view of the corpses."

He peered through the binoculars.

"Good. No one I know is swinging above the treetops today, may Allah have mercy on them all."

He sat down on the steps, handing the binoculars to Ali, who he knew would need support soon. Ali turned the lens, bringing the bodies into focus. Odd. They looked tired, as though weary of hanging midair, asking to lie down, and longing for the dark rest of a coffin. He wondered whether he was emotionally detached or if the sight were too surreal to absorb. What became of these bodies after their public humiliation was complete? Did the family claim the bloated and stinking corpse? Or were they too afraid for their own safety to come forward, leaving the government to dispose of the shells?

He studied the face of the nearest body, a man who looked to be in his 50s; how his head tilted to the left, causing his long, gray beard to droop sideways. His eyes were vacant, boring a cold stare into some world the living couldn't see. They were unsettling. What had they seen at the moment of death? When their light flickered and sputtered out, did those eyes see heaven, or were the religious clerics correct that this man had sinned against the God of Islam? Then where had his soul gone?

Confronting mortality's certitude made Ali queasy. He'd never given thought to who would see his dead body. How would he die? He'd never given it any serious consideration. But somehow he'd make sure it didn't involve a crowd watching him swing from a crane. Nor would he let Nema see him staring into a cold nothingness.

Manu studied his trembling brother.

"Are you okay?"

"Of course, I'm fine," said Ali, but he thought, I've got to get hold of myself, and shifted his gaze to the second body, a young man, maybe 20, and clean-shaven. His body was battered to a pulp. Even at this distance Ali could see signs of torture. His eyes were swollen shut. So young. Too young. Ali grasped for a straw of rationale. What had the kid done to deserve this? He needed to find logic in the brutality. Maybe this was a stupid kid who mouthed off to a guard, saying something negative about the revolution. Well, kid, look where your false bravado got you. If you'd only lied, pretended to switch allegiance, you could have lived out your life. Who would that have hurt? Was being true to your beliefs worth the punishment you endured? What did dying accomplish? This kid had as much as asked for his fate. Blaming the victim granted Ali emotional relief.

"I'm fine," he told Manu.

"Good, let's go," Manu said.

"One minute." He swung the binoculars over to the last body and grabbed the railing. Clearing his throat, Ali took a noisy breath and looked again. This body was female. Her uncovered head showed her hair crudely chopped off at the nape of her neck, the indignity of which was offensive enough, but what crumpled his knees were the large bloodstains below the waistline of her smock.

Ali couldn't move. Outrage paralyzed him. It seared his insides, seeping out his skin as cold sweat. His face drained of color and bile rose in his throat. He forced himself to swallow it.

Manu saw his brother lose control and grabbed him.

"We're leaving, man. Right now. I'll carry you."

"My head's clearing. I can walk. Let's get out of here."

"Good, I'm right behind you. I've got your back in case you get woozy again."

Ali stumbled his way through the crowd in the direction of the Tehran Taxi.

Manu lagged a step behind, making sure his brother stayed on his feet. A voice in the crowd called out his name.

"Captain Nassiri!"

Manu paused. The voice sounded familiar.

"Captain Nassiri, is that you?"

Manu turned around.

At first, Ali didn't hear the commotion. He was too bent on reaching the car. But when the noise finally drew his attention he glanced over his shoulder to ask Manu what was going on, and then stopped.

His brother had vanished like prey snatched by an eagle's talons. Ali scrambled atop a pile of sandbags. He scanned the street with the binoculars until he spotted the crowd making way for a handful of soldiers to pass. They had arrested someone and were leading him in handcuffs to an unmarked van. Ali tried frantically to get a glimpse of the man's face but they were walking away from him. Just before getting into the vehicle, the man turned and looked in his direction, pure helplessness written across his face.

They had arrested Manu.

Ali was hysterical by the time he reached home. Leyla had difficulty understanding his story. He kept repeating, "It's my fault. What can I do? How can I save him?"

"Save who?" she asked again and again.

When he was finally able to spit out, "Manu – they took Manu – the hangings," she pieced the fragments together.

Her heart screamed, "What were you doing there in the first place?" But he was too distraught.

Instead she said, "Let's see how the Sultans can help. They must know people."

Soraya immediately phoned Mehdi. After explaining the situation to him, she listened carefully to his response, nodding and glancing at Ali.

"That's what I was thinking, too. Thank you. I love you," she said and hung up.

Soraya sat back down at the kitchen table, taking Ali's hand but avoiding his panicked face by looking at Leyla.

"You understand that we are on the wrong side of the Islamic Republic, and in danger ourselves."

"Yes, Mrs. Sultan, but who else can we turn to?"

"You did the right thing, Leyla. Mehdi and I would like to give you 360,000 rials. Perhaps you can bribe some government officials for Manu's release."

"No, it's not right to ask you to do that, Mrs. Sultan."

Ali was torn between gratitude and a manic desire to demand a larger amount.

Leyla stepped in. "You two have been good to us for thirteen years. We could never take money from you."

Ali held his breath.

Soraya leaned into them. "We care about you. Mehdi and I have talked and it's settled. We'll be insulted if you do not take the money."

Leyla nodded feebly. "Thank you."

For a moment, Ali was relieved. Then he buried his head in his hands.

"What if it doesn't work?" he moaned, his voice soaked in anguish. "It's my fault that we were there. First I tell Manu he shouldn't visit the execution site. Then I change my mind and have him drive me there. I don't understand how they found him. Who turned him in?"

"It doesn't matter, Ali," said Soraya, "and don't blame yourself. Manu had been taking a calculated risk. Someone must have seen him there on a regular basis. He simply went one time too many."

Ali was inconsolable. Leyla spoke for him.

"You're most generous. We'll never forget this, no matter what transpires."

"There's not enough time," said Ali.

"You don't know that for sure, Ali," reassured Soraya.

"I'll have the cash for you tomorrow afternoon. I can't withdraw the entire amount in one day from our bank because they've frozen most of our assets, and taking out a large amount would raise suspicions anyway. But I can withdraw some of it and ask Mehdi's relatives to lend me the rest. I'll get it to you as quickly as I can."

"Then we'll go to the government offices tomorrow. I'll go along with you, Ali, for support," said Leyla.

"No. I put my brother in jail and I'll be the one to plead for his release. A man is stronger in these situations without a woman to distract him."

The table went silent as the women bit their tongues. Even when the men needed their women the most, they brushed them aside. Leyla stood and took Ali's hand.

"Then let's go home," she said. "You need to prepare yourself for a very lonely, emotional experience tomorrow."

Chapter 18

Bribes and Lies

Offices of the Islamic Republic,
Tehran, April 19, 1979

"WHO?" demanded the young soldier at the front desk, squinting near-sightedly at Ali. The soldier's beard was so unkempt and thick it sprang like fireworks from his chin.

"Manu Nassiri and he was arrested yesterday."

"And so? Do you have any idea how full the jails are right now? How should I know where he's being held?"

"But surely you keep records," said Ali, trying to sound reasonably calm.

"What crime did he commit? His name alone is a crime. He is related to General Nematollah Nassiri?"

"No, he's not," Ali lied. He wanted more than life itself to reach across the desk and strangle this young man. "It's true, he was serving in the regular army, but he never committed a crime against the Islamic Republic."

"Except for supporting the so-called 'Shadow of God,' the Shah, and killing revolutionaries." The soldier spat in the general direction of the trashcan, stroking the spittle from his beard and wiping it on his shirt. "Most of the filthy imperialists like your brother are being held in Qasr. Maybe they know who your brother is and where they've jailed him, if he's still alive."

The soldier started randomly shuffling papers. From the way he thumbed through, sorting them into disorganized piles, Ali realized the man was illiterate. There was nothing more to be learned here, and he'd already presumed that Manu was in the nearby Qasr Prison. He hurried over there, running up the front steps to its main office.

"His name is Manu Nassiri and he was arrested yesterday. Are you holding him here?"

The man who stood before him now was no uneducated soldier. His wire-rimmed glasses gave him an intellectual aura, even a bookish appearance, like a university professor. His hair was neatly combed and his beard well trimmed, but his cold eyes made Ali despair. Here was a man newly entrusted with the power to decide men's fates and clearly he was enjoying the position.

"Well, now, Mr. Nassiri," the man said in a well-modulated voice, "I personally notate the arrest of each criminal, so if he's here and has not yet been convicted and executed, he'll be on my list."

He smiled blandly, expectantly. It took Ali a moment to

understand, but when the man put out his hand Ali quickly pulled some rials from his pocket, dropping them into the man's palm.

"Ah, that helps my memory. Let's see, yes, I remember where I put yesterday's list," he said, opening a desk drawer. He spoke with pleasant, disingenuous grandeur. "I am the guardian, the warden here, you know. This is my building and what I say, goes."

Ali nervously fingered the money in his pocket.

"Let's see ... Nassiri ... Nassiri ... what was the first name again? Oh, yes, Manu ... Manu Nassiri. Oh, Captain Manu Nassiri. Perhaps he was personally responsible for martyring some of our revolutionaries."

Ali was quick to respond. "Oh, no, he was a numbers man and his was strictly a desk job. Very bad with weapons, so bad, they stuck him out of the way at a desk."

The man's cordial façade cracked. "Not according to one of his own men, who rejected your brother's corruption to join the revolution. He told us where we'd find him. "

Ali blanched.

The warden lit a hand rolled cigarette with deliberate languor, blowing smoke in Ali's direction.

"You lied to me," he said. "Bad things happen to liars."

Ali's legs shook. He would grovel if that were his only

chance to awaken some empathy in this man.

"Please, sir. I'm sorry, I'm sorry. I know you excel at your job. It's obvious why the highest authorities have put you in charge. You deserve respect. It's just that Manu is my little brother. You understand family loyalty, I'm sure. I'm convinced Manu never intended to hurt anyone. You'd try to protect your own brother or sister, wouldn't you?"

The man stared at the ceiling, intently admiring the artistry of the smoke rings he was blowing.

Ali's heart pounded.

"Please, just tell me if he's still alive."

The man waited. Ali gave him more money, which he quickly slipped into his pocket.

"Ah, let me check the records again."

Adjusting his glasses, he glanced casually at the papers on his desk. "Why yes, here it is. Your brother is still being held here. Pity. The Revolutionary Court is backlogged with traitors, you see, or he would have already been tried."

Ali could breathe again. He gasped for air. "May I see him, please?"

"No, it is not permitted."

"But, you said ..."

Ali pulled out the rest of the money from his pocket. Trying to stay in control, he attempted a soothing voice.

"Perhaps this might unlock his cell door? I respect the

power you hold in this building, sir, but surely the government wouldn't miss one prisoner. You said yourself the jail is overcrowded and that the courts are terribly backlogged. Perhaps releasing just that one prisoner would do everyone a favor, don't you think?"

The warden slipped Ali's money into his pocket.

"It is not my decision to make. I am not a shah who makes life and death decisions with the snap of his fingers. Go down the hall. Three doors on your left is the office of Chief Justice of the Revolutionary Court, Sadegh Khalkhali. Just yesterday he passed death sentences on the entire Pahlavi family and all their former officials, to be carried out as soon as they are extradited to Iran. Interesting. I wonder how you will persuade him to release your brother. As they say, 'Other than you, may God give your children some intelligence.'"

Ali panicked. He recognized the name. Khalkhali was notorious and feared, known as the "hanging judge." Without an exorbitant amount of money to bribe him, all would be lost.

"May I come back tomorrow? I've given you all I have. I need to go home and collect more "persuasion."

"There is no time." He stamped something next to Manu's name. "Your brother's trial is tomorrow."

"But you said the court was backlogged. You said you

control these things."

"I do, which is why I'm giving your brother special treatment so he won't suffer in prison."

"He needs a lawyer. I need time to retain one."

"No lawyer defends corruptors like your brother."

Ali's hand twitched involuntarily with the impulse to bash the man's head onto his desktop. He turned and walked down the dark hallway. He was out of ideas and money. How would he save Manu's life? He prayed like never before, for Allah's help. "Tell me what to say, Most Merciful One, I beg you."

The office door was closed. He stared for a moment at the sign: Jurist Sadeq Khalkhali. Taking a deep breath, he knocked. No answer. Ali slowly cracked open the door and looked inside.

Khalkhali, a 53-year-old hard-line Sharia cleric, sat behind a fortress of a desk piled high with papers. His short stature was overwhelmed by the fat squishing from out the sides of his swivel chair. He wiped away beads of perspiration from his forehead with a large white, monogrammed handkerchief, acknowledging Ali with a vague wave of the damp fabric. Ali stepped inside.

Khalkhali sipped from a glass of what looked like water, but Ali could smell the alcohol. Some Muslim, he thought. The judge smiled a smile of disturbing sweetness, given his well-known pleasure in meting out executions.

"Why are you here? I can help you, how?"

Ali delivered his words in a deliberate and measured tone. "With the greatest respect I stand before you, *Agha*, begging for mercy. You are a just man, I know, a man with great power and I pray to Allah that you will use your power to free my brother, who is innocent of all charges against him. The warden at the front desk must agree with me or he wouldn't have sent me to see you, don't you think?"

Khalkhali mopped his forehead again.

"They're all guilty or they wouldn't have been picked up. Who is your brother?" He looked down at a pile of binders on his desk.

"His name is Manu Nassiri."

"Nassiri? You are related to Nematollah Nassiri, head of SAVAK?" He chuckled. "You have brightened my day. I will arrange for your brother to die the same way the general did." He shook his head sadly. "The man made a poor decision during his trial. He saluted when the Shah's name was spoken. I immediately had that arm cut off. He didn't salute again." Khalkhali emitted an oddly girlish, high-pitched giggle.

"No, no. Please, I swear, we are not related."

Sadeg Khalkhali leaned back in his chair and squinted

suspiciously at Ali.

"Really. And how are you employed?"

Ali had to quickly distance himself from any occupation that could link him to the general.

"I'm just a chauffeur. I drive for a family, that's it."

Khalkhali took another sip of alcohol, licking his lips.

"Tell me why I should free your brother when I free no one else. If he's innocent he'll be freed after his trial. But, they're never innocent, which is hardly my fault."

Ali knew what Khalkhali wanted, but all of the Sultan's money was already in the warden's pocket. He felt like an idiot. Now he had nothing to offer, unless he could strike some sort of bargain. He wracked his brain for something he could offer in trade for Manu's life.

"I'm sure my brother would provide you protective services if he were set free."

The proposal was so weak it fluttered to the floor. The judge giggled again, that high-pitched, unsettling giggle. Then he turned serious.

"You really have nothing to give me to help me feed my family? I've donated all I have to the Revolution."

Now Ali had to stifle laughter at the egregious lie. But the danger in alienating Khalkhali was too real. That was a game Ali wouldn't win and his options were dwindling.

Khalkhali knew it too. He spoke encouragingly. If only

his words hadn't been so treacherous.

"Why not offer me information? You're a driver, you say. You must know Tehran very well. What have you seen that we might want to know about?"

Ali went numb. "Nothing. I'm no one. I only chauffeur for the Sultans." He'd never meant to say the Sultan name, but his mouth had formed the sounds before his brain realized they'd been uttered. He back-pedaled, speaking fast and loud, as though he could drown out the information.

"Why don't I become your driver, sir? I'd be proud to serve you. Please allow me to drive you for free in exchange for my brother's life."

Khalkhali shrugged impatiently.

"I don't need you. I have a driver. Come back when you have something I want. Now go away."

"But my brother's trial is tomorrow. I only have today. What can I offer you? There must be something."

Now Khalkhali had him where he wanted him, so he played with him like a cat toying with a mouse.

"You say you're the chauffeur for this Sultan family. They must be very wealthy. In what kind of car do you usuualy drive them? Which is their favorite car?"

Ali swallowed hard and choked out the best and only response he could conjure.

"Uh, nothing. It's not fancy." He cleared his throat to

buy time. "It's a foreign car they've had a long time. It's just a family car."

Khalkhali's expression hardened.

"Tell me or your brother dies without a trial."

Ali spit out the words.

"A Daimler. A Daimler DS420 Jaguar limo."

"Really. How unique. Now tell me about the Sultans."

"They're good people."

Khalkhali went in for the kill.

"I said tell me about them. Now."

"They have a young son, uh, Mrs. Sultan's very refined, and, well, Mr. Sultan's business is importing marble ... I don't know what else to tell you."

"I assume they supported the Imperial regime?"

"I don't know."

"Of course you do."

"I suppose ao, I'm not sure. Mrs. Sultan's a Muslim, pretty much, but not completely observant and he's ..."

Ali clenched his teeth to stop the words from coming out of his mouth.

Khalkhali let Ali suffer in agony for a moment before saying in a soft, deadly earnest voice, "... and he's ... what?"

There was no place to hide.

"Mr. Sultan is a Bahá'í. But he's already left the country. He's not here so he can't be arrested."

"Interesting. He leaves his wife and child behind."

"It's not like that. He's a fine husband and father."

"He's an apostate."

Ali squirmed.

"I guess you could say that. Look, why don't I promise to bring you the Daimler? You can keep it. I'll make up a story for Mrs. Sultan. Please, let my brother go."

Ayatollah Khalkhali slowly finished his drink. Rubbing his hands together, he thought briefly, plotting something.

"You've done well enough for today. I'll postpone your brother's trial until we explore what the Sultan family can contribute to the Islamic Republic. Now leave."

He swiveled in his chair, turning his back on Ali, who asked one question out of desperation.

"Do I have your word that you'll postpone the trial?"

Khalkhali swung back around.

"What did you dare to say to me?"

"I said thank you, Justice Khalkhali, for your gracious leniency in the matter of my brother."

Ali backed out of the office and hurried outside.

What he had done was done. He couldn't undo or un-say anything. He could only pray: In the Name of Allah, the Most Compassionate and the Most Merciful, save Manu.

Ali drove around aimlessly for an hour. The Tehran Taxi smelled of his brother: Cigarettes, half-eaten food and gun grease. It was such a familiar scent that he expected to hear his brother crack a joke or stick his head out the window to yell funny insults at strangers.

As the elder child, Ali had gotten his headstrong sibling out of trouble often during their childhood. But now he'd put him into the worst situation imaginable. His brother's blood would be on Ali's hands if Manu were executed.

Three blocks from home he pulled the car over to think. He had to decide on how much he'd share with Leyla and Mrs. Sultan. He was too ashamed to tell them the whole story, but it wasn't a lie to say he'd persuaded the judge to postpone Manu's trial, pending further review. And he could thank Soraya for the money, which had gotten him from one place to the next. Beyond that, he'd volunteer nothing.

Ali was struck by a dreadful realization: His brother's life was in danger because someone he trusted had betrayed him. Now Ali had betrayed people who trusted him. What ripples of bad karma had he set in motion?

Chapter 19

Fate and Karma

April 20, 1979

H E NEVER TOLD Leyla that he'd visited Mrs. Sultan again late that night. Soraya had been eager to hear what had transpired, but was perturbed to learn that he wanted more money.

"How much more do you think is required?

"His fate is in the hands of Jurist Khalkhali."

"Oh, no, that devil? No, we cannot leave Manu in that man's evil hands. I'll ask Arash for the money. Pick it up here after breakfast."

Once his pockets were re-lined with cash the next day, Ali returned to the Islamic Government offices. He'd purposely planned a route avoiding the "hanging street," but a burning dread pulled the steering wheel to the left.

He parked the car. He would walk to the government offices from here. He tried to keep his eyes away from the cranes, yet he felt compelled to take a quick glance. If Manu wasn't there, then he was still in prison, alive and relatively safe. Ali took along the binoculars. Gawkers were lining the street, as they always did these days. Laughter floated by Ali, making him livid. How dare these people disrespect the martyrs with inappropriate and macabre humor? Its grotesqueness stabbed at his heart. He spat at the men who were joking. They responded with obscene gestures.

Climbing the steps of the doorway to the same place he'd stood that day with Manu, he adjusted the lenses. The same three cranes, but with different bodies hanging from them. How many bodies had hung there since the revolution? How many families had wept?

One corpse was very tall. Thank God, one less tortured face to view and one less chance that Manu was dead. Ali leaned heavily against the railing. He was queasy already. The second body wasn't Manu's either. One more to go. He began hyperventilating ... it would be okay if only ... Ali studied the third body ... about Manu's age ... about Manu's size ... but not Manu's face. He wasn't here. Unless Manu had been shot, he was still alive.

Joy poured from his every cell. Manu wasn't swinging from a hook. Today others could grieve for their loved ones; he didn't care. Dread's mantle slid off his shoulders. There was still time to negotiate for Manu's life. He would go to Judge Khalkhali's chambers offering whatever was necessary to save his brother. Hope cushioned Ali's feet as he walked. Throwing his head back, he laughed loudly.

Chapter 20

Betrayal

April 23, 1979

O N A FRIDAY MORNING near the end of April, a chapter in Soraya's charmed life came to an ugly end. It was a fairy tale ending, except that in this instance, the princess bravely faced down the villain and lost.

The day began with a literature class she regularly taught to the compound's children. Tehran's schools had yet to reopen. Teaching did not come naturally to Soraya, but she loved the written word. Today she was reading to the compound's children from Antoine de Saint-Exupéry's "The Little Prince," sharing its magical world with obvious delight. The children were entranced. She paused to explain the text she'd just read.

"When we feel sad, there's still beauty to be found if we keep looking for it. All right, skipping down the page ... yes. The pilot is carrying the little prince while he sleeps. He looks down at the prince's face. He feels like he's carrying a fragile treasure and says, 'I said to myself, What I'm looking at is only a shell. What's most important is invisible.'"

Soraya lingered over the line. She hadn't really noticed it before. It sounded vaguely religious and therefore, quite foreign to her. The author seemed to be suggesting that the unseen was as or more real than the seen, which was mumbo jumbo to her, but she did find it poetic. She considered her explanation before speaking.

"I believe that Saint-Exupéry is telling us that the love we feel is more important than the way we look." Close enough. "Et maintenant, en français, oui?"

It was important that the children learned some French. "Ce quie je..." She stopped abruptly and looked towards the foyer. A thundering noise was approaching. What in the world was coming up their driveway?

"Fatima ...?"

"I'm on my way," the nanny said.

But Mohsen beat her to the door, worry written on his face. He put his hand on the doorknob and braced himself for whatever was on the other side. It couldn't be good.

Fatima peeked out a window. Military trucks were lining up like dominos behind a jeep – their driveway was in the midst of a military invasion.

"Don't let them in," she urged Mohsen. "We have to get the children out of here first."

"I'll stall them as long as possible, but what in the world could they possibly want from the Sultans?"

Fatima ran back to the schoolroom, clapping her hands.

"Classes are over for today!" she said. "Mrs. Sultan, shall we declare an impromptu holiday? We have important visitors arriving at our front door, so why not give the children a free afternoon?"

Soraya's eyes screamed questions. Who was at the door? Was there a threat? Could she charm her way out of the situation? She was feeling more indignant than fearful. Turning to the children she nodded.

"Aren't you lucky? Quickly and very quietly now, let's go. No, sweetheart, we're walking out the back door today. Hurry, now. Darius, go with Nema. You can play at his house for a few hours. Come home for lunch."

The children happily grabbed their books.

Killing time, Mohsen slowly and grandly opened the front door. A burly captain leaned insouciantly against the doorjamb, puffing on his cigarette and clad in a dirty, threadbare and ill-fitting uniform. He didn't bother introducing himself. His authority emanated from the weapon slung over his shoulder. Mohsen sized him up, and what he saw frightened him, but he engaged the officer with a voluminous amount of snail-paced verbiage.

"Good morning and welcome to the Sultan household, kind sir. I am the butler here. Please allow me to introduce myself to you. My name is Mohsen. And you are ... so that I may announce you properly?"

The officer ignored him. Mohsen cleared his throat.

"Again, welcome. Please, sir, tell me how I may help you today. I will do my best to serve your needs. I see you brought along reinforcements. Unnecessary. We are very peaceful people. I assure you we pose no threat to anyone."

The captain's face sweated arrogance.

"Who is inside the house right now?"

"Well, sir. The only people present at this particular moment are Mrs. Sultan, the nanny and myself. The rest of the staff is enjoying a long weekend."

Discovering that the mansion was largely deserted emboldened the officer. He almost smiled.

"Stand aside, we're coming in."

Mohsen widened his stance to delay the soldier's entrance, but he kept his tone deferential.

"Truly sir, I can better assist you if I understand the business you require from the family today."

The officer said sourly, "I will take whatever business I require without your assistance. Your long weekend begins now. Go home, butler."

He motioned Mohsen down the driveway. The butler heard the kitchen door gently click shut in the background. The children were safe. He walked slowly down the long driveway leading toward his house, counting eleven trucks along the way.

Soraya came around the corner just after Mohsen had disappeared from view. She glanced right and left, surprised he was nowhere in sight.

"Good morning, sir. I am Soraya Sultan. Welcome to our home. How may I help you?"

"Why is your head uncovered? Put something on your head immediately. You offend me."

Soraya was startled. No one had ever spoken to her in that tone of voice before and it made her angry. She bit her tongue hard before she almost retorted, "I'll tie a pillow on my head. Then it will be covered. Would that work?"

Fatima came into view, further agitating the officer.

"Why are the women in this house not dressed in hijab when someone comes to the door? Where is your modesty? Are you whores?"

The women were shocked by his insolence, but they now grasped the gravity of the situation they were facing. They were in real danger, yet they were all alone, two females in a male-dominated society.

Fatima deflected the insult.

"I assure you, officer, my employer is a very modest woman of Islam. The fault is entirely mine. I'm dismayed to say you caught me in the middle of doing the laundry. All of our proper, outside clothes are in the washing machine."

She turned to Soraya.

"My deepest apologies, Mrs. Sultan, for putting you in this embarrassing situation; however, I did put away some regular scarves in your dresser. Why don't we run upstairs to cover ourselves more appropriately for our guests?"

Well played, Fatima, Soraya thought. That would give them a minute to discuss the situation. They had to discern what the soldiers wanted from them.

Soraya's composure kicked in and she said sweetly, "Fatima, you think of everything. Please excuse us, sir. We don't want to offend such honored guests. And do please come in," she added with a tinge of sarcasm, since raggedy soldiers in mismatched uniforms were already streaming through the door.

Soraya worried whether these men belonged to one of the rogue *Komitehs* she'd heard about: Street gangs who wielded unilateral authority, and all of it brutal.

The captain ran his eyes over the mansion's riches, a gleam rising in them as he took in their opulence. This was a greater cache than he'd hoped. Knowing he was here to confiscate everything made him feel powerful.

"Take a detailed inventory of each piece of furniture, the carpets, every painting, every statue and every light fixture before loading the trucks," he instructed his men, who began measuring items and marking them with stickers.

Upstairs, the women overheard his order. Without saying a word, they began grabbing jewelry from Soraya's jewelry box, shoving it into bed pillows, inside loose drapery hems and into their bras.

Downstairs, the officer stopped and looked up. The women had been gone too long. His eyes narrowed.

Turning to his men, he shouted, "Go to the master bedroom. Now!"

They found Soraya and Fatima standing in front of a large gilt mirror, demurely adjusting their head coverings.

The captain eyed them warily.

"Search every inch of this room."

Soldiers flung open the walk-in closet doors and stopped, blinking at the ordered magnificence before them. The closet was so large they thought perhaps they'd opened the door to another room. Their superior snapped.

"What's wrong with you? Move!"

The men piled inside, ripping clothes off hangers, pushing aside shoes, emptying boxes on the floor, shoving expensive ties into their own pockets, and checking inside each one of Soraya's many purses. A soldier dumped her favorite purse, an ostrich skin Hermes Birkin, from its orange flannel dust bag and onto the floor, drawing an involuntary groan from Soraya.

The captain caught her reaction. He grinned with

nefarious interest and picked the purse up off the floor. He minced his way back over to her. "So, this is your special bag, perhaps the one you carry when you and your rich friends go out? The leather is very soft. Here, take it, hold it, it's yours after all, yes?" he said. Then he whispered in a confidential and friendly tone. "Tell me about this purse and what's special about it. What kind of leather is it?"

Soraya groped for a noncommittal response.

"It's no more special than any other purse. I think it may be snakeskin, I don't recall, no, I don't think so, but I like the extra pockets inside; you see how it has specific pockets for lipstick and sunglasses. And I'm sentimental about it because it was a birthday present from my husband."

"What a thoughtful gift ..." the officer said, snatching back the bag, "... for my wife's birthday next week. Now it's her special purse." He left the room.

Watching the soldiers open her bureau drawers was like watching her world flayed before her eyes, exposing the sinews of her life. She gasped. They were rifling through her underwear – tossing panties, hosiery and bras like litter on the carpet. Humiliation turned her face away from the sight, but her stomach wrenched knowing their grimy hands were touching garments that had touched her most intimate places, as though their hands were violating the places themselves. She was amazed to hear herself shouting.

"What are you doing? You are observant Muslim men, aren't you? Don't touch private things of a woman. Stop it."

"We are devout Muslims, praise Allah. You, obviously, are not. Women like you are not treated like women of Islam. This is how we treat infidel whores."

The soldier twirled her silk panties in the air on his finger, leering. Pressing the crotch to his face, he inhaled deeply, smirking at her and licking his lips.

Soraya shivered, raped from across the room.

Fatima quickly took Soraya's hand in her own.

"Squeeze my hand as hard as you need to," she muttered under her breath. "Pretend it's his you-know-what and squeeze it until it falls off."

Another soldier held up a bag of cash he'd discovered in Mehdi's nightstand. He laughed.

"So this is how they get their money. They plant it near their shit and it grows in the stink of their manure."

He tucked a handful of bills inside his pockets before handing the bag off to the soldier with the notebook.

"Count this and enter the amount. The Sultans have not been paying enough taxes. They owe our government."

Soraya nearly fainted remembering that Mehdi had taken with him the Kitáb-i-Aqdas, his Bahá'í scriptures, from that very nightstand when he left. What if the soldiers had found it? What if he'd been here? What would they have done to him? They could have the damn money. She didn't care as long as Mehdi was safe.

But seeing the bag also reminded Soraya about the money sash in the bathroom vanity's bottom drawer. The soldiers hadn't gone in there yet. More important to her than the money were the two diamond rings hidden inside: Her grandmother's wedding ring and a Van Cleef & Arpels pearl and diamond ring Mehdi had surprised her with in Switzerland. She decided to sacrifice her lesser jewelry to protect the rings.

"Before you tear up the rest of the bedroom, why don't I just tell you where the jewelry is?"

"Why? We're going to find it anyway."

"I understand." She'd salvage what she could. "But this will save all of us time and I'll have less to clean up after you leave if I simply tell you."

"Why would we trust you?"

"Because I'm only going to help you here in the bedroom. This is my sanctuary and I don't want your dirty fingerprints all over it."

They took the bait. She kept indignation in her voice for good measure.

"You haven't found my jewelry box yet. It's in the top drawer of my dressing table. Take it and leave the rest of my bedroom and my personal items alone. I'm begging you."

Soraya turned; she had no strength to watch the theft. Releasing Fatima's crushed hand, she whispered to her, "Bottom drawer – bathroom vanity - money sash - hide in the toilet tank."

Fatima nodded imperceptibly. She'd secure it while the soldiers were otherwise occupied.

Soraya strode downstairs to confront the captain.

"Sir," Soraya began speaking from the staircase.

At the sound of her voice, the captain turned around with an arched eyebrow.

"Did I invite you to speak?"

"No, you did not. But this is my home. I invited you in with the spirit of *tarof* in my heart. But instead of reciprocating, you are stealing my life. On what grounds? What have I done to harm you?"

The officer sneered.

"You may have spirit, but not of *tarof*. You've stolen from the people long enough. We are from the Foundation for the Dispossessed. We take what is ours."

"How can you possibly need a Steinway piano?"

"It cheers up the soldiers before battle."

He snorted at his own joke.

"This is only happening because I am a woman. You would not dare do this if my husband were home."

"If your husband was home, I'd shoot him in your

driveway. Don't you know how we treat Bahá'í scum? You're very lucky. You'll not become a widow today."

Soraya was shocked. How did he know so much about Mehdi? The room whirled around her as she tried to reconcile the impossible with the apparent. His knowledge was too extensive to be random.

She finally muttered, "I have to make lunch for my son. He'll be home any minute."

She desperately needed to think. Making as much noise as possible in the kitchen so the soldiers wouldn't check on her, she yanked out pots and pans, clanked utensils and slammed drawers. Pulling off her wedding rings and bracelet, she threw them into a soup pot, filled it with water and turned on the flame, adding bouillon, rice, peas and chicken. She slammed the lid on. The gold and diamonds would survive a good boiling.

She mentally scanned the room. There were some of her mother's sterling silver servers in the kitchen drawer. She hid them behind a leg of lamb in the freezer and barricaded them with a large bag of lentils. And the everyday china: She stacked what she could fit behind the cleaning closet's supplies. At least the soldiers wouldn't get the complete set. She took her everyday purse from the kitchen table and stashed it inside a garbage bag in the broom closet.

Darius burst through the kitchen door. "Mama, what's

happening? I was watching through the window. They've sawed off the piano's legs and now they're trying to carry it out the front door. Why are they taking things? Are they taking my toys, too?"

She threw her arms around him.

"I'm so sorry, Darius. I don't know why they're doing this, but I can't stop them. We have to be brave, like we were that day on the plane. We were very brave then and we can do it again."

Except that today was different. Today thieves were scraping the paint off the canvas of their lives. Today, memories were being confiscated. Today was different.

Soraya quickly ladled some of her jewelry-flavored soup into bowls. Darius looked puzzled at the thin, flavorless soup, but then he'd never seen Mama cook before so maybe this was her best effort. They sat at the kitchen table listening to the sounds of their home being dismantled and their belongings taken to who-knew-where to be used for who-knew-what. Soraya buried her head in her hands. Darius patted her shoulder.

"It's okay, Mama. Daddy will bring me more toys. I just hope they leave my Bee Gees poster alone."

Soraya sighed. This truly was theatre of the absurd: Degenerates stealing their expensive and irreplaceable heirlooms, neither caring nor cognizant of their quality, carting them away in broad daylight, with the authority of a brutal revolutionary government that had taken her king. Now they were dismantling her life.

Swear words resounded in the entryway. Soraya and Darius went to look. Soldiers were trying to manually hoist one of the large bronze nymphs in the foyer. It slipped from their hands and dropped onto the marble floor with a cavernous bang. Soraya watched a spidery web of cracks appear in the marble floor. The men grimaced with pain. She was happy they'd hurt themselves. It made the ruined floor worth the sacrifice.

The captain came strolling up the driveway. She was surprised to see Ali walking alongside him, yet was glad to see a friendly face and a male one at that. She tried to catch his eye, but apparently Ali was absorbed in his conversation with the captain.

"Ah, Mrs. Sultan, or shall I call you Soraya?" he said. "I feel I know you so well now. I've been talking with my friend, Ali. Oh, that's right, you know him. He drives you everywhere, doesn't he?"

Ali's eyes dug holes into the ground.

"He's told me about the safe in your husband's office. Did you forget to tell me about it?"

Soraya was infuriated. What had Ali done?"

You will write down the safe's combination." He thrust

paper and pen in her face. She glared at Ali.

Now she would forfeit her heirloom pearls, a ruby bracelet and a large sum of cash.

The officer put his arm around Ali.

"And now my new friend, I need the keys."

The keys? Soraya wondered, keys to what?

"Please, sir, no," Ali begged. Hanging his head, he said to Soraya, "I didn't know they'd take everything."

The captain was growing impatient. He had another house to loot today.

"You specifically offered the judge their limousine. Give me the keys right now."

Ali fumbled in his pocket.

Angry tears spilled from Soraya's eyes. Of all people, the traitor was Ali. He'd brought the revolution to their front door by selling them out, inviting these men to cart off their identity, one piece at a time. How much were they paying him? Is that how they knew Mehdi was a Bahá'í? How did Ali find out? Mehdi must have confided in him. If so, then a man they'd embraced as family had rewarded that confidence by destroying them. May he be damned, she thought, may he rot in hell forever.

She looked directly at him. "You're fired."

The captain slapped his thigh, laughing.

"You're no longer his employer. He works for me now."

Soraya ignored him.

"Get out of my sight," she said to Ali.

"Mrs. Sultan ..." Ali pleaded. He couldn't explain the deal he'd made right now.

"You and your family may no longer live on this property," Soraya said. "You'll vacate the house by the end of the week."

"But Mama," said Darius, who'd finished his soup, "What about Nema? What about my best friend?"

Soraya stalked upstairs.

Ali's conscience cried out for attention, but he would have to beg for mercy later. Right now he needed to confront the captain, who already was sitting in the limo's front seat, spinning dials, pushing buttons and savoring the gentle purr of the Daimler's engine.

His voice quavering, Ali said, "You have what you wanted and you took much more than you said you'd take, but it's done. I've completed everything required of me. Now it's time to keep your end of the bargain. Release my brother from prison."

"Oh, your brother is already out of jail," the captain said dismissively, shutting the car door and turning up the radio. Ali rapped on the window until the officer rolled it down part of the way.

"You said that my brother Manu's already been freed?"

The captain repeated. "I said your brother is no longer in jail. What was promised is done." He pressed a button and rolled up the window in front of Ali's face. Ali watched his own breath condensing on the dark glass. The captain slipped the car into gear and rolled away, the Daimler gliding like a swan through the back gate of the compound, gone forever.

Something felt very wrong. What was that inflection he'd heard in the captain's voice? He replayed the sounds in his head: "Your brother is no longer in jail."

The words stank with rancid ambiguity. Ali bent over, bracing his hands on his knees. He'd let his head clear first before going home to tell Leyla they were moving.

When the soldiers finally left, Soraya called Mehdi.

"He did what?" Mehdi said in disbelief from the living room at their vacation home in Villefranche-sur-Mer on the French Riviera. "Ali wouldn't betray us. Everyone in the compound is 'bread and salt' to us. And we just gave him money to help rescue Manu. For him to betray us would be obscene behavior from a man I've trusted for years. Why are you so convinced he's the informant?"

Soraya gripped the receiver tightly. The ordeal was over but adrenaline still coursed through her veins.

"Do you suppose I'm making this up? The two of them acted like old friends and Ali refused to look me in the eye.

And Mehdi, he told them where the safe was, and worst of all, he gave them the keys to the Daimler. It's gone. The very sight of that soldier's arm over Ali's shoulder was so appalling it would blind Mohammad. Yes, I'm certain."

"I'm just shocked, darling. I'm sorry." His voice throbbed in anger. "I'm enraged ..." Mehdi paused to control the emotion filling his chest. "It's unspeakable. I would have beaten Ali's face until it was pulp."

"Naturally I fired him on the spot. He is forever dead to me and I will never again acknowledge his existence. But please, please tell me whatever possessed you to tell him you're a Bahá'í?"

"What are you talking about?"

"They knew. Ali must have told them."

"That's impossible."

"Well, today somebody performed the impossible. Who else could or would? It had to be him. He's hung a death sentence around your neck. The soldiers would have killed you if you'd been here today. They told me so."

Mehdi went quiet. Then, with barely contained fury, he said, "I'm baffled about how they found out. Ali and I never discussed religion and I wouldn't have told him anyway, since he's a devout Muslim. Somehow he must have inadvertently discovered it. Why else would he have been friendly with the revolutionaries?" Mehdi tried to digest the unthinkable. "So Ali has turned informant." His voice sagged. "This tragic history of Persia – producing generations of informants who betray friends and family regardless of who's in power. What will become of us?" He stared out the living room window at the Côte d'Azur without seeing it. Worry obscured its beauty. He went on, too angry to care if the phoneline was tapped.

"I've been working through conventional channels to get you out of the country, but it's taking too long. Now we're getting you out of there, whatever it takes. There are ways, unconventional means, of escaping. Look, darling, I know people who know people, who know people ..." His voice trailed off. "I just want you and Darius by my side, safe and sound. If I arrange this kind of escape, it will be the hardest thing you've ever done. Can you be really tough? It will be dangerous."

"Don't you realize what I've already been through? Are you a Muslim or a Bahá'í, because you sound like a typical Muslim male. What is it your precious Bahá'u'lláh says? 'The world of humanity has two wings - one is women and the other men. Not until both wings are equally developed can the bird fly. Should one wing remain weak, flight is impossible.'"

Mehdi shook his head.

"Why is that the only Bahá'í quote you remember?"

"Maybe it's the only one I like. You are too Persian to understand the strength of my wing, Mehdi. I can fly, too. Stop treating me like a china doll."

"But you're that precious to me, darling. I didn't mean to insult your dainty wing."

"Mehdi, today I endured illiterate goons confiscating the life we've built, piling it into their trucks and driving away with it. Just arrange what needs to be arranged."

"How will you get by in the meantime? What are you using for furniture?"

Soraya sighed. "Well, they left our mattresses and the kitchen table, plus some kitchen gadgets. And apparently, the government doesn't need toilet paper. They probably don't use it. Praise to Whoever, they left behind the Bee Gees poster. Arash has brought over an extra couch and some side chairs. He's coming back with sheets we can use as curtains for now. The family will take good care of us. They don't seem to be targeted, for now. We're all right."

"You can slowly buy some more furniture. Don't take out too much money at one time or they'll freeze the rest of the accounts."

"I'll let the staff go. There's nothing for them to do."

"But keep Fatima on for Darius, of course, and best to keep on Ebi. You don't want the garden's flowers to suffer under the wrath of your lovely but dreadful black thumb."

"Really, Mehdi, today of all days, you tease me? Honestly, I think you'd poke fun at me at my funeral."

"What makes you think I'd go to your funeral?"

He could find humor in the darkest moments. It was an infuriating, if endearing, trait.

"You win," she said.

"That's my girl. My darling, I mourn that you faced this alone. I should have been there."

"If you'd been here, I'd be mourning your death right now. Better that you're the one mourning."

After midnight, since sleep spurned her, Soraya padded down the hall, careful not to awaken Darius and Fatima. Near the bottom of the stairs, she switched on the foyer chandelier. Light sprang onto the walls, fractured by the crystals into thousands of luminous, dancing diamonds. It was resplendent, dazzling and oddly comforting. This chandelier remembered yesterday and last week and last year. It still shone, unfazed, across the entryway's empty expanse of red marble, bereft of its tables, the sitting chairs and priceless artwork, looking less like a foyer than a skating rink made of red ice.

Soraya wondered if the idiots who'd taken the antiques had damaged them. She walked across the foyer to where the soldiers had dropped the bronze statue. Cracks were still creeping away from the point of impact. She knelt, running a finger along the jagged lines.

This is like my life, she thought, fractured and I don't know where or when the cracking will stop.

She sat for a long time on the cold marble, aching, wondering, grieving, and trying to grasp this new reality. Losing the family heirlooms that for so long were markers of her family's history was too painful. She'd grown up surrounded by these carefully preserved and treasured objects, lovingly curated by her ancestors for her generation and the ones to come. Now they were lost forever.

She wandered over to the corner where the piano had been tortured, its legs amputated before the soldiers figured out that they could be unscrewed. The soldiers had taken all the silver frames with the photos in them except for one lonely frame, which lay face down. Soraya picked it up, slivers of glass falling to the floor, with hope in her heart that a piece of their life remained. She flipped the frame over. It was the wedding snapshot Uncle Mahmud had taken, but it no longer held joy. She surmised it was left behind intentionally because it delivered a clarion threat to Mehdi. Someone had used a piece of glass to slit his throat. The frame dropped from her hands.

Her soul ripped open with an agony so raw – and from a rending so deep – that no sound could escape. Her body crumpled like a child's, shaking with noiseless sobs.

Chapter 21

Manu's Message

April 24, 1997

ONCE AGAIN, the Tehran Taxi drove itself to the hanging street. Ali kept thinking to himself, No, I'm driving straight to the government offices to find out when they released Manu. He'd repeatedly phoned his brother, but Manu wasn't answering. Five times Ali called and each time he got the message: "This is Manu. I'm either not here or I'm doing something more fun than talking to you. Leave a message after the (beeeeeep)."

Ali had left four messages, each one more urgent than the last. Where was his little brother?

The Tehran Taxi maneuvered its own way down the street. Ali was powerless, led by a mounting anxiety that wouldn't subside until he could disprove it.

The Morbidity Mongers were getting their daily dose of gruesomeness. Ali was forced to park six blocks away.

He'd already walked four blocks before realizing he'd forgotten to bring the binoculars. The crowd was too thick to fight his way backwards. The way was gridlocked.

All right. He'd walk another block or two, working his way over to a side street. He was searching for an alley when his eyes accidentally swept past the hanging bodies.

He stopped. The crowd continued right around him, unconcerned. But Ali stood there, staring at Manu, who was hoisted high above the street, like a hummingbird hovering midflight, hanging with his calloused hands tied behind his back and dried blood coming from his ears. Ali didn't need the binoculars to know who it was. He yearned to be wrong, but he knew his brother's build, his broad shoulders and distinctively bowed legs, and there was no mistaking his khakis and blue tee shirt or his close-cut military hair with the precision-trimmed sideburns.

Still, a small chance remained that he was mistaken, Ali thought wistfully, until something happened – something impossible to a man who didn't believe in the supernatural: He swore he heard Manu talking. Was his brain playing a trick? Was this a manifestation of shock? He not only heard Manu's voice clearly, he felt Manu resting a brotherly hand on his shoulder. Ali whipped around to see who was touching him, but no one in the crowd had stopped walking. They flowed around him like he was a rock in a stream. Yet Manu's reassuring baritone voice filled his ears.

"Ali, my brother. The bastards were every bit as nasty as you'd expect, but I didn't break. I was glad when the end finally came, but I took their worst and spit it back in their faces. Be proud of me, brother. And look, this was not your fault. I know you're blaming yourself. Stop it. Don't come closer to my body, don't look at it again, and don't ever come back here. Forget you saw me like this. Go home, Ali. You know you have no stomach for this kind of thing."

Ali ran. "No!" It was the only word his mind could form, the only word that pushed away reality. He screamed it over and over again.

The gallows crowd was used to hearing similar cries of fresh agony. They casually eased aside, making way for yet another devastated relative. Ali ran, not caring where he was going, only trying to outrun the horrible sight before it seared itself into his memory.

Eventually exhaustion forced him to slow down and reality caught up with its victim. The moment his rubbery legs pulled him down, the pavement branded him with the hot iron of grief and his heart came unhinged.

Ali vomited repeatedly until bile dribbled down his shirt. He must have fainted because he opened his eyes to a young woman shaking him.

"Are you alright?" she asked, looking concerned.

"Yes," he mumbled, just to make her go away. He realized he was lying in his own vomit. He didn't care. He could think of only one thing: That Manu was wrong.

Of course this was his fault, all of it, from the moment he'd asked Manu to bring him to this ghastly street, to informing on the Sultans in the effort to save him. He had started a horrid chain of events, tempting fate, flaunting it, and believing he could control it. Now, despite bribing government officials and selling out his employers, Manu was dead. Furthermore, the Sultan's household had been looted; the government knew Mehdi was a Bahá'í; Soraya had fired him so that he no longer could provide for his family; Leyla's relationship with Soraya was destroyed and so was Nema's tender boyhood friendship with Darius.

This was entirely his fault. If his brother only knew what had transpired since the arrest. Ali had ruined the lives of everyone he cared most about, and the awful truth was that he couldn't come up with one reason why anyone should forgive him, nor could he make things right and redeem himself. He sat on the sidewalk watching Respect and Hope walk away from him in utter disgust.

Chapter 22

Ripples of Devastation

The Sultan Compound

L EYLA SOBBED in Soraya's arms. The Nassiri living room was dimly lit and filled with pain.

"But I don't know why he would betray you. That's not the kind of man he is. He respects you. We've tried to show you how much we appreciate working here. Please give Ali a chance to explain. What if he was tricked?"

"I've thought of that, Leyla. And while Mehdi and I know how desperate Ali is about Manu's imprisonment, that's not a conscionable excuse for his actions. Ali is dead to me. But, I have changed my mind somewhat. I'm not going make you homeless. You may live here until Ali finds new employment and then you'll move. Nema is always welcome to play with Darius at our house, but Darius will not be allowed to play at your house. Third, I never want to see Ali's face at my front door again."

"I understand. I'm sure Ali will too. Thank you, Mrs. Sultan, thank you for not throwing us out. I'm grateful, we're grateful to you for everything you've done. This day is so horrible, so painful, it's impossible for anyone else to understand."

She dissolved into tears again. Soraya had no more tears to spill. She patted Leyla's hand and left. As she strolled through the willow trees toward the mansion, she considered humanity's many shortcomings: How quickly Ali sacrificed people who had treated him like family and how Leyla felt only her own pain and not the pain Ali had inflicted on them. She'd given Ali money and he'd sold them out. Leyla's house hadn't been invaded and stripped. Where was the sympathy for what Soraya had suffered?

Ali returned home near midnight, lugging a heavy duffel bag that he dropped on a living room chair. Leyla threw herself into his arms. She'd been frantic for hours. Having Ali safely home reassured her that he'd smooth things over with Mrs. Sultan. Leyla was quick to share the encouraging news that they could stay in the house for now and Nema could still play with Darius.

Leyla made tea. Then she blurted out her frustration.

"Ali, where have you been? I've been terrified. What's been going on with Manu? You're not sharing with me. Is he doing okay? Most of all, I don't understand - why did you turn in the Sultans to the Islamic Republic? Does it have anything to do with Manu? Just tell me. I'll explain it to Mrs. Sultan tomorrow. I'm sure she'll forgive us."

He stared into the steaming mug, absently playing with the handle.

"It's done, Leyla. There's nothing to explain, not to you, not to the Sultans. It's over. There is no good way to share bad news. Manu's dead. I saw him ... I saw him ... hanging ... it was definitely him. Accept it."

"Oh, Ali, no. You can't be sure." She reached for his hand, but he pulled it away.

"I said to accept it."

He poured his tea out and picked up the duffel bag.

"I have things to do before bed."

Leyla searched his face.

"I'm so very sorry about Manu. It's barbaric."

She waited for him to break down. He didn't.

"How are you handling it?"

He didn't answer.

"Will we get his body for burial?"

"No."

"How can I help you?"

"You can't."

"But we have to go through this together."

He picked up the bag.

"What's in there?" Leyla asked.

"Things from Manu's apartment. I'll store them in the garage for now and decide what to do with them later."

Ali was gone when Leyla awoke the next morning. Even as she tied on her bathrobe, he was in Manu's apartment, inhaling his brother's scent, standing mostly in the closet, where there was the comforting, masculine mixture of sweat, aftershave and dust.

There was no doubt this was a soldier's apartment. It was sparsely furnished and drab except for a psychedelic black light poster of Jimmy Hendrix on the bedroom ceiling. Nearly devoid of food, it was also in dire need of vacuuming. Manu's bed sheets stretched tautly across the mattress before they were turned down precisely at the top. A gray blanket lay smoothly folded at the foot of the bed. His toiletries in the bathroom were lined up and evenly spaced with the labels uniformly turned outward, like new recruits facing front and center. Ali slipped the aftershave into his back pocket.

Amassed on the bedroom bookshelf was an army of athletic trophies, standing at attention like China's Terracotta Warriors. Tucked between them were black and white photos. He slid one out. It showed Manu winning the Tehran High School decathlon. In another, there he was accepting an award as the school's top all-around athlete.

Ali remembered the exact moment the next photo was taken – the two of them sitting under a tree, grade-school-aged, arms slung around each other and with mischievous grins across their faces. In another shot they were standing up (against the rules, he recalled) in a paddleboat on Eram Amusement Park's lake. Manu was feigning losing his balance, mugging for the camera.

Ali pulled out all the photos. Excepting for the few athletic images, these were a testament to brotherly love, rather than a shrine to Manu's accomplishments. Manu had never been demonstrative, so Ali hadn't known how deep his affection had run.

Ali felt an odd sensation of warmth, as though someone stood behind him, not unlike the presence he'd felt yesterday. He turned around. No one was there.

"Don't get all sentimental and full of yourself."

Just the way Manu would have talked, thought Ali. How was this possible? He must be insane with grief.

"Believe me, I enjoyed being the big man at school. I had one healthy ego. I just cared about you more. I looked up to you, big brother. You didn't know that, did you? Ali, I'm telling you that this wasn't your fault. Do you hear me?"

Ali was sure he was hallucinating, except that the voice seemed very real. But surely he was talking to himself; projecting his own thoughts into a ghostly manifestation.

"No, you're not crazy," the voice said. "Well, a little. The only thing I regret is that I never had children. But you did, Ali, and there's no greater treasure. Listen, I'll always be looking out for you, like you did for me."

The room went cold. Whatever had been there was gone. Ali tucked the photos in his shirt pocket. He looked around the room, imprinting it into his memory. As he closed the curtains he decided to continue paying Manu's rent for the time being. Finances being tight, they could live here if Mrs. Sultan threw them out of their house.

Meanwhile, Soraya wasn't giving Ali a thought. She and Fatima were sharing an afternoon snack. After suffering so much loss, they needed a frivolous release.

"Oh, Fatima, please don't hesitate to tell me," said Soraya, between bites of warm barbari bread with poppy seeds on top, and spread with feta cheese and fig jam.

"I don't remember the last time I heard good news." Fatima set down her cup of rose petal tea.

"This will shock you, but I've met someone special."

"That's wonderful! Of course I'm shocked! You've always been so picky that I feared the man who could please you didn't exist. This is thrilling news! He must be very special. Who is he and how did you meet him? Tell me everything, from the very beginning."

"I met him, oh, probably a year ago at the downtown

supermarket, where he's the manager. I noticed he always appeared to ring me up, no matter what line I stood in. We had the chance to flirt a little. But since the revolution I haven't dared go to the supermarket, so I assumed I'd never see him again. Then about two months ago I ran into him near the fabric store. I guess he decided not to waste the opportunity, because he asked me to coffee then and there. Now we see each other at least twice a week. He's wonderful, smart, funny and a hard worker."

"What's his name or are you keeping that a secret so I can't have him checked out?"

"His name is Jamal." She laughed. "But I'm not sure I should tell you his last name. You're right, I'm afraid you'll have him checked out."

Soraya nodded.

"You may assume I'll have him checked out before you get too involved. No one gets to hurt you."

"He's made it clear his intentions are honorable. I think you'll like him."

"You're leaving out important information. I hope he's good-looking? Tall, short, fat ... which?"

Fatima blushed.

"I think he's beautiful. I can't believe he's interested in me. Let's see, he's tall and on the lean side with kind eyes. His voice is deep and soothing. I feel safe when he talks, but he's shy until he gets to know you."

"Well, he's going to have push right past shyness if he's going to survive visiting this household."

"I've already warned him! And he knows he's going to have to pass muster with you and Mr. Sultan before we decide anything serious."

Soraya was delighted to be thinking about nuptials instead of death and loss. It was rejuvenating.

"Then we'll invite him to dinner, even if we have to eat on TV trays with plastic forks. You'll tell me when he's free and I'll cook for him. Oh dear, saffron rice is the only thing I know how to make. Well, then I'll make him the very best saffron rice he's ever eaten. No one makes saffron rice better than I do, unless Alaleh is here, then she'll make it. Her saffron rice is better than mine."

Fatima's happiness was making her silly.

"Wait a minute, that makes no sense. You say that Alaleh makes rice better than your rice, which is the very best saffron rice, except for hers, which is better? I believe you've eaten too much saffron and have gone daffy."

Even Soraya had to chuckle. What a glorious change from all the pain. The stress made them both punchy – they didn't know whether to laugh or cry. Today they chose to laugh, because they could.

"Now Nanny," said Soraya with mock sternness, "as my

employee, you're not allowed to confuse me with my own words, easy though that may be, since my mind blows around like a feather these days. There's too much strain, too much ugliness ... but it's not too soon to start planning your wedding, I hope?"

"Oh, goodness. That's way down the road, I'm sure."

"But let's keep talking about happy things, anyway. I can't take any more bad news. We could at least start looking through bridal magazines, for the fun of it."

Fatima shook her head solemnly.

"I understand the Islamic Republic has confiscated all magazines showing 'depraved' Western clothing. Maybe they'll publish a wedding magazine for the fashionable, but devout, Islamic Republic girl. That would be one sexy cover, wouldn't it?"

The thought of it tickled Soraya so much that she answered before swallowing her mouthful of toast. "You mean you don't have a subscription to 'Burqua Bridal?'" She guffawed at her own joke, spitting fig jam all over the kitchen table.

Fatima had never, ever seen Soraya lose her composure. The nanny laughed at her employer's breach of manners until tears rolled down her cheeks.

"Perfect. 'Burqua Bridal' works," said Fatima, gasping for breath. "I can choose between the black burqua on page

16 or the white one on page 17."

Soraya was beset with an undeniable case of the grade school giggles. She buried her face in her hands, her shoulders shaking with mirth until coming up for air.

Fatima looked cross-eyed at her employer.

"Yes, definitely too much saffron! Careful or you'll laugh yourself to death!"

Soraya further succumbed to the giggles. The harder the women tried to compose themselves, the more they lost control, reaching a crescendo of unapologetic hysteria.

Arash walked in through the kitchen back door. He took one look at the duo and shook his head. He would never understand women. But at least they were happy and he was pretty sure Soraya would be even happier in a minute.

"I have good news," he began.

They looked up in surprise to see him.

Soraya said, "More good news? I'm allowed two pieces of good news in only one day?" She looked at Fatima. "I don't believe that's legal under Sharia law."

Fatima agreed. "I'm quite certain it's illegal. Says so in the fine print. One may receive only one piece of good news per day, and only every other day. Sorry, but you'll have to come back day after tomorrow, Arash."

"Girls, do you want to hear the news or not?"

"Fatima,'" said Soraya. "Please get my brother some

saffron so he can laugh himself crazy like us."

They collapsed into hilarity again.

"Soraya, come on! I need to tell you something."

"Of course, Arash," said Soraya, inhaling deeply to smother a developing case of hiccups.

"I spent the day knocking on government doors. I think I've found a way to reclaim your belongings."

Soraya became serious.

"What? You're not teasing, are you?"

"No, I'm not. Unlike you, I haven't eaten too much saffron. Here's the story: The government auctions off almost all confiscated property; however, you're allowed to go before an official and plead your case for reclamation if your property is still in the warehouse and you can prove it's yours. I've made an appointment for you on Monday at the Foundation for the Dispossessed. I'll accompany you, of course, and you're going to have to wear the dreaded chador for modesty's sake."

Soraya threw her arms around him.

"Arash, you're my hero, thank you! Fatima, did you hear? Is this possible? I'll have to start praying again to the Most Merciful, if he still remembers me. May our ancestors plead with Allah to give us back our things, our family history, our artwork! I must call Mehdi."

Arash kissed his sister before looking sternly at her.

"Tomorrow you and I will practice what we're going to say, and for once, you're going to follow directions."

Soraya looked meek. "I promise."

"Hmm," he grunted. "I've seen that look on your son's face right before he disobeys. Now it's clear to me where he learned it. I'm holding you to your promise, make no mistake, sister."

"Yes, Arash, of course. I'll be a little lamb."

"Heard that one before, too," he tossed over his shoulder as he closed the kitchen door behind him.

For a moment the women basked quietly in the news. Then they looked at each other and jumped up and down, hugging, laughing and screaming like schoolgirls.

Chapter 23

Power and Manipulation

April 29, 1979

Morning sunlight filtered through the old sheets they'd hung over the windows after the soldiers had ransacked the mansion. Soraya came downstairs around 10:00 a.m. The house was so quiet these days she no longer bothered rising any earlier. Last week she'd let go all the employees except for Fatima, Alaleh and Ebi. Although Poolak had offered to stay on at a substantial pay cut, there was simply nothing for her to do. There could be no parties without furniture, china or silverware. Fatima offered to do most of the housework and Alaleh said she'd continue cooking on a budget if she could stay. Ebi kept the house lovely by arranging flowers in empty marmalade jars.

Passing through the foyer to the kitchen, Soraya saw a piece of paper slipped part way underneath the front door. She unfolded the hand written note.

Dear Mrs. Sultan,

I know nothing I can say or do will make me worthy of your forgiveness. All I can do is apologize. You and Mr. Sultan were so generous in giving me money in the effort to save my brother. One day I will pay you back, somehow. Thank you for letting us stay in the house until I find work and thank you for letting Nema and Darius remain friends. It pains me to tell you that Manu is dead. They hung him like a slaughtered animal. Since I can't forgive myself, I don't expect you to forgive me. What I have done – to my brother, to your family and to mine, causes me great anguish.

I'm sorry,

Ali Nassiri

Soraya blinked, hoping the words would be different when she opened them again. Impossible. Ayatollah Khomeini's government had executed Manu, he of the ready smile and broad shoulders. Horrific. The world had gone mad. She dialed Mehdi and read him the letter.

"What do I do, Mehdi?"

"You can tell him you forgive him."

"I won't forgive an employee who purposely betrayed us, even under duress."

"Soraya, I'm not sure any of us knows what we're capable of if we're desperate enough."

"Mehdi, you didn't watch our lives being stolen."

"*Soraya-joon*, you have a tender heart. You'll feel differently once the shock of being robbed isn't fresh."

His tone of voice changed and Soraya knew whatever he said next would be in code. "I do have some good news to share with you. Yesterday I saw our friend, Henri, and he's just bought a lovely home in Villefranche-sur-Mer."

Oh, my goodness, thought Soraya. Henri was their French realtor. Mehdi must have sold their vacation condo for the cash, probably to buy her way out of Iran. Oh, how she would miss the French Riviera.

"How lovely. I'm sure they'll enjoy the town."

"Yes, Henri was quite pleased about the purchase and I, for him. When I told him that you had donated our household to the new government, he felt as I do, that you and Darius deserve a little vacation. I really think you should entertain the thought."

Soraya was uncertain how to respond. She wanted details about the plans he had for them but had to pose her questions in a way he could answer.

"Will you make the reservations for us, once we decide where we'd like to go, or shall I have Fatima do it?"

"There's no need to trouble Nanny. I'll be happy to do it for you. As you ponder your vacation, go ahead and think about items you'd want to pack, just for the fun of it. By the way, have you visited the government offices to start the process of recovering our household possessions yet?"

"Arash and I have our first appointment tomorrow."

Then, for the benefit of anyone who might be listening in on the line she added, "I'm positive it will go smoothly. As soon as the government understands our situation, I expect our things will be returned within a few days."

"That's wonderful, darling, good news all around. I'm flying to New York tomorrow to handle some business matters. It seems that our marble is not reaching the plant in Tehran, so I'll be speaking with my colleagues in America. Hopefully, we can break the logjam in Tehran or else begin setting up a new business in the States."

Oh no. The government had confiscated his business. There went their main source of income. No wonder he'd sold the vacation home. Mehdi continued cheerfully.

"After the trip to New York, I'll be putting down some roots in Washington, D.C."

So the United States Capitol would be their new place of residence. It made sense. After all, he had business connections to a number of Washington politicians. She thought it sounded exciting.

"Oh, and dear Soraya, please do me a favor. Make my memories happy - will you please enjoy a big handful of pistachios for me? The ones here in France aren't as large and tasty, but at least they make me think of you."

What he was trying to tell her? She finally inferred he wanted her to try and hold onto the pistachio farm. In their one stroke of good luck, Ali had forgotten to inform the government about it. It would be their main source of income for now.

"With pleasure, Mehdi. I will. I love you. I wish we were all together."

"When the time is right." He sounded lonely.

"It can't come soon enough. We miss you."

"Same here. Kiss Darius for me."

Soraya hung up with the thousand questions she couldn't ask. How soon would they be leaving? How would she and Darius slip away unnoticed? How would they get their airplane tickets? Memories of being pulled off the Pan Am flight still made her shudder. Who was he bribing to pave the way? Who would contact them? Was it prudent to leave Tehran just when it appeared she would be reclaiming their possessions?

The last question was answered the next day at the Foundation for the Dispossessed, which turned out to be a single small room with a desk and some chairs. The room's one window had a large crack and was so dirty that only a bit of light made its way through the glass. Fluorescent ceiling lights made everyone in the room look green, which was how Soraya felt as the official began the interview.

"My name is Zero Wasem. I am handling your case." He looked at Arash. "Who are you?"

"I am Arash Cyrus."

"And who is this?"

"This is my sister, Soraya Sultan." Wasem's stare made her uncomfortable.

"So, Arash Cyrus, you claim that the government mistakenly took items from your home?"

"No, Mr. Wasem," Arash replied, "I believe the government purposely removed nearly everything from my sister's home."

"We have taken what is ours. The question is: Are you hiding anything more from us?"

He studied Soraya.

"Where is her husband? Why does her brother come with her instead?"

"You see, sir, her husband has business overseas and was not there when this errant confiscation occurred."

Soraya was angry. This Zero Wasem was pretending she wasn't in the room. Wasem glanced at his clipboard. Flipping through several pages, he let out a bored sigh and tossed the clipboard on the desk.

"I see nothing improper here. Did you bring proof of your belongings?"

"Yes, sir, of course we brought proof," began Soraya.

Arash's commanding hand gripped her shoulder. His tacit "Shut up, Soraya," rang in her head. He'd made her promise she wouldn't speak unless she was directly asked a question yet she'd broken the promise mere seconds into the interview. He'd have more to say to her later.

"Yes sir," answered Arash. "We've gathered a few photos and some receipts. We would have brought further proof if the soldiers had not taken all my sister's photo albums, so I can only show you photos from my own collection of our family gatherings. And we've spent hours writing descriptions of the Sultan household items to be matched with your warehouse inventory."

Wasem crossed his arms and sighed once again, unimpressed.

"This case is problematic without hard proof and without this woman's husband present. You will try harder and come back next Monday with better proof."

Arash struggled to respond to the irrational.

"But, I ... we will do our best. Thank you for hearing our case, Mr. Wasem."

Over the next week Arash and Soraya drew pictures of the furniture and wrote histories behind the artwork, the only method of further proof they could devise. These they gave to Wasem on the following Monday. He perused the drawings with an oily smile – seemingly pleased they'd been made to work so hard.

"Ah, now some of these begin to look familiar to me. I will check in our warehouse and see if they've already been auctioned off. You will come back next week. Then I will see what I can do."

From then on, every meeting ended the same way.

"Are you hiding anything more from the government? No? Then come back next week and I will see what I can do to return your things. Come every week or there will be no progress for you."

But that progress never materialized. Soraya was disheartened and irritated. Months passed. Finally she begged Arash to let her speak at the next meeting.

"Nothing's happening anyway. Why not let me try? Then he'll have to acknowledge I exist, and I'd get satisfaction out of that, at least."

Arash shrugged. He couldn't argue the point.

"Most of the stuff is already gone, I'm sure. Likely we've not much to lose. But be careful not to provoke him."

So the first Monday in June, Soraya, wearing her most modest dress and her most beguiling smile, asked, "Mr. Wasem, today may I please be allowed to speak?"

Wasem refused to look at her, directing his question to Arash.

"The woman is the one who asks the questions now?"

Arash quickly responded. "I've insisted Soraya speak today. She is so modest she didn't feel it was her place, but I explained that her house is the one in question and therefore she must bear responsibility for regaining its contents. She is too shy to speak in public but has agreed to do so to please me."

Wow, thought Arash, that's the biggest lie I've ever concocted. Soraya was thinking the same thing, and was impressed that he'd managed to keep a straight face.

But before she got to speak a word, Wasem cut her off.

"Well, since this has become a woman's matter, her brother can wait outside."

They both stared at him, dumbfounded. This was unthinkable: A Muslim woman alone in a room with a man not related to her? It was highly improper. Panicked by a situation fraught with dangerous unknowns, they realized they had no choice. Arash walked to the door.

"This is scandalous, Zero Wasem. I am holding you accountable for my sister's modesty. If she is insulted or harmed, I'll move heaven and earth to make sure you are properly punished."

Wasem's oily smile slid around his face, from cheek to cheek and up and around his eyebrows, it seemed. Soraya wanted to scrub it off with detergent and a hard wire brush. Wasem turned his full attention to her as soon as they were alone, looking her directly in the eyes with a gaze utterly devoid of respect. It was so disquieting she actually wished she were invisible again.

He circled her chair, staring and rubbing his chin.

"So, Soraya Sultan, whose husband has deserted her, what have you done to deserve this fate?"

"Nothing, sir. I've done nothing. I am innocent."

"Really?" He picked up his clipboard. "I have all the details right here, how your husband fled the country because he is an infidel Bahá'í and, oh yes, right here is the inventory of everything collected from your house."

Soraya looked up, shocked.

"You have the inventory list? Then why did you require proof of ownership from us? You've known from day one where our things are?"

"Of course."

"Then why are you putting us through this?"

"Because the Sultan household is up to its neck in the camel dung of Imperial Iran. You knelt at the feet of the demon Shah Pahlavi, stooge of the Americans. You are complicit in the exploitation of the Iranian people and the glorification of Western corruption."

The smile spread across his face again.

"Besides, I don't like your brother. You, I don't know about yet. We'll see. Come back next week. I'm sure we can recover your items. At least a few of them."

Arash was too furious to talk on the drive home, but Soraya persisted.

"It's our only chance. Let me keep trying."

"He's disrespecting you as a Muslim woman. How do I protect you if I'm not in the room?"

"Don't forget how loud I can yell."

"You're in danger."

"I know." She hesitated, then began, "Arash, I need to share something, but you can't repeat it to anyone."

"I already know. When are you leaving?"

"How ...?"

"I'm your brother. And you don't have a choice. Iran is entrenched in anarchy and you're in its cross hairs. Tell me how I can help."

"I don't want to endanger the family, but I could use some cash for the flight. I assume we're flying, anyway, but I'm not really sure how or when we'll be contacted with more information."

"It's not like you've done this before. I'll give you whatever I can. Anything else?"

"Well, I fired Ali Nassiri two months ago for destroying our lives and I don't regret it, mind you. But he hasn't found a new job. I don't know how they're eating. Nema looks thin and sad. Please, I need help finding Ali a job."

"Ali's not going to find a job. There's little work and he has the wrong last name. No one named Nassiri is going to be hired under our grand new Islamic Republic. Killed maybe, like his SAVAK relative or his brother Manu, but not hired. Let me talk to Uncle Mahmud. Perhaps Leyla has a saleable skill Uncle can utilize. So you hate Ali but worry about the family?"

"Leyla says he's no longer himself. I do worry."

"You're a marshmallow at heart."

"No, I'm not. All right, perhaps I am."

Ali sat at his workbench in the garage, cleaning Manu's M1911 Colt .45. He shifted the semiautomatic pistol from hand to hand, feeling its weight, sensing Manu's touch on it, wondering how many times his brother had fired it and if he'd killed anyone with it. Manu had taken him once to a firing range but the ease of unleashing its deadly force unnerved Ali, so he'd declined another visit. Now he was fascinated by its mechanics and how it echoed the American gunslingers of the Wild West. He only brought out the gun while Nema attended school at the Sultan's mansion and Leyla was out of the house. Ali had tried hard to find work the first month, lost enthusiasm the second month, and stopped looking by the third. Luckily, Leyla was doing housework and running errands for Soraya's uncle. They had survived for a little while, living for free on the compound. He was still paying the rent on Manu's apartment, but they'd either have to move into it or let it go next month. They needed the money.

He pushed the Colt's release button. The clip dropped into his hand. He set it down and pulled back the slide to double-check. The chamber was empty. Maybe he'd visit the shooting range again in honor of his brother. He slid the gun back into Manu's duffel bag, pushing as far as possible under his workbench. He didn't want Nema finding the gun by accident. Ali definitely did not need any more bad karma.

Chapter 24

An Orderly Drawer

September, 1979

SORAYA'S EYES flew open. It was pitch black outside, yet the phone on her bed stand was ringing. She lunged at the receiver, her heart pounding. On the other end she heard a breathless Arash.

"I just had a call from Mehdi."

"What's wrong? Oh my God, is he hurt?"

"No. He's fine. He said he was thinking of you but didn't want to wake you up any earlier than necessary so he called me instead."

Soraya was confused.

"So you hang up and call me right away. Thank you for the extra ninety seconds of sleep. Why didn't he call me?"

"He and I caught up on some things first. He says he's been thinking of your beautiful garden and he has asked you to think of him when you next cut flowers."

Uh oh, thought Soraya. Here we go again, but nothing made sense, especially since she abhorred dirty hands, and had never cut flowers from the garden, and Mehdi knew it.

"All right, that's a sweet idea. I'll have Ebi cut some flowers for an arrangement and we'll send Mehdi a picture of them."

"No!" said Arash. He quickly lowered his voice.

"Mehdi asked if you would please gather them yourself this morning, as early as possible because he's thinking of you. Maybe you could do it now, since you're already awake, and the flowers are asleep, poetically speaking, and whatever you do, definitely do it before Ebi arrives. Mehdi also asked that you put them in the wicker basket he bought you in Qom years ago."

Soraya slowly pieced together the puzzle. She had to use that old basket with the broken handle? Apparently there was something in it he needed to get to her.

She consciously answered in a playful tone, in case someone was listening in.

"Well, that's my Mehdi, so romantic he can't wait until the dawn to send me flowers from my own garden. And aren't you the poet? I did not know that flowers snoozed at night. Thank you, Arash. Why don't you come over for breakfast and I'll show you my lovely floral arrangement? But please, wait until the sun rises."

The clock read 4:40 a.m. She yawned. Grabbing the bedside flashlight, she threw on her robe, slipped on a pair of flats and tiptoed out the front door, creeping across the compound to the gardening shed. Mehdi had specifically indicated the basket and she hoped the ratty old thing was still there. She'd have to look for it. Ebi used a tin bucket when he cut flowers. Who even knew that he hadn't thrown away the basket?

Soraya opened the shed door slowly. She'd not been in here for a long time. Its earthy scent was refreshing, reminding her to enjoy the garden more often. She left off the ceiling light, fearful its glow would attract attention at this hour. Gangs had taken to roaming the streets at night.

It was troubling to know that apparently someone had climbed over the compound walls undetected and entered the gardening shed without waking the guard dogs. The compound was more vulnerable than she'd imagined. She checked the shed's perimeter to make sure she wasn't being watched. The very thought made her skin crawl.

Shining the flashlight slowly around the room, she spotted the basket on the highest shelf, stuffed in between some cracked pots. It was well above her reach. She laid the flashlight on top of a pair of rolled up gardening gloves, angling it upwards to illuminate the shelf.

Now she needed something to utilize as a stool. A large, upside down flowerpot was in the corner. It was heavy and scraped loudly against the floorboards as she pushed it into place. Freezing at the noise, she waited for the dogs to bark, but the compound stayed quiet. They needed new guard dogs. Carefully, and as quietly as possible, she moved the pot. Standing on its base, she could just reach the basket.

She looked inside the sorry-looking thing, finding an envelope. Written on the stationery inside it was a phone number with the name, Zamani. She tucked the card into her robe pocket, replaced the basket onto the shelf exactly as she had found it, and gently pushed the pot back to its corner. Zamani must be her contact, or perhaps the very person who would spirit them out of Tehran to a joyful reunion with Mehdi. The difficulty of keeping this information secret dawned on Soraya. She'd best not share anything with Darius. Secrets were not his forte.

Fully awake now, she abandoned the notion of going back to bed. She walked back, when somewhere between the garden shed and her front door, the reality of leaving behind home and country hit her like a bucket of ice water. The walls of her house suddenly became more precious than any of her jewels.

Brewing a pot of jasmine tea and setting a bowl of almonds on the kitchen table, she decided to create a list of preparations for the trip. Already feeling nostalgic, she took a new notepad from the kitchen's notepad drawer.

The drawer itself was a family joke, with origins two years earlier, when Alaleh had rebelled against the numerous lists and notepads Soraya left scattered everywhere about "her" kitchen. One evening, the chef had cleared out a drawer of kitchen gadgets and neatly stacked Soraya's collection of notebooks, some partially used and others brand new, inside the drawer. With a recipe card and felt tip pen, she'd created a label reading: Soraya's Notepad Spa and Resort, taping it onto the drawer front before closing down the kitchen for the night.

The next day, as family and staff noticed the drawer, laughter began to echo through the mansion. Soraya finally came downstairs to investigate the levity. When she walked in the kitchen, it went quiet. The staff was afraid of her reaction. Bewildered, she finally saw the label, read it, and opened the door to examine its contents. Then she roared with laughter.

As she left the kitchen, she'd quipped, "You're going to need a bigger drawer." They'd laughed at the "Jaws" reference, and now she was feeling sentimental about that silly kitchen drawer. Leaving was going to be much harder than she'd imagined, she realized, as she wiped away a tear, but getting organized with a list would help.

The back door opened and Arash stuck his head in. "How's the newly-appointed horticulturist doing?"

"It's still nighttime, you goose. Go back to bed."

"Not sleepy. Where are the flowers?"

"Oh please, Arash, seriously? Now tell me why Mehdi called you instead of me."

She pushed a bowl of nuts toward him. He chewed thoughtfully on a handful of the almonds.

"He wanted to inform me about what's transpiring and didn't want to risk giving out the information on your phone line. You're going to need my help, sister. You can't up and travel without a male escort. And vanishing without somebody noticing isn't going to be easy. We're trying to anticipate where things could go wrong."

"So you know more about the plans than I do?"

"No, not really, except that I'm going to travel with you as far as I can, but at some point you're going to be on your own. Mehdi says he's arranged for the safest, most comfortable and streamlined way out."

"How long will it take? Did he say?"

"No more than three or four days. What was in the wicker basket?"

"A name and phone number."

"Good, that's the man who contracts the smugglers. The whole garden shed ruse was an experiment to establish a secure way for getting information to you, if necessary. Hide the paper or better yet, let's memorize the information and shred the paper. We'll phone him ... what's his name?"

"Zamani."

"Okay, we'll call him from my office this weekend."

A sleepy Fatima stumbled into the kitchen.

"I heard noises. Why are you up, Mrs. Sultan? Is everything okay?" She yawned without covering her mouth, blanching when she noticed Arash. "Oh no, I didn't see you there, Mr. Cyrus. I'm barely awake. My hair isn't even brushed. Please don't look at me!" She covered her face with her hands.

He couldn't resist needling her.

"I'm sorry, Miss, but have we met? My name is Arash. You are ... ?"

Soraya threw an almond at him.

"You pig! Fatima, your timing is perfect. Our 'vacation' plans are falling into place."

Arash quickly cautioned them, "You must realize that things probably won't happen immediately. This is just the first step. Smugglers wait until they have enough people to make the trip profitable. They also make certain the timing is right before setting things in motion, so the actual 'vacation' will happen somewhat last minute. Be ready to throw your things into a suitcase and vanish."

Fatima was staring at the floor, but Soraya didn't notice at first and kept on planning.

"Fatima, we'll do this together. And will you please help me decide ahead of time what Darius should bring? I don't want him to know about our plans yet."

Fatima avoided looking at her.

"Of course, Mrs. Sultan, but I'm not sure ... now that things have changed in my life. I mean, Jamal and I ... it's just, I don't think I want to leave now ..."

Soraya jumped in.

"Of course, dear Nanny. What was I thinking? You're in love. One must never walk away from happiness. You'll be all right here in Tehran. Just don't tell anyone you worked for us and they'll leave you alone. Jamal is a good Muslim, yes?"

"Yes, but not a revolutionary. Don't worry, though, I'll stay here with you until you go." She teared up. "How do I tell Darius goodbye? I can't bear the thought."

"You will say 'I'll see you soon,' because you'll come to visit us, wherever we end up. Think more about the sweet reunions. And we'll return as soon as the Shah is restored to power." She hoped.

Arash grabbed a handful of nuts to go and stood.

"Well, as delicious as these are, Raya will make me a more complete breakfast than you've provided. I know she suspects what's transpiring, but she's smart enough not to ask questions. I'm grateful to have a very trustworthy wife."

Soraya hugged him.

"Thank you, Arash."

"You're welcome. For now, just go about your lives. Pretend nothing is different. It may be days, weeks, even months before this happens. But be ready to move when it does." He looked at Soraya. "I'm afraid we'll have to keep showing up to Wasem's office. He'll be suspicious if we suddenly lose interest in recovering your things."

Soraya set her jaw. "I'm going to get something back from him if it kills me."

Unfortunately, as week after week of meetings with Wasem went by, his behavior slid toward the lascivious, setting Soraya on edge. Her worst fears materialized in the middle of September.

"My dear woman," Wasem began, as Soraya took the seat she'd come to hate so much, "it pains me to see you walk into my office alone each week."

"I wouldn't walk in alone if you'd allow my brother to chaperone, as is proper."

Soraya was more nervous than she let on. His voice had a dangerous tone.

Wasem eased his way behind her. She nearly jumped from the chair when he started to massage her shoulders.

"You're still a young woman, too young to be without a husband. You do understand, don't you, that yours will never be able to come back to Iran, and if he dares to try, I'll personally make sure he meets his fate?"

She didn't answer.

"Why, *Soraya-joon*, you're trembling. I can't possibly frighten you. Or do I?"

He laid out his agenda.

"It would be so much easier for me to retrieve your possessions if you and I were married. My household would be your household, as yours would be mine. Just think of it, you'd have all your pretty things back. I'd be very good for a woman like you."

Soraya was on the verge of screaming for help, but she wanted to beat him at his own game.

"I'm shocked that such a devout Muslim would want to marry a woman who has stared him in the face," she began, "and a woman who has observed his lack of size through his pants." It was a wild guess, based on his overblown bravado. She had to push him to the edge of the cliff without inviting violence on herself.

Wasem was taken aback. She'd hit a nerve. He was self-conscious about the size of his penis. His buddies had teased him about it since high school. He pressed forward on the offensive, angry.

"My dear, my other wife will testify to my prowess in bed. This is a good offer I make today. You ungrateful bitch, you're like all the other ungrateful bitches. That's why there are so many more women in hell than men. They are disrespectful to men. The Qur'an says ..."

She cut him off, her voice rising with indignation. She hoped Arash could hear the commotion. She might need protection at any moment.

"Don't you quote the Qur'an to me. You think I haven't counted the times you've ignored the call to prayer while interrogating me week after week? Perhaps I'll share your blasphemy with your superior."

Wasem shouted. "No one would believe you. You are a woman. You are nothing! You wouldn't dare to ..."

The office door flew open and an older man strode into the room. Zero Wasem leaped away from Soraya and stood at attention. This obviously was Wasem's superior, and he was angry. That thrilled Soraya. She wanted nothing more than to see Wasem chastised.

Except that the man wasn't looking on Wasem, he was glaring at her. Shaking a piece of paper in her face, he said, "You have not been forthcoming, Mrs. Sultan. You have withheld from us knowledge of your farm property, despite weekly requests for information regarding all of your assets. You have lied to us and tried to cheat the government, but it's no matter. The Islamic Government has taken control of your farm. You, Soraya Sultan, are in much trouble."

He slammed the door behind him. Wasem stared coldly at her. "Well, my lovely rose, it seems you have hidden thorns. What shall I do with you?"

Soraya panicked.

Wasem grinned. He had the upper hand now.

"Perhaps you don't have the options you did a few minutes ago. What's that? I'm not hearing your insults anymore. My offer is looking more generous, I suppose, since it may save your life. As they say: He who wants a lovely rose must respect the thorns. Decide carefully, my rose, or I will prune you with one snip."

Soraya didn't tell Arash about Wasem's threats. They would only infuriate him more and the situation would explode. Things were bad enough as they were. From that day on, Wasem's interviews were brusquer, harsher, and always concluded with a demand for her answer to his marriage proposal. Soraya strung him along, pretending she wanted to marry him but that she her father opposed the match. How much longer, she worried, could she keep this disgusting man at bay without causing dire consequences?

Chapter 25

Politics

October 22, 1979

IT WAS A GRAND celebration. Today was Uncle Mahmud's 70th birthday and the entire family was gathered at Arash's house. The copious flowers, streamers and balloons befitted Mahmud's jovial nature. As usual, he was having more fun than anyone. Jokes continuously rolled from his mouth, by-passing his happily inebriated brain.

"Okay, here's another good one," he said.

The family groaned good-naturedly.

"I want to hear it!" said Darius.

"Good boy!" said Mahmud. "But first I'll just ..."

He drained his champagne glass.

"Okay. Here it comes: An American and an English-speaking Iranian board a plane from Tehran to LAX.

The Iranian sits next to the American, who asks him:

'What kind of 'ian' are you?'

What?' asks the Iranian.

'I said, 'What kind of 'ian' are you?'

'I don't understand your question,' says the Iranian.

'Stupid! Are you Cambod-ian, Ind-ian or Iran-ian?'

'Oh! I am Iranian,' our countryman answers.

Two hours pass without a word.

Finally, the Iranian asks, 'What kind of 'key' are you?'

'What?' asks the American.

'I said, what kind of 'key' are you?'

'I don't understand your question,' says the American.

'Stupid! Are you a mon-key, don-key, or a Yan-kee?'"

The room erupted in a chorus of boos.

"More champagne!" said Arash. "I'm not drunk enough for these jokes!

Mahmud lifted his empty glass.

"That's because I'm way ahead of you, nephew, but if you bring me another bottle I'll show you how it's done."

The room was still vibrating with merriment when Ardeshir walked downstairs, his face ashen. He held up his hands, eliciting quiet.

"Please, everyone. Give me your attention. I'm sorry, but I must share something important. Shah Pahlavi has left Mexico. He's in the United States."

He had their attention.

This was surprising. The Americans had refused the Shah asylum, so he'd moved nomadically from Egypt to Morocco, from the Bahamas to Mexico. He'd sought medical treatment in the United States, but had been rebuffed, cut adrift by the Carter administration. Even though former President Richard Nixon and former Secretary of State Henry Kissinger remained supportive, overall, the Shah had been vilified to the Americans, both by the Administration and by the press, which had embraced Khomeini's rise to power.

"There's more," Ardeshir continued. "Our king has been admitted to New York Hospital for emergency cancer treatment, but they're saying that his medical care over the last few years has been misguided and shameful."

Almost impossibly, the Carter administration hadn't known that the Shah had non-Hodgkin's Lymphoma until a few days before allowing him into the country. He'd somehow kept his illness a secret.

Ardeshir had difficulty getting the next sentence out.

"The Shah is dying."

Grief crushed the party's gaiety. How had the Shah remained stoic even while millions in Iran called for his death? How was Empress Farah Pahlavi holding up? And the children: How horrific to watch their father dying in a fog of pain.

Ardeshir lifted his glass. "To our leader, a man of great courage. To Mohammad Reza Shah Pahlavi."

Soraya bit her lip to keep from crying. There went any chance of his return.

Even Uncle Mahmud, former prisoner of the Shah's prison, lifted his glass in a toast to his ruler.

"To our Shah."

Later that night, Soraya called Mehdi.

"I'm ready to leave. If the Shah is not returning, there is no Persia and I have no country."

"I know, my darling, I know," was all he said.

Chapter 26

The Hostage Taking

American Embassy, Tehran, November 4, 1979

A T 5:30 a.m., the handful of remaining U.S. Marine Security Guards still stationed at the American Embassy in Tehran was alert and extra vigilant. Students and Revolutionary Guards had been casing the embassy grounds from the neighboring rooftops over several days, stressing out the embassy's staff, which already was living under the clawing shadow of Ayatollah Khomeini's new and hostile Iranian theocracy.

They'd been instructed to destroy the embassy's Intel in the event of any security breach. The State Department was well aware of the threats surrounding the embassy, where once more than 300 people had lived and worked before the Shah's exile.

But now only about 100 workers remained. Most of the American staff, including William H. Sullivan, American Ambassador to Iran, had gone home. The most senior official remaining was Chargé d'affaires, Bruce Laingen, who began this day at the Iranian Foreign Ministry Office.

Laingen was scheduled to meet in the afternoon with State Department Vice Consul Richard Queen, who had come into work early this morning. The clock on his wall now read 7:00 a.m.

As Queen briefly scanned the street, the ubiquitous handful of anti-American protesters were milling sleepily in front of the gates, carrying their usual signs, which demanded the extradition of the Shah to Iran. It was a pretty normal morning in an abnormal situation.

Unbeknownst to him, a few blocks away at Tehran Polytechnique, a massing of students soon to be known as the Muslim Student Followers of the Imam's Line were receiving their instructions. Ali Zahmatkesh was in charge of today's planned attack on the embassy. He spoke to the huge gathering of students, his "troops," with passion, fanning the flames of their zealous anger over the United States' admittance of the "Most disgraceful king."

Despite the Shah's illness, they would accept nothing less than his immediate extradition to Iran to stand trial for his "oppression of the people." Naturally, then they would execute him. But unless these demands were met, they promised that America would pay for giving him sanctuary.

The students were eager to begin their march on the embassy, which, as informants on nearby rooftops had assured Zahmatkesh, was grossly understaffed. While the students spilled out onto the streets, a brief but significant event took place: He handed a pair of metal cutters to a female student, who tucked them underneath her chador.

Around 10:00 a.m., the embassy employees looked up from their desks, startled. The marines were shouting. Something untoward was unfolding. Running to the office windows, they witnessed a terrifying scenario: A seething mass was converging on the embassy, shouting, *"Marg bar Amrika,"* "Death to America."

Staff Sergeant Michael E. Moeller barked orders. The number of embassy guards had been reduced to this tiny nucleus, and typically they were stationed inside of the buildings and not around its vulnerable perimeter. Now they were facing down an uncontrolled mob coming down the street. The marines would stand their ground until they were either overpowered or killed. Clearly one of these two fates was fast approaching.

As one marine watching the advancing mob said to a fellow marine, "Man, we're going to have an Alamo."

Inside the offices, cries of "Destruct, Destruct!" rang out. Workers grabbed stacks of paper and ran to the burn furnace, reaching over and across one another to throw sensitive information into the flames. Other employees placed frantic phone calls to Washington.

The soldiers repositioned to form an outside buffer

that they hoped would buy the staff a few minutes.

Someone yelled, "Barricade the doors!"

A female staffer shouted, "The papers aren't burning! The furnace isn't working. Damn it all to hell! Try the paper shredders!"

Expletives flew as thick as the stacks of papers. The documents were repeatedly shoved into the inexpensive government shredders, which proved too lightweight for the large volume of papers. The machines jammed.

Staffers heard the students shaking the gates.

"Oh, my God, they're trying to climb over the walls!"

The Americans were out of time. They weren't going to be able to destroy sufficient paperwork. Sensitive U.S. documents were about to fall into the hands of the students and important intelligence was going to be compromised. Now the employees began wondering whether they would live or die through this disaster.

Among the sheets of paper, one in particular, which remained in pristine condition, fell to the floor. It was a copy of a letter the American Embassy had sent to the State Department, warning that they would be in grave danger should the Shah be admitted to the United States before the embassy was secured by a stronger military presence.

Outside the compound's gates, the student with the metal cutters pulled them from underneath her chador and handed them to Zahmatkesh, who easily snapped the lock on the front gate. With that, the deluge of students, perhaps thousands of them, rushed inside, overrunning the twenty-six acres of official American soil.

News organizations quickly got wind of the students' incursion. The takeover was a massive humiliation for the United States. To the eyes of the whole world it had exposed the superpower's impotence. The once mighty Americans were now at the mercy of students. Sixty-six hostages already were being paraded before television cameras, blindfolded and with their hands tied behind their backs. American flags found in the rampage were being dragged through the dirt and burned for the cameras.

Three other Americans were also taken hostage at the Iranian Foreign Ministry Office, including Bruce Laingen.

Khomeini, who at first labeled the Embassy "a den of spies," changed his mind a week later and let go all non-U.S. hostages. He also released all but two women, and all but one African American man, asserting that they weren't culpable because they had already felt the "oppression of American society." Richard Queen would be released eventually, about nine months later, after falling ill with multiple sclerosis.

But the remaining 52 Americans were just beginning 444 days in captivity: One year, two months and two weeks would be ripped from their lives, nearly 64 weeks with time spent in handcuffs, or blindfolded, sometimes in solitary confinement and frequently subjected to mock executions.

The world held its breath for all 444 days. The Islamic government turned its focus to the students' triumph and the worldwide attention they were garnering, leaving former targets like Soraya Sultan more or less ignored.

Mehdi called on Thursday, November 22nd. Soraya had just finished a late-night snack when the phone rang.

"Happy American Thanksgiving from Washington, D.C., darling. At least it's Thanksgiving on this side of the world." he said. "How are you, my dearest Soraya?"

"I'm fine, darling. Thanksgiving? Isn't that the day the Americans eat turkey?"

"Yes, and I've been invited to a Thanksgiving dinner this evening. Because of the focus on the hostage situation, many congressmen are flying their families to D.C. for Thanksgiving rather than going home. The country is in an uproar over the crisis, as you know. President Carter has embargoed Iranian oil. Now he's also frozen Iranian assets. I don't think he can figure out how to rescue the hostages." Mehdi sounded like he didn't mind being near the action.

"Isn't it dangerous for you to be there, as a Persian?"

"No," he said, "I come highly recommended by my contacts, and the congressman who issued the invitation wants my perspective on Iran. I'm happy to oblige. He's an interesting man. He fought in World War II."

"Oh," said Soraya. "That does sound interesting." But she wasn't very familiar with World War II.

"I know you prefer Persian history, Soraya, and nothing here in the States has the *gravitas* of King Cyrus and the Cyrus Cylinder, but this man is powerful, and happily for us, he's familiar with some condos for lease nearby."

So Mehdi was looking at places for them to live.

"Oh, my."

"Well, I may rent for a while and see if I think you'd survive the cold winters. Then you can 'vacation' here if it works out. Otherwise, I'll meet you in California. We know its winters are mild, and apparently many expats live there."

California! Soraya hadn't imagined living near movie stars and cowboys. And the beaches!

"Would you rent in Hollywood? Or near the ocean?"

"I don't know the areas yet. I'll try D.C. first."

"Did you get the pictures I sent you of Darius?"

"Yes. He's such a little man. I can't believe how much he's grown. Speaking of growing things, are you spending much time in the garden?"

"Not lately, with the recent cold snap. The garden looks pretty barren."

"That's why I was thinking it's time to let Ebi go. Tell

him you'll hire him back next spring, but that money is running low right now. Ask him to find another job."

Her head was spinning. Mehdi was either clearing the way for them to disappear, or he wanted her to have easy access to the garden shed for messages. Or both.

"All right, darling. I'm sure he'll understand. Our cash flow is definitely tight. Without Arash helping us out, I couldn't keep Alaleh on, that's certain."

"I think you should let her go, too."

Soraya's pulse raced. They might leave that soon?

"You're going to make me cook? All right, my love. Just be glad you don't have to eat it."

Ebi and Alaleh accepted the news graciously. Ebi said not to worry, and that a gardener could always find a garden to tend. Alaleh cried, but thanked Soraya for keeping her on as long as she had.

At midnight, Soraya stole outside to the garden shed, assuming there was a message in the basket. There was. It read, "Be in Zabol no later than December 15th. Bring one suitcase per person. Call when you arrive in Zabol." The letter was signed, "Zamani."

No wonder Mehdi was looking at places to live. The time for them to vanish into thin air had come.

Chapter 27

Sweet Memories

Manu's apartment
Friday, November 23, 1979

MANU'S LANDLORD shook Ali's hand. "Leave the key on the floor when you're completely out," he said. "The place looks fine." He lowered his voice. "I'm real sorry about your brother. He was a good man. Didn't deserve what he got."

"Thank you," said Ali.

"There's too much grief in Tehran these days. I hope your pain eases over time."

"Thank you."

The landlord sighed, at a loss for consoling words.

"Okay, then. *Khodahafez.*"

"Goodbye and God be with you, too."

Ali and Leyla were officially done paying rent on Manu's apartment, although they had another week to vacate. Leyla offered to take time off from work today to help him finish the emotional task of removing Manu's personal property, but Ali had declined. He preferred to be alone here and frankly, there wasn't much left to do. The place was nearly empty since he'd been coming several times a week for a month. He'd already sold the bedroom furniture, the television, sofa, table and chairs and disposed of Manu's small library.

Now he sealed up the last box of sports trophies, thinking how impressed Nema would be to learn that his uncle had earned four large boxes of them.

Nema was beginning to show real athletic talent. He was fast, just like his uncle, but track took second place to soccer. He was looking like a striker. They'd signed Nema up for a youth soccer program, and after watching him play, the coaches had moved him into a higher age bracket where he could face stiffer competition.

It was Ali's dream that one day his son would play on the Iranian National Team in a World Cup competition. Wouldn't that have made Manu proud! The two were very much alike. Ali had boxed up a cross section of Manu's trophies for Nema, hoping to inspire his boy.

Ali looked at the boxes lining the living room wall, three-fourths to give away and the rest to be saved for posterity. They comprised the last of Manu's belongings. As a dedicated soldier and one who chose a life devoid of serious romantic relationships, Manu's apartment was sparsely decorated and thus was easy to vacate. Ali had labeled each box, indicating where it should go.

Manu's desk and roller swivel chair were still in the living room, though, the only remaining furniture. Ali had needed someplace to sit down and read through papers or look at photos, or just to take a break from the packing. He'd arranged for the desk to be picked up tomorrow. But he hadn't cleaned out the kitchen yet. As he suspected, there wasn't much in there, and nothing of value, although Ali decided Leyla might like the hand-held vacuum. Besides that, the kitchen consisted of two dirty dishtowels, an inch of liquid dish soap in a plastic bottle, a torn sponge, mismatched plates, a few bowls and an assortment of silverware. In the cupboard he found what he termed 'guy' food: Stale lavash crackers, dates, a bag of walnuts, and jam. There were apples on the counter and cheese in the fridge.

Ali snacked on the food that wasn't spoiled, and then, remembering his brother's sweet tooth, checked the freezer. He was right. There was a large carton of Manu's favorite dessert, *bastani-e za'farani*, Persian ice milk made with eggs, rose water, saffron, vanilla and pistachios.

I know my brother well, he thought, rinsing off a spoon and digging in. It was delicious. His brother had bought the version with frozen flakes of clotted cream, the best kind. He set the carton back into the freezer. This would be his reward once he was finished loading the boxes into the car.

Up and down the stairs, back and forth to the Tehran Taxi he trudged, fitting the boxes with precision into the trunk. When that was full, he filled the back seat. By the time he'd finagled the last box into the front passenger seat, the car was sagging. He wondered if the junker had enough muscle to even reach the speed limit.

Pushing down the door locks and forcing the door closed, he gave the car a pat on its "head." The Tehran Taxi had a personality of its own and he figured it deserved a little praise at long last.

"You're a good vehicle."

He headed back up the stairs. Time for his reward.

Plopping down at Manu's desk, he set the carton of *bastani* at his right hand and leafed through the photo scrapbook he'd assembled over the weeks. He downed more of the custard-based ice cream. He and Manu had eaten a lot of *bastani* over the years: At the bazaar, during the holidays, birthdays, celebrating Manu's athletic victories, and all summer long. He only wished he had those thin, crispy waffles that turned the *bastani* into ice cream sandwiches. He dug out another scoop of the creamy gold sweetness and lifted it heavenward.

"Here's to you, little brother."

Finishing up the rest of the album, he lingered over the last photo, the one of Manu and him with their arms draped around each other. They looked so happy. They had always been happy together.

For the first time since Manu's death, Ali was at peace. Reaching into his coat pocket, he removed Manu's pistol. He nuzzled it under his chin and pulled the trigger.

Chapter 28

Ten Women in Shiraz

L EYLA LEANED against the kitchen counter lest she fall. The note she was holding was unbearably heavy. She stared at it, not comprehending the words at first, then resisting their dawning understanding, and ultimately emitting a guttural cry of anguish.

Ali had written his goodbye on a sheet of high quality stationery, as though intending to compose an eloquent farewell, but failing to find the words, had given up and scrawled, "I'm sorry."

She found herself on Soraya's doorstep. She didn't remember walking here, but she had, and obviously she'd rung the bell, because Soraya was standing at the door.

"Leyla, are you all right? You're pale."

There was no answer.

"Leyla! Dear, look at me, I'm asking if you're all right. Come in. Tell me what's happening. Is Nema okay? Are you sick?" She took her by the hand, sitting her on the couch. "Tell me what has happened."

Leyla looked at Soraya and dropped the crumpled sheet of stationery in her lap. Soraya smoothed the paper to read it. She looked up, shocked.

"Leyla, has Ali left you?"

"No. Yes." Her tears trickled down like quiet rain.

"No, it can't be! Is it another woman?"

"I wish. No, I don't mean that, except that anything would be better than the truth. He's committed suicide, Soraya. I just know he has, better than I know my own name. And I'm angry. Does that make me heartless?"

"No, Leyla, you're mistaken. Ali wouldn't do such a thing to you and Nema. You are the jewels of his heart. He loves his family. Look how hard he tried save his brother."

"That's just it. This is all because of Manu. I knew Ali was spending too much time at the apartment, that it wasn't healthy, but what could I do? I had to go to work; I had to take care of Nema. You know that Ali blamed himself for Manu's arrest. But I was certain that we meant enough to him ... obviously I was wrong."

Soraya hugged her, fighting off pangs of guilt.

"No, I won't let you think that. Ali didn't know what he was doing. He was crazed with grief. I promise you he loved you more than anyone else in the world."

Leyla stared down at her lap.

"I noticed a different look in his eyes this morning. I offered to help him finish up at the apartment, and when he said he didn't need me I agreed because he seemed so normal. He's been depressed since the execution, but this morning he looked much better. I assumed the clouds were parting, but I misread him. I think I wanted to believe that after eight months, he was healing."

Soraya offered a tissue. Leyla wiped away tears.

"How was I so stupid? How could he do this to us?"

The doorbell rang. It was Arash, along with a policeman.

"I'm looking for Leyla Nassiri," he said. "Mr. Cyrus said we'd probably find her here."

Leyla quickly blew her nose and appeared at the door. The policeman could see that she already knew. "I'm sorry for your loss. Did he leave a suicide note?"

Leyla handed him the paper. She needed to ask a question even though she didn't want to hear the answer.

"How did he ..."

She couldn't finish the sentence.

The policeman had been through the process countless times. He saved her the pain of asking.

"One bullet, Ma'am. He never felt a thing. I'll need someone to identify the body, but I'd advise someone going in your stead. It's too difficult."

Arash spoke up.

"I'll handle everything, Leyla. I'll identify him at the morgue, see that he's washed and purified and I'll make sure that he's wrapped in a proper *kafan*. I'll do whatever it takes to make sure the washers won't talk about how he died. Once the body is wrapped in the *mustahab*, no one will be able to see how it happened. I'll have him buried tomorrow. He will face Mecca, Leyla."

"But I have to say goodbye to my husband."

Arash's tenderness sought to console.

"Figure out a better way to say goodbye," he said. "Seeing your husband like this will only create an ugly memory. Hang on to the beautiful memories instead. I promise to bring home a lock of his hair, his wedding ring and personal effects. Leyla, be kind to yourself."

Soraya looked at her brother. What a big-hearted man he was. She recalled all the baby birds he'd rescued as a boy, how he'd befriended classmates no one else liked, and as an adult, how he made regular visits to children's hospitals. No wonder she and everyone else adored him.

She compared Arash's kind heart to her immutable anger toward Ali. But, she reminded herself, her anger was justified, and furthermore, she hadn't shunned Leyla or Nema. Still, she wanted to hide. What if she'd shown him the largesse of mercy instead of her righteous anger? Unimaginable, but what if she had? Would Ali still have pulled the trigger? She'd never know.

"Leyla, I insist that you and Nema stay here tonight,"

she said. "We'll help you get back on your feet. Later on tonight we'll plan for your future."

After dinner, Leyla showed Soraya those passages from the Qur'an condemning suicide. It was a punishable state of disbelief. Ali's suicide would cast shame across her and Nema. The women fabricated a storyline for Ali's death.

"Here is our story," said Soraya. "Poor Ali simply had a heart attack at Manu's apartment. Agreed? Good. We will never utter the word 'suicide' to anyone, family or friend. I'm sure Arash can offer you an organizing job at his office to supplement your work at Uncle Mahmud's."

She didn't add that Arash would also be giving the police officer a healthy check to alter his report.

The next afternoon, at the hour of Ali's burial, Soraya and Leyla carried flowers to the farthest corner of the compound, where Ebi, who'd come immediately to help, had dug a symbolic grave, giving Leyla a place to grieve. The women laid their flowers inside the hole and pushed the dirt back inside with their bare hands, patting it into a traditional mound. Leyla recited passages from the Qur'an, while Soraya scented the freshly turned earth with rose water. They stood there for a while and cried, one from grief and the other out of guilt. When their tears were spent, Soraya placed a few stones next to the grave before leaving Leyla to mourn alone.

Darius took Nema under his wing. Nanny had explained to him how sad his friend was, and Darius responded with gusto, keeping his buddy occupied all day and having him sleep over in case he had nightmares.

All the while, Soraya tried to manage her own stress. She, Darius and Arash had to be in Mashhad, a city 450 miles northeast of Tehran, no later November 30th, a date only five days away.

One night after the household was asleep, Arash and Soraya met outside the kitchen door to plan their escape.

"A bus? No!" Soraya wailed, then lowered her voice. "Why should we take a bus? It's only an hour by plane!"

"Soraya, it's not possible. I drove by the airport today. Have you forgotten what security was like the last time you tried to fly out of Tehran? And believe me, this time you're on 'the list.' It's the same issue with the train station. But they won't expect you to take a bus."

"Well, of course they won't. I've never even been on a bus. How long will that take?"

"With stops and a transfer, about fourteen hours, but the bus is the least of our worries. Even with the helpful distraction of the American hostages, we must leave town well before our next Monday appointment at the government offices. They're so preoccupied with the Americans, they may not care if you don't show up, but it's also possible that Wasem will start scouring the departure points out of Tehran. We'll leave tomorrow night."

"But it's not possible to get ready in one day, Arash. I'm leaving my whole life behind!"

Arash rubbed his forehead. "I do understand, Soraya. I really do, and if it were in my power to change events, I would, but I can't. I warned you this would be difficult and sudden. You have to be out of town long enough before your appointment so that we're too far away for them to track us down."

"And I have too much to fit into one suitcase and not enough time to pare it down."

"Pack an extra bag and I'll carry it on the bus. We'll sort through your clothes in Mashhad and I'll take home the unnecessary things."

"Think of how difficult this will be for me."

"Soraya, the Islamic Republic just hanged ten Bahá'í women in Shiraz. Think of the consequences in this political climate if they catch you trying to flee the country again."

Chapter 29

Vanished

November 30, 1979

SORAYA TIPTOED into Darius' bedroom a little after midnight. Fatima was just shutting his suitcase. Soraya's bags were downstairs with Arash, who waited patiently.

"Did you fit everything in?" whispered Soraya.

"After sitting on it, yes. Please let me look at him for one minute before we wake him. I can't imagine how I'm going to let him leave." She fought back tears. "I promise I won't let him see me cry."

"On my honor, Fatima, this will not be the last time you see him. We'll speak of you every day to keep his memories fresh until you can see him again. But I do wish you were coming with us."

Fatima memorized his chubby face and mass of curls.

"I know. I hope we can move to America some day. Thank you for letting me care for Darius all these years. It's been an honor. Please send me lots of pictures."

"We couldn't have asked for a better nanny."

Fatima's breathing was shaky, but she grit her teeth.

"Okay, I'm ready."

Soraya crooned, "Wake up, Darius." She patted his hand until he stirred.

"What?" he mumbled, rubbing his eyes open, and sitting up in surprise. "What's wrong?"

"Nothing, darling," said his mother. "Actually, it's very exciting. We're going on a trip."

"Yes," said Fatima. "And you'll never guess where."

"I'm too tired to play a guessing game," said Darius, flopping back down on his pillow.

"Then I'll just tell you," Soraya said. "We're going to America to be with Papa. Tonight!"

Darius was wide-awake.

They headed to the kitchen for a quick breakfast. Except for some packaged snacks in Soraya's purse, this meal would have to hold them until they changed buses in Shahrud in the afternoon. Darius chattered endlessly about meeting the Bee Gees in America.

Soraya excused herself. She wanted to take one last walk around her beautiful home. She imagined it the way it once had looked, stylish and filled with artwork and heirlooms. She relived bringing infant Darius home from the hospital, thought about all the family birthday parties and gloried in the dazzling soirées that had filled this house with prestige. Running a finger down the staircase's banister, she thought about how many times she'd walked up and down the stairs. Memories flooded her heart, of the immediate family and business friends; of large events and private emotions.

Soraya realized that her nostalgia represented a futile longing to glue back together a life already broken into a million pieces. And since it was gone, she had to go, too. Still, the thought of leaving behind these remnants of happiness tore at her heart.

It was nearly 2:00 a.m. by the time they walked out the front door for the last time. Darius noticed that Nanny wasn't carrying a suitcase.

"Nanny, where's your bag? Hurry, we have to go."

Fatima knelt down in front of him.

"My sweet boy, I'm going to stay here because I'm getting married. I won't see you for a little while, but I'm going to write to you every day and you're going to send me lots of pictures."

"No!"

Fatima pinched her arm hard to hold back her tears. "It won't be for long, and you're going to be so excited to see your papa and the Gee Gees, or Bee Bees or whatever their name is, that you'll forget about me."

"No I won't!" said Darius, starting to cry.

She hugged him tightly. Grief was threatening to overtake her. She had to make a clean break of it, right now.

Cupping his chin in her hands she looked into his eyes and said, "Darius, I love you, up and down, and all around; forever and for always. Okay, it's your turn."

He tried.

"I love you, up and down, and all around ..."

His lip quivered. She hugged him one last time.

"Forever and for always! Now you need to hurry. See how I've slowed you down. Arash is already putting the luggage in the trunk and Raya's sitting in the driver's seat. Go, my darling!"

He turned and ran to the waiting car. Fatima closed the door quickly; afraid she'd run after him. When she heard the car driving away, she pulled aside a curtain, just a bit, for one more glimpse of her boy. He was staring back at the house from out the rear window, wiping tears on his coat sleeve. Letting go of the curtain, she let go her own tears.

Raya dropped off the trio at the bus station three and a half hours before their scheduled departure, getting them out of the neighborhood lest early risers see them leaving the compound carrying suitcases.

Once inside the station, Soraya and Arash chatted animatedly. They'd constructed a story about taking this bus to attend their cousin's wedding in Mashhad and how wonderful it was going to be, but they quickly exhausted their improvisational skills and by the time the bus arrived at 5:15 a.m. they were silently staring at the walls.

Waiting in line to board the bus, Arash whispered urgently in Soraya's ear.

"Please pretend like you've ridden buses your whole life. If you show discomfort or disdain we'll look suspicious. We've already drawn glances because your beauty screams 'aristocrat' no matter how common you to try to look."

Soraya tossed her hair.

"Oh, please, Arash, I'm fine."

But although she tried her best to act casual, the bus interior stank of old food and sweat. The seats were ripped and the chipping paint was scratched with graffiti. Two factory workers sat down directly across from Soraya, wearing company jumpsuits that smelled as though they'd been washed in an outhouse.

Arash patted her hand.

"You're making a face, dear sister."

She blew her nose, trying to blow away the stench.

"Don't touch anything, Darius," she muttered.

Four stops later, the bus was filled to capacity and Soraya was beside herself. A baby screamed incessantly, a filthy mongrel sat on the seat next to his grizzled master, and a boy parked his battered bicycle in the middle of the aisle next to her. Her face was turning green. Arash hastily opened the window for fresh air before she threw up.

Darius, on the other hand, was having a ball meeting passengers, until Arash whispered a reminder of the story they'd concocted about the wedding. Darius pouted. He thought going to America was a much more exciting story. He couldn't understand why he was being instructed to lie. All his life he'd gotten in trouble for fibbing and now his uncle was telling him he was supposed to lie. Grownups.

Shortly after noon the bus pulled into Shahrud, where they gratefully stretched their legs and located a nearby café serving decent food.

"We're half-way there," said Arash. "I'm going to find a pay phone and call my buddy SattAr to tell him we're about to make the transfer. He's picking us up in Mashhad."

Much sooner than Soraya wishsed, they boarded the bus that would carry them the rest of the way.

"How are you handling your adventure, sister?" Arash asked quietly.

Soraya wasn't going to give him the satisfaction of sharing her real feelings. "I'm absolutely fine with it," she said. "In fact, I've decided to invent a new perfume. I will call it, Eau de Puant."

Darius knew enough French to translate. He looked at his mother, puzzled, to ask, "Stinky water?"

It's a joke, darling," but she turned back to Arash, saying dryly, "We can distill it directly from the odors in this bus."

She was ecstatic when they arrived at the Mashhad bus station. It was now nearly 7:30 p.m. Thankfully, SattAr was still waiting for them in the parking lot. He swept them into his car and less than an hour later, they were seated in his dining room devouring a home cooked meal.

"So you're still a bachelor, SattAr," said Arash. "I suspect you're a hopeless case by now."

"That's all right with me. I like the single life," SattAr replied. "Darius, my boy, would you like to watch TV?"

"That's a wonderful idea," encouraged Soraya. "Adult conversation is boring."

Once Darius was settled in the family room, Arash opened up the discussion. "Thank you, my good friend, for facilitating my sister's escape. You are gracious and brave to take us into your home. You'll understand that it's urgent for Soraya call her contact in Tehran right away. He has further instructions."

Soraya dialed Zamian's phone number. A gruff voice answered. "Tell me your name and where you are."

He began giving her information. Soraya furiously took notes, her eyes getting bigger with each passing minute. By the time she hung up, a mixture of confusion and panic filled her eyes.

"Now we have to get to a village on the outskirts of Zabol to meet the men who will take us out of Iran. Zamian mentioned that Mehdi had bought us the "Cadillac" escape, whatever that means. I was assuming we'd fly out of the country from here, but Zamian said something about needing Pakistani passports before flying out of Karachi to Portugal. I think there's been a mistake, don't you?"

"No, I don't. Did he give you the date to meet your escorts?" asked SattAr.

"December 8th."

"So you have about a week, time enough to rest for a day or two. There are more than 500 difficult miles between here and Zabol. The drive will take two days."

Arash was worried.

"What do we do? She can't drive that distance alone and I have to get back to work before people suspect I'm part of their disappearance."

"Why don't we take the bus?" Soraya asked, shocking even herself. Disgusting though the bus had been, she'd discovered the pleasant diversion of eavesdropping on other people's conversations.

"Not possible," said SattAr. "There are only short regional bus routes between Mashhad and Zabol, and even if you could navigate the dozen transfers, most of those routes only run biweekly. Do you really want to sleep in bus terminals?"

"Perhaps we could hire a driver?" suggested Arash.

"Dangerous. He might turn them in. Better you buy a cheap piece of junk here and abandon it in Zabol. I'll drive them close to the town, but in the end, she'll have to meet the smugglers unaccompanied, because they'll kill me first and ask who I was afterwards. My cousin lives west of Zabol. We'll spend the night of the 7th at her house. On the 8th, she can drive you and me back to my home where you can catch a bus. Soraya's on her own for the last twenty-five miles."

Arash looked doubtful, but hadn't a better solution.

"Thank you. You've done good deeds for us. May Allah send you blessings for your *savab*."

"It's what we do for each other, yes? 'The happy heart delights to beat for others.'"

"We'll somehow repay your kindness," added Soraya.

It had been a long day and she was exhausted. She excused herself but quickly reappeared in the doorway.

"SattAr, what do you think Zamian meant by the 'Cadillac escape route?'"

"He was telling you that your husband paid extra to ensure you won't have to travel inside an empty oil tanker truck, since people have died inside them."

The color drained from Soraya's face.

"Oh. How thoughtful of him."

Chapter 30

Driving into the Unknown

December 8, 1979

DAWN LAY CURLED up beneath the horizon when Soraya and Arash exchanged their private farewell. "Hand over your list," Arash teased. "I know you have at least one."

She grinned sheepishly and gave him three.

"Here's an itemization of the clothing you're taking back with you to Tehran. I'll get you our new address as soon as possible so you can ship them to me. Here are the phone numbers of our former employees. And here are the numbers to our bank accounts. Use your judgment, Arash. I trust you. Your name is on all the accounts."

He tucked the papers into his shirt pocket.

"Soraya, you'll always be my favorite sister."

"You only have one sister."

"Sure, but I could always leave the category blank." Then, taking her hands, he spoke earnestly. "You can do this. You have strengths you've never been asked to use, but they're inside of you. I believe that with all my heart.

Hopefully, this will be a short, easy journey, but if things go wrong, don't panic. Remember, you've survived a bus."

She smiled ruefully. "Actually, I'm most terrified about driving the car into Zabol. It's been forever since I drove."

"You had a decent practice session behind the wheel yesterday, if you don't count backing into the tree. Go slow, don't over-steer or hit the brakes too hard. You'll be fine."

"I'll try. You're a good man, Arash. What would I do without you?"

He kissed her on the forehead.

"You're in my prayers every day and branded on my heart, always."

An hour later, SattAr and his passengers turned onto the road in a blue, undistinguished Chevy Nova. The car rattled and moaned. Soraya doubted it would make it all the way to Zabol.

SattAr explained why they wouldn't be turning on the air conditioner.

"Using the air conditioner in this wheezer will suck the tank dry. It would be very dangerous to run out of gas between here and Birjan. I've stored two gallons in the trunk, but they're only for an emergency."

Sweat soon trickled down Soraya's back. Darius had started the day buoyantly, but the heat and monotony soon defalted his enthusiasm. "I miss Nanny," he complained.

"She'd make me laugh. Are we almost there? I'm so, so, so bored, Mama."

"We'll be stopping in Birjand, *Naz Nazy*. It's a good-sized city and quite pretty, I hear. They have pine trees there, if you can imagine that in the middle of the desert! We'll get something to eat and walk around to stretch."

Darius groaned and lay lengthwise across the back seat. There was nothing to see out the window anyway.

The respite at Birjand revived their sagging spirits. They found some simple but tasty food. The pine trees were lovely and the mountains rising just beyond city limits were impressive. Soraya suggested they do some sightseeing, but SattAr pressed her to continue.

"There are only so many escape routes from Iran. The authorities are getting wise to them, so we don't dare delay reaching my cousin's house."

Heading out of town they saw their first nomads alongside the road. Darius pointed to the cluster of tents.

"Mama, look! Nomads and camels! I wonder what it's like inside the tents. They're very dirty on the outside. Mama, do you see? Those kids aren't wearing any shoes! How do they walk on the hot sand?"

Soraya was wondering the same thing. She'd never seen nomads in person, only in pictures. Their lifestyle was as inconceivable to her as was living in Siberia, or being poor.

"Aren't you glad your mama wasn't a nomad, Darius?"

He tried to picture his mother living in a tent, but couldn't, even using his wildest imagination.

SattAr's cousin was not at all pleased to see them arrive. Apparently this wasn't the first time SattAr had used her home as a way station for refugees.

"Let's just say I've known other people who needed to leave the country quickly," he said.

Soraya and Darius slept on cots that night. Darius woke up crying from a nightmare around 1:00 a.m.

"I miss Nanny! I need her!"

"But I'm here, my son."

It wasn't the same and Soraya well knew it. She wished Nanny were here too, because Fatima was Keeper of the Secrets when it came to Darius. Had hiring a nanny driven a wedge between her and her only child? She needed the help, certainly, given her duties managing the compound's staff. But truth be told, Fatima knew Darius better than she did. Well, she had plenty of time to spend with him now. Soraya dabbed at his tears with her linen handkerchief.

"Oh, Darius, I'm sorry Nanny couldn't come. Why don't you tell me what to do? Maybe I can help."

"Well," he said, sparking to the idea, "first, she'd wipe my face, like you did. Then I'd have to blow my nose."

"I'll be right back," said Soraya, returning with two handfuls of tissues. "Will these be enough?"

Darius cracked a thin smile.

"We need a lot more people for that many tissues."

He blew his nose.

"So what comes next?" Soraya asked.

"Well, then Nanny would make me smile, like you just did. You're doing very well, Mama!"

Mama was proud of herself.

"Let me see if I can guess what she'd do next."

"Yes! We play lots of guessing games!

"I'm guessing that Nanny would pull you in close."

"Yes."

"And then she'd sing you back to sleep?"

"Nope, we'd talk until I got sleepy."

"All right, we can do that," said Soraya.

"Huh-uh. We talk because she's a terrible singer, but you have a pretty voice. I'd rather hear you sing."

This wasn't so difficult after all, Soraya thought.

The next morning she awoke next to her boy for the first time ever. It felt so cozy; she was loath to wake him. Soraya studied his sweet face, so like his father's. Darius would garner his fair share of attention from girls.

She sat up. It was time to focus on the drive to Zabol, with those twenty-five terrifying miles she had to drive by herself looming ahead. Arash, SattAr and his cousin had departed earlier this morning. She and Darius wouldn't leave until afternoon. Her instructions were to be there at 5:00 p.m. At least she had time to practice driving again.

But the afternoon arrived before she was ready. Darius sat in the car, eager to begin the final leg of their journey. Meanwhile, Soraya rifled through the kitchen. Assuming she'd never see SattAr or his cousin again, she decided to "borrow" snacks for the trip, taking her pick from the cupboard before donning a chador and heading to the car. Sliding behind the Chevy's wheel, she took a deep breath.

"Are you okay, Mama?" asked Darius.

"Of course, darling. I have everything under control," she said, but the first lurching mile suggested otherwise.

By the time the hilly, outlying village appeared in the distance, she was a mass of exposed nerves. Her curled fingers gripped the steering wheel as though glued to it.

The late afternoon sunlight draped across the dirt streets separating clumps of square houses. Wispy shadows inched up the ancient walls. Day was plodding methodically into evening, but Soraya was nearly hysterical. Darius hadn't ever seen his mother like this, but then again, he'd never seen her drive. He desperately wished for a chauffeur.

"Everything's under control," Soraya muttered again, whipping around a corner like a stone from a slingshot.

Whether "under control" referred to the car or their fate, she was mistaken. The car was nearly driving itself at will; and as for whom they were about to meet and what would happen next, she hadn't a clue.

Soraya's hair blew out the open window, snapping back against her cheeks like tiny whips, punishing her for her poor driving skills. The car darted erratically in and out of the shadows.

These roads were barely more than alleys. Where was this mythical town square? A flock of chickens scattered a few feet in front of their bumper. Darius gasped and covered his eyes, certain that his mother was going to crash.

Miraculously, she didn't. Soraya came upon an open area, which she concluded was the center of town. Slowing to check her wristwatch, she was horrified to discover it was only 4:45 p.m. They were fully fifteen minutes early. How had this happened? She always ran late, a privilege of the privileged, but today she'd overcompensated.

"Bishour!" she mumbled. Idiot! She braked to a hard stop. There was a decision to be made and she was incapable of simultaneously thinking and driving.

Her fingers fluttered along the curve of the steering wheel. There were only two choices: Wait here or drive around some more. It was too dangerous to wait. Someone undoubtedly was noticing the strangers in their village and soon they'd come around, asking questions.

Dropping her foot too heavily back onto the gas pedal, they lurched out of the square, looping through the alleys and creating parachutes of billowing dust in their wake. After thirteen minutes, they returned to the square. She snapped off the engine, threw open the door and hurried to the trunk to retrieve their bags.

"Mama, may I close the trunk? I can reach it."

"No." His mother's voice sounded pinched. "Leave it open. It's a signal."

Handing Darius his suitcase, she picked up hers, her fingers squeezing the gold-plated handle. Darius watched her knuckles rise like white peaks across her soft hands and was shocked by her strength.

At precisely five o'clock, a dented black Land Cruiser screamed into the square. Three men wearing black clothes and masks jumped from the vehicle. They threw the two suitcases into the back and shoved Soraya and Darius inside the SUV, flooring the gas pedal before the two of them had even buckled their seat belts. Five minutes later they stopped in an alleyway behind a run-down house.

"Get out," said the driver, who hurried them through a small doorway into a dim living room. Dust particles hung motionless in its stifling air. Furniture was sparse, but dirty dishes were piled everywhere. The stench of moldy food was nauseating. She clamped her hand over her mouth.

A frail, gray-haired woman with greasy lips hobbled to the middle of the room. The deep lines on her face painted a portrait of her hard life. She shoved aside a rickety dining table, peeled back threadbare remnants of a Persian carpet and lifted a trap door. The men motioned to Soraya and Darius to go down a rickety stairs into the basement. One of the men followed behind them.

"Stay here, " he said, in locally accented Persian.

Soraya and Darius waited, shellshocked, at the bottom of the stairs, until their eyes adjusted to the olive-brown gloom. Darius was the first to see that they were not alone, and that the others sat on the damp earthen floor, staring back at them. When Soraya saw them, she nodded curtly, guiding Darius to an open space where they sat down.

The man surveyed the group. His accent made him difficult to understand, but she caught enough words to follow. It seemed that she and Darius were the last to arrive. The man addressed them.

"Wear as many layers of your own clothing as you can. Whatever you don't wear, you leave behind. Our hosts will be happy to use what you don't take." He smiled thinly. "They especially like jewelry and nice suitcases."

Reaching for a cardboard box, he dumped a pile of used, dirty, sorry-looking clothes into a heap on the floor.

"Put these on over your own clothes," he said. "We don't want you to look too well-dressed, in case we run into trouble. Most especially, take whatever looks warm."

A mixture of contempt and worry flitted across his face. He wheeled around and climbed up the stairs. The trap door slammed with an air of finality, followed by the soft thud of the carpet dropping, then the muffled scratching of the table sliding back into place.

The group followed his instructions like obedient school children. Darius cocked his head to ask a question, but his mother touched her finger to his lips.

"Don't think about it," she urged, pulling shirts, pants and socks from his suitcase and handing him an armful of clothing with a tight look on her face.

He was terribly confused. Who were these people? What were they doing here? He scrutinized the group. There was a family consisting of a mother, father, an adolescent girl and a grandmother in one corner, a young married couple with a toddler, and a tall, good-looking man who seemed to be alone, plus he and his mother. Ten of them, total.

Shirt under sweater, under another sweater, under a bigger shirt under a coat, layer upon layer, people ballooned up until they couldn't pull another layer one over the previous. They looked silly, but no one laughed, too nervous for humor. An awkward silence ensued as everyone wondered what to do next. One by one, they sat down again. Tedious hours limped by. Perspiration soaked the inner layers of their clothing, but it was a cold sweat, born of a growing fear that they'd been abandoned.

No one came to offer water or food. Hunger invaded their empty stomachs, filling them with thundering hunger pangs. People stole wary glances at each other, inhaling the dank air and exhaling into the rising humidity.

Soraya folded her chador into a makeshift pillow to cushion their behinds from the dirt floor.

Darius wriggled. "Mama, I have to 'go.'"

"Don't think about it."

Everyone was trying not to think about it, but "mind over bladder" had its limits.

Necessity finally trumped both stoicism and modesty. Grandmama began the parade. She struggled to her feet and surveyed the room. Selecting the least populated corner, she waddled over like a duck, hiked up her many layers of apparel, squatted and peed, loud and long.

"Huh," she grunted. "Better."

Darius couldn't stifle his giggle. The sight was pretty funny, after all. His laugh tickled the stale air, easing the tension long enough for everyone to laugh. One by one, everyone made a pilgrimage to the impromptu toilet, until the mounting human waste began to foul the air with an overpoweringly acrid bouquet.

The teenaged girl gagged.

"I'm going to throw up."

Her mother swept the girl's long hair off her neck and fanned her with a rag. Darius held his breath. He covered his nose with his hands. He pulled his sweater over his face, but nothing helped. He was miserable, and so hungry his stomach cramped. He hugged his knees against the pain.

Soraya combed her pink fingernails through his wiry curls, murmuring, "Soon, *Naz Nazy*, not much longer, my darling. Someone will come get us, I think, soon."

As it turned out, no one did, not for twelve anxious, stinking, hungry hours of uncertainty.

Chapter 31

The Orange

Registan Desert, "Country of Sand," Afghanistan
December 9, 1979

T HE NEXT MORNING, heavy footsteps shook awake the basement's occupants. Darius and Soraya clutched each other as the trap door flew open. Four unfamiliar but identically shrouded men talked over one other in Sistani, a version of Persian that Soraya didn't know; however, clearly it was time to leave and do so quickly. She tossed the damp chador over her shoulders, and with one last, longing look at the Dior suitcase she was leaving behind, took Darius by the hand and rushed with the others up the narrow staircase, jostling their way out of the choking confinement.

As she hurried through the living room, Soraya had her arm grabbed from behind. She whirled around to find her face mere inches from the weary-faced old woman, who now hissed in Soraya's ear.

"Take," she said, pressing a stale loaf of bread into Soraya's hands. It was as hard as a rock. Soraya recoiled at the sight of holes dug into it by the woman's grimy fingers.

"No, no. Thank you ... but no. I don't want it. No."

But the woman insisted.

"Hurry up!" the tall, thin, hooded man ordered. Everyone else was already outside and climbing onto two pickup trucks.

She took the loaf and ran. The clean, rich morning air helped clear her head, but she struggled to climb up onto the flat bed. The handsome man stretched out his hand. His grip was strong and she couldn't help noticing how beautifully he wore his masculinity.

"Let me help."

"Thank you so much."

She noted that he hadn't covered up his nice clothes with the rags. The man, who looked to be about forty, wasn't easily intimidated. Impressed, Soraya wondered about his background.

He easily lifted Darius up into the truck behind her. The boy's eyes grew big.

"Mama, look." he gasped. "There are bullet holes in the windshield."

"It'll be okay," said the man. "Don't think about it."

Darius scrunched his face and whined. "Why does everyone me not to 'think about it?' It only makes me think about what I'm not supposed to think about even more."

The trucks drove toward the open desert. People held onto the truck's sides as potholes and sharp corners began tossing them about. Skirting around the edges of Zabol, they soon left the paved road, driving directly into the sandy vastness without a stop or explanation.

As night fell, the drivers eschewed their headlights and the world faded into darkness. Their pace slowed.

The eldest of the smugglers, a heavyset man, rolled out of the lead truck to jog ahead. With great effort he led them, waving a white rag for the trucks to follow. Soraya wondered if he had an invisible map in his mind, for there was no road. However, she did know that somewhere in this endless desert lay the boundary between Iran and Afghanistan.

Darius was in great pain. His back kept slamming against the side of the truck bed and the bruises were becoming unbearably tender. He cried out with every rock and rut. Soraya tried to wedge him against the side of the truck bed, but she wasn't strong enough to hold him in place. When she found blood on his clothes, she frantically examined his body for its source.

The handsome man pointed to her arm.

"The blood is yours."

Soraya stared in disbelief at a long gash on her arm. Somewhere along the way she'd been cut. She blinked away the rising tears. They would only further upset Darius, and she needed to help him handle this situation like the man he wasn't. She had to take everything in stride. She severely doubted that she was up to the task.

Human misery can make Nature weep. At least that's what Darius decided when a soft raindrop tapped his cheek. Maybe, he thought, Nature felt so sorry for him that she was crying. The thought was comforting, except that he'd mistaken hesitation for sympathy. The black, moonless sky was concealing the building storm clouds. After those few initial, caressing drops, Nature began squeezing out the spaces between them, until sheets of water poured from the sky and rivulets of water snaked around the truck tires.

The heavyset man, whom Darius mentally nicknamed Mr. Fatfingers, was soaked to the bone and too tired to wave his rag. It hung limply at his side. His shoes were weighted down with muck and he struggled just to walk. The thin man screamed for the old man to get moving and wave the damn rag, but Mr. Fatfingers was panting heavily. Soraya feared his heart would give out.

In a small measure of justice, the lead drivers were getting soaked as well, for when their truck hit a deep rut, its bullet-hole-weakened windshield had shattered.

The second truck ground to an inglorious halt, stuck in the wet, gooey clay. Mr. Fatfingers fell to his knees, his chest heaving, desperate for the rest.

The young driver of the entrenched truck made a bad decision. He gunned the engine, spinning the tires deeper into the mud, which flew everywhere and further mired his vehicle. Feeling stupid, the teenager walked around the truck, assessing the situation, pretending he knew what to do. But he hadn't a clue, so he kicked the driver's side door instead, using words Darius had never heard. He wondered what they meant.

The masked men gestured for the males in the group to help free the vehicle. They rocked the truck back and forth, coaxing it from its trap. Luckily, the storm was abating and the floodwater beginning to drain. The wheels came loose with a loud sucking sound, and the truck was rolled onto firmer ground.

Mr. Fatfingers looked sadly at the freed vehicle; obviously wishing it had remained stuck a while longer. Shaking his head, he lifted the white rag anew, taking them ever deeper into the desert.

Tiny lights flickered off in the distance. Mr. Fatfingers squeezed back into the cab of the lead truck. The drivers adjusted their course directly toward the lights. Wherever they were supposed to be, Soraya thought, they were arriving. It was three in the morning, it was cold, and after nine hard hours of travel, the group needed a rest stop.

A horrid smell assaulted their noses as they rumbled to a halt. Camel carcasses lay nearby like marooned ships listing on a dark ocean. They belched the stink of rotting flesh. Still, the travelers gratefully crawled out of the trucks, staggering like drunken sailors until they readjusted to solid ground. Everyone scattered upwind of the camel carnage to relieve their bladders.

The two men with the lanterns also wore hoods. These human smugglers had made absolutely sure the refugees could never identify them.

Soraya led Darius to a large rock. They leaned wearily against it, hoping to feel a reservoir of warmth from the day's sun. There was none, but before despair could set in, Soraya reached between the layers of her clothing, magically pulling out a small thermos of water. She reached in again, pulling out something round.

An orange! Darius was ecstatic, letting loose a yelp of joy. Soraya shushed him. Better they feast unnoticed in the dark before the sun rose and others could see their riches. As she peeled the fruit, a fine mist of juice sprayed Darius' cheek. He inhaled its fragrance, sweeter than his mother's most expensive perfume. He had a most clever mother. Soraya meticulously separated the segments, giving her son an extra one. He nibbled the orange, savoring its pulp to prolong the feast. No gourmet meal had ever tasted better.

"Mama, where did you get the food?"

"Let's just say that SattAr's cousin shared."

He wondered what other wonderful snacks she had.

Soraya poked around inside her clothes, reassuring herself she still had that loaf of stale bread the woman had forced on her. It would be a last resort, because she'd also stolen crackers, nuts and another piece of fruit from SattAr's cousin. Yes, she thought, I'm a thief. She'd lowered her standards to steal. But they would eat.

She yanked a thread off her raggedy clothing and sighed. She'd had a closet filled with Hermes, Gucci, Versace, Chanel and Dior. Now look at her.

Darius studied the outline of her delicate frame in the darkness. She held herself like an empress, he thought, involuntarily shivering as mountain ranges of goose bumps rose across his body. The wind had kicked up and the sand was swirling like it wanted to devour them.

"Oh, no, a sand storm. What else can happen? Why do we deserve this misery? Come here, darling, let me protect you," Soraya said, scooping him into her lap.

She draped herself on him like a sock on a foot, pulling her chador around them both in an attempt to shield him from the piercing cold. Guilt sliced through her heart. What kind of danger was she visiting on Darius? Maybe they should have stayed in Tehran and faced the revolution.

Here, they were at the mercy of mercenaries. She wished that she could pray, like Mehdi did. But praying required faith in something she couldn't see, and without tangible evidence, Allah was a figment of someone's imagination.

Still, a voice in her head whispered that their survival required strength greater than her own. In response, she fabricated a tentative faith in a vague greater Power, in whose existence she remained skeptical, but in whom she would temporarily believe. Her face stung from the flying grains of sand, yet creating a "Someone" who cared about them gave her a whiff of hope.

"Why are these men making us stay here, Mama?"

His whisper was hoarse. He was utterly fatigued and his back hurt. He shut his eyes tightly against the assault.

"I don't know. As they say, 'If Ali is the camel driver, he knows where to rest his camel.' I guess we have to trust the men who brought us here."

"When will the sun come up?"

"Soon, my son."

"Why didn't they drive us to a hotel in a city?"

Soraya hadn't the answer or the energy to engage.

"Too many questions. Let curiosity take a nap."

But Darius couldn't help it. Although his body was freezing cold, his mind burned with questions. He shifted his attention to the guards about forty feet away, fearful of the spiny outlines of their weapons. They, too, huddled together against the sand storm. He heard them talking, but the wind blew away their words before he could decipher them. Or perhaps he was only hearing the sandstorm groan. He couldn't tell. He only knew he hated the men. Two weeks ago his life had been as beautiful as fine porcelain and now it was smashed to pieces.

He flung a defiant glare in their direction, but either they couldn't see his bravura or it didn't frighten them, because they completely ignored him. No matter. Darius was sure that his courage had generated an invisible bubble of protection around him and his mother. He'd made things safe for them, for now.

Soraya was observing the men, too, except that she watched how their bodies twitched with overly taut nerves. She noted how their heads swiveled, scanning the landscape for danger. They were anxious. It did not inspire her confidence in them.

Generally, Soraya was on a first name basis with anxiety, but tonight anxiety was not her overriding emotion. Tonight she felt utterly inconsequential. While she'd experienced betrayal and had been introduced to persecution, out here she was simply irrelevant, a bundle of flesh, bones and blood, being transported from here to there by human traffickers. She wouldn't have put up with this back home. Being unremarkable was difficult to accept. Fine, she thought, I'm unremarkable, but only for a few days. She spit onto the sand, watching the bubbles of saliva. It made her feel better. She spit again.

The wind was abating. One of the men came over with some cheese and stale pita bread. He ordered them not to wander away, "... because we will not look for you and then you will die out here alone and we won't care anymore than the desert does. Do you understand?"

She nodded yes. She understood the words if not the hostility. It hardly mattered, anyway.

Darius munched on the cheese and slid down in her lap to look up at the sky. She followed his gaze. The heavens were studded with pulsating lights. Even without a moon the sight was shockingly beautiful. She looked down at Darius to share the moment but his eyes had closed.

When the sun poked its head above the horizon, Soraya still cradled Darius in her lap. She let him sleep until afternoon, when the men urgently pointed to the distant horizon and leapt up, shouting at the group to load onto the trucks. People with a car and several camels had appeared on the horizon, heading straight toward them, probably roving bandits, who preyed on caravans.

"Darius! Wake up!"

Pushing him off her lap, Soraya grabbed his hand and

dragged him toward the trucks.

Darius opened his eyes, bewildered. Gathering his feet under him, he began running alongside her.

They didn't know to where, but they were on the move.

Chapter 32

Treacherous Paths

Chagai Hills, Afghanistan/Pakistan
December 11, 1979

THE TRUCKS RACED across the sand, trying to put as much distance as they could between them and the bandits. The smugglers argued among themselves, gesturing wildly while pointing in different directions, as they tried to determine the best escape route. Grandmama screamed over them that she was about to bounce out of the flatbed. The handsome man held tightly onto Darius. Soraya gripped the sides of the truck with all her might.

The tall, thin leader made the decision. Arguing ceased and the trucks headed for the rocky hills rising before them.

Soraya yelled over the loudly screaming old lady, "What do you think we're going to do?"

The handsome man thought about it for a moment. He yelled back.

"Mostly, the bandits probably want the trucks, gas cans and any jewelry we might be wearing. I think we have a chance to beat them. The rocks ahead are the Chagai Hills.

We'll be doing some rugged walking if I'm right."

"Walk up those mountains? Are they insane?"

"No. It makes sense. Regardless of what they say to us, they don't want us harmed. It's bad for business."

The trucks screeched to a halt at the foot of the rugged granite range. They'd bought a little time with their speed, but the pursuers were approaching fast. The smugglers pulled their charges from the trucks and pointed the way. Two of them brought up the rear, herding the panicked group and prodding the slow ones to move faster.

Even though the path looked terrifyingly difficult to traverse, at least the jagged walls quickly swallowed them up from sight.

"What if they follow us?" Soraya was already gasping for air. She'd never exercised.

"Unlikely," answered the man, "not once they have the trucks and gas cans. That should be enough for them."

But the hapless group was unprepared for such treacherous climbing. Their shoes slipped on loose rocks and their arms scraped against craggy walls. The higher they went, the cooler the air, which felt good at first, but soon they needed every layer of clothing they had. Their guides must have walked these hills before, because they followed the semblance of a path. It was narrow and steep, but it hinted of a purposeful destination. Soraya's feet already hurt. The soles of her fine shoes were thin and each piece of rock dug deeper into them. She wasn't sure how long she could keep walking. She could feel the bruises and blisters forming on the bottoms of her feet. Darius was faring better because Nanny had put on his practical shoes for the journey, but his short legs were tired. After an hour he finally whimpered to her.

"Mama, can't we stop for a little while?"

The leader turned and looked at him, then checked the sun's position. It was dropping toward the horizon.

"Five minutes. Not a minute longer. Everyone sit."

They all sank wearily to the ground. Soraya removed her shoes. Holes polka-dotted their fine leather soles. She waved her right shoe in the air. The sole had detached from the upper and flopped like a fish out of water. She knew she was in trouble, but wouldn't complain, because everyone else was exhausted, too. The little girl's father had carried her for the last hour. His arms ached. Grandmama looked like she was going to need carrying soon.

The leader stood up. His imposing height and steely voice didn't allow for bargaining.

"No more resting. We must find shelter before dark."

Shelter? Soraya couldn't believe they thought she was going to spend the night on this freezing pile of rocks. It wasn't possible. She saw that the men had grabbed water bottles and ropes from their trucks, but there were no tents or bedding. She thought about the snacks she had still hidden in her clothes. She'd sneak Darius away from other hungry eyes, or they'd be forced to share what little food they had.

The path became steeper and rougher as they ascended, demolishing what remained of Soraya's lovely shoes. Her blisters were bleeding and the bottoms of her feet were red. She pulled them off in disgust.

"I might as well toss these and go barefoot."

Mr. Fatfingers stopped her.

"No. Anything on your feet is better than nothing. If the snow up ahead doesn't give you frostbite, the rocks will strip your skin from the bones."

He pulled out the white rag he'd used earlier to lead the trucks, ripping it into strips and wrapping them around her shredded shoes, neatly tucking in the ends to secure the wrapping. She nearly wept at his kindness. The cloth even cushioned her battered feet a bit.

"Mama, your poor feet!"

"I'm fine, darling, really." She sniffled. "Darius, you have warrior blood. I know you're tired. Can you keep walking?"

He set his jaw, growing up before her eyes.

"I'll be fine, Mama," he said, but his voice cracked.

Grandmama plopped down on a rock. She was done.

Her mental toughness had succumbed to her frail body and she couldn't take another step. One of the smugglers sighed and stepped forward.

"Come on, old lady. I'll carry you on my back."

She grunted. "Old lady? I'll whip you for calling me that, because these legs have walked to places you've never even dreamed of. You son of a bitch, I'm like a fine vintage wine, worth more than you can afford. But I'm going to let you carry me, just so some of my wisdom can rub off on you."

"Fine," he said, "But promise me you won't flap your gums in my ear, or I'm liable to drop your fine, vintage body over the side of a cliff."

She grunted again before climbing on. She was careful not to talk, however.

Half an hour later, the leader halted the procession.

"We are near the cave where we will sleep tonight, but the path ahead is very dangerous. We must reach the cave before dark. You will follow my instructions without complaining, doing exactly as I say. If you argue, I will leave you behind in these hills and let your dead body be eaten by scavengers."

"I'm in a horror film," muttered the teenager.

Darius was terrified. Soraya would have begged his forgiveness if she'd thought it would help the situation. She clenched her teeth. Gravel-sized rocks lined the footpath, making the going slippery and progress slow. It was dusk when the lead smuggler stopped them with his hand.

Up ahead lay a sharp curve to the left. What was around the corner, Soraya couldn't see, but what she could see was horrifying enough. At the bend the path abruptly fell away, melting down to a few inches ending in mid-air, as though a giant cleaver had sliced off a slab of granite. The sheared rock face plunged into a deep crevasse. A fall would mean certain death.

The leader removed several of ropes from his waist.

"There has been more erosion since the last time I was here. The ledge is narrower. I will go first, as I know what's on the other side. Two of my colleagues will follow me. The others will stay on this side, to help bring you around one at a time. I will loop the rope over this," he said, pointing out a ledge jutting out, about ten feet above them. "If you lose your footing, the three of us might have a second to save you from falling all the way. Do exactly as you are told or you will die. I have told my men to save themselves first. I need them more than I need one of you."

He indicated Darius and the toddler. "The two children will be carried around the corner. Then we'll send the girl." He pointed at the teenager.

"Why don't we simply take a different route?" asked the toddler's father. "Why must you put all of us at such risk?"

"You will not question me. The cave that can shelter us from tonight's freezing temperatures lies just beyond this curve. There isn't enough sunlight left to take another way."

With that, he edged, around the corner, slowly, sideways, hugging the rock wall. Lifting his right leg, he wiggled his left foot along the ridge as close to the corner as possible, his chest glued to the vertical rock face, while his fingers searched for dimples to use as fingerholds. Swinging his right leg around the corner, he paused. Debris tumbled into the crevasse below. Slowly, he inched his right foot along the blind side of the path as far as he could, until it widened. His arm and leg disappeared. Two of his men carefully followed him, each one causing small avalanches that tumbled down with frightening crashes.

"We're all going to die," said the teenager, the only one brave enough to say what they were all thinking.

Soraya's mind raced. How could she let them take Darius around that corner? If Darius fell, she would leap after him; she couldn't go on living if she caused his death. Not unlike Ali and Manu, she realized.

"Give us the little girl first."

One of the smugglers held open his arms while another worked the end of the rope that wrapped around the rock ledge above them. He made ready to tie a makeshift harness around the small child that he could secure to his back.

"No," said her father, shaking his head. "You'll not test the ledge with my child. I'll go first, to show her it's okay and that I'm waiting for her. I go first or we're not going."

The smuggler shrugged. "It's your choice."

The old woman mumbled prayers under her breath.

"Shush, Grandmama, things are bad enough without your stupid prayers," said the teenager, rolling her eyes.

The father kissed his wife and hugged his little girl. The smuggler, who threw one end of the rope back over to the other side, harnessed him. Groaning and sweating, the young father gripped the rock, wiggling his toes, bit by bit. It took ten minutes before finally slipped from view. The group collectively held their breath. Once they heard his cry of triumph from the other side, they cheered.

"*Joonam*, my very precious life, do you see what Daddy just did?" The mother cooed to her toddler. "Listen, he's calling for you. This nice man will wrap you up snug and safe, and then off you go to see Daddy!"

But the toddler was scared of the man's mask and shrieked. The handsome man stepped forward.

"Let me try. I have a thorough knowledge of knots plus she's more familiar with me." He stroked her hair. "Hello, sweetheart, our *Joonam*." She shrank back, but stopped crying. He touched her cheek and pretended to pull a coin from behind her ear. She stared at him in wonder and a look of delight brightened her face.

He laughed and kept chatting while looping the rope around her to secure the harness.

"Good enough," said the smuggler. "Stand behind me and tie her to my back. I'll pull up my hood in the back so she can see my hair. I'm a father. I understand."

While her mother fearfully sank to the ground, the ropes were tightened and knots checked. The gentleman followed behind the unlikely pair, engaging the toddler. At the turn, the smuggler slowed his maneuvers along the razor thin ledge while the toddler's father called to her. The group froze, petrified at the sound of falling debris.

"I'm holding her in my arms! She's safe!" The father was jubilant. The mother sang praises to Allah.

All eyes turned to Darius. Soraya placed her hands on his shoulders, fully intending not to let go.

"No!" she said. "It's too dangerous. He's not going."

"There is no choice. Stop arguing, woman."

Darius lifted his face to his mother. His chin trembled, but his words were firm. "Mama, remember what Papa told me at *Chaharshanbe Suri*. I have to face fear by running straight at it. I can do this."

Soraya was floored by his courage. "Oh, Darius. You shame me with your bravery. You're right. Let's concentrate on the way you leaped over that fire without fear."

The men knotted the rope around Darius. He closed his eyes to concentrate. Soraya feared her heart would beat its way out of her chest and that she'd fall dead in front of her son. They began inching around the corner.

"I can see you and Papa running right at the fire!" she managed to say weakly.

Darius responded. "I can feel Papa holding my hand."

Soraya knelt in the dirt, her face buried in her hands. She couldn't watch. She tried to pray, but couldn't focus.

A low rumble came from nowhere, then a loud crack and the crash of rocks falling thousands of feet. The ledge was crumbling. Soraya's eyes flew open and she ran toward her son.

"Mama!" Darius screamed.

"Darius!"

The falling rocks drowned out Soraya's cries. "No! No! Darius!" She pounded on the rock wall until her hands bled. Then came a deafening silence.

"Someone over there," Soraya screamed. "Someone, talk to me! Is my son alive?"

There was only rustling, moaning and swearing. A male voice finally answered. It was the little girl's father.

"They made it," was all he said.

"Mama?" Darius' voice was thin as water.

"*Aziz Talah*, my precious child. Are you alright, Darius?"

"I don't know. It hurts."

"They hit the cliff hard before we pulled them up," said the young father. "They're checking him and nothing looks broken. But he's got nasty cuts and bruises."

Soraya could at least breathe again. "Praise Allah! You jumped over very high flames today, my darling. I'm coming right away."

Mr. Fatfingers' called to his comrades in their local dialect. After a lengthy and animated exchange, he shook his head and spoke to the group.

"No more. The ledge is gone. It's a miracle they were able to grab them. Your son fared better than my friend. His arm and some ribs are broken."

"*Mersi*, a thousand times over, *mersi*, thank you," Soraya shouted in gratitude to the man on the other side.

Then she turned back to Mr. Fatfingers.

"What do you mean, no one else goes? Of course I'm going. My son is over there and he's hurt."

The little girl's mother sobbed.

"My husband and child are over there. We have to go." Mr. Fatfingers threw up his hands.

"Do you think I can build a bridge, or fly you to the other side? Don't you feel the temperature dropping? We must figure out how to avoid freezing to death tonight. Tomorrow we'll go back down to the desert floor and find a different, but longer way. My friends are sending over some flasks of water for us."

"Then," Soraya said, "we will take the longer route. Tonight. Let's leave right now."

"I agree," said the toddler's mother.

"No. The night winds up here blow like knives."

"Even more reason to get going," said the teenager's father. "I can carry my mother."

The old woman's ire was raised once again.

"I'll out walk the lot of you. Why these legs have ..."

The gentleman interrupted her in a calm voice, but one too authoritative for her to keep complaining.

"Our chances of finding suitable shelter tonight are negligible. Even if we do, and even if we then head back to the desert, what are the odds someone will find us? Moving keeps us warmer, and finding a route to meet up with the others gives us a reason to survive. Our best chance lies in reuniting with the others as soon as possible."

Mr. Fatfingers looked dubious.

"I have only one flashlight and it won't last all night."

"Let's utilize the rope," said the gentleman. "You lead with the front end and I'll bring up the rear and everyone in-between holds on."

Mr. Fatfingers rubbed his chin. "Well, I am pretty familiar with these hills ... first we'd have to hike higher ..."

"Then it's settled," said Soraya.

Mr. Fatfingers was still unconvinced.

"You do know it'll be dawn before we reach them, and that's only if nothing goes wrong."

"It's always best to play the odds, don't you agree?" asked the gentleman. He was persuasive.

The others nodded. Fatfingers shouted the plans to the men on the other side of the rock wall. Water flasks were hoisted over the ledge. Before leaving, the two mothers tried to encourage their offspring.

"My beautiful little daughter, sleep in Papa's arms tonight and I'll see you in the morning," said the toddler's mother.

"Brave Darius, it's Mama's turn to jump over the fire. I'm coming, I promise."

"Pretend that I'm holding your hand, Mama," Darius answered in a feeble voice.

Her heart wilted.

That night would remain a blur in Soraya's memory forever. Her right shoe came off somewhere along the way but her feet were too numb for her to notice. Her fingers cramped and froze around the rope. She couldn't have let go if she wanted to. The group shuffled slowly up and around the craggy hills beneath a heartless moon. But if they kept moving, they just might live to see another day.

Chapter 33

Mr. Fatfingers

Chagai Hills, Pakistan
December 12, 1979

SORAYA WAS so intent on putting one foot in front of the other that she missed that ephemeral moment when dawn tentatively probes the horizon with light. The teenager announced the good news.

"It's morning!"

"We made it," chortled the old lady. "I told you so."

Soraya looked up. Morning's frail light kissed her eyes. She shouted ahead to Mr. Fatfingers.

"Where are we? Are we close to the others?"

He stopped to study the terrain.

"I need more light. I'll know in a few minutes, but I think we're close. Let's stop and watch the sun rise. You've earned it."

Mr. Fatfingers displayed more humanity than the other smugglers. He even lifted the front of his hood to better enjoy the dawn himself. Those who took a quick peek at his face were pleased to discover that his was a very kind one. He'd be remembered with gratitude.

And such a sunrise they shared, a most glorious ascent of the sun god in his golden chariot. Soraya turned her face toward the light like a sunflower. Of all the sunrises of her life, this one was a miracle. Together, they had survived.

The remaining water canteen was passed around. Soraya fumbled inside her clothing until she found the loaf of stale bread. She was starving, but the bread was hard as the rocks around them. Finally she whacked it against one of those rocks. She popped a broken piece into her mouth. It tasted as delicious as éclairs from her favorite Paris patisserie. She was about to devour more when she saw the ravenous looks on her companions' faces. Feeling selfish, she took one more bite and passed the loaf on to Grandmama. Her companions took no more than a bite or two before passing the bread along to the next person.

They still didn't know each other's names, but they'd been to hell and back together. This level of intimacy was a novel experience for Soraya. While she didn't quite know what to do with it, it touched her.

Mr. Fatfingers climbed atop an outcropping to survey the hills, lining them up in his mind with the sun and the desert below. He pointed.

"Yes! I recognize the curve of the foothills! If we keep going this way, we'll reach the others in about two hours,

I'm almost sure of it."

The group struggled to their feet, anticipation refueling their energy. "Let's go!" "Who's tired? I'm not tired!"

Mr. Fatfingers, every bit as excited as they were, coiled the rope, hooking it to his belt. They didn't need it in broad daylight. He was pretty confident he'd located their destination. Yes, he thought, we'll arrive in about two hours, maybe a little longer.

Forty-five minutes passed. Mr. Fatfingers decided to try hailing his colleagues.

"Helloooo!"

The others echoed him. "Hello! Can you hear us?"

Mr. Fatfingers quieted them with his hand.

"Stop calling and listen."

They waited.

"Alright, let's try it again. They may be afraid we're the bandits. Hellooo!"

They waited.

"Look," said the teenager, pointing. Someone was waving a shirt in their direction. A voice floated upwards.

"Is it really you?"

"Yes! Put out markers and we'll find you, " said Mr. Fatfingers, who now appeared five years younger and ten pounds lighter than yesterday.

"All right," he said to the group, but he didn't move. He

just stood there, looking at them.

"Well done," he said, and no more, but they'd caught the look of respect in his eyes.

He turned, leading them toward the bright clothing being heaped on the rocks below, southeast of their current location. The group chattered happily on the path.

Minutes later, Soraya stumbled for no apparent reason. Struggling to get her balance, she realized that her right foot felt cold and numb. She looked down and recoiled. Her toes were as white as pieces of frozen chicken. She screamed.

"Help me! Oh, my God, what's happened? Where's my shoe? My toes!"

The gentleman reached her first.

"Sit down. Let me see. Please, sit down. I can help you." He examined her foot. "I'm going to press on your big toe. Don't look at your foot. Just tell me when you start to feel any pressure."

"All right, I feel it now," Soraya said. "Is this going to spread? Will I lose my foot?"

He pressed on her little toe.

"Which toe am I touching now?"

"The little one, I think." She was hyperventilating.

"That's an excellent sign. You're doing well. Do me a favor, though. I'd like you to consciously slow down your breathing. Do you normally have high blood pressure?"

"No."

Mr. Fatfingers knelt over her to evaluate.

"I'll make a bandage," he said to the gentleman. "You warm up the foot."

The man lifted Soraya's chin until their eyes met.

"Since your foot is about to meet my armpit, shouldn't I know your name?"

"Soraya. Soraya Sultan."

"Well, Mrs. Sultan. Your toes have frostnip, and we need to get the circulation going again."

"Thank you, and your name is …?"

"Why don't you just call me Asad."

"Thank you, Asad."

She closed her eyes, trying to block out a burning sensation, and after ten minutes, the color began slowly returning to her toes. Mr. Fatfingers wrapped the foot in his t-shirt, which he'd torn into pieces for her.

"You'll carry her on your back?" he asked Asad.

"Of course."

The sun was nearly overhead when the intrepid group arrived at the cave. The young father sprinted up the path with the toddler to reunite the family.

"Mama!" the little girl said, reaching out.

Her mother burst into tears, kissing her all over.

Soraya looked around for Darius. He hadn't come out to

greet her. Asad sensed her anxiety and lengthened his stride so they reached the mouth of the cave first. Soraya slid off his back and limped into the cave's gloom.

"Darius?"

"Mama? Is that you?"

"Darius, where are you? I can't see you, my love."

He waved his arms from where he was leaning against the wall. "I'm over here. Can you see me? Why are you limping, Mama?"

Dropping to her knees, she crawled to him, taking his face in her hands and pressing her forehead to his.

"My son, my son. I thought I'd lost you. They should cut off my arms before I could lose you."

Darius buried his face in her shoulder.

"I was so scared when you walked away last night, I was afraid that ..."

He started crying. They hugged each other.

Soraya checked his body.

"Where are you hurt? Your pants are bloody."

"I banged my knees on the rocks when the men stopped us from falling. Oh, Mama, the path was there one second and then it wasn't, and we fell, but the men held on to the rope — they had it wrapped around a big rock. The rope stopped us so fast that it jerked hard. It hurt so much when we banged into the side of the cliff. Then they had to pull us up over really sharp rocks."

Soraya carefully rolled up his shirtsleeves. He was scraped from fingers to shoulders.

"My poor baby."

"My knees hurt too much to walk, my arms hurt and my neck is sore. But Mama, why is your foot wrapped?"

"It's quite a story, but not nearly as traumatic as yours. My shoe fell off on our walk and I didn't even notice! I deserve a beautiful new pair of shoes, don't you think? My toes got too cold and I have some blisters, but I'll be good as new by tomorrow."

"Me, too," said Darius. "By tomorrow, or maybe the next day, for sure."

Across the cave, the lead smuggler was tending to the man who'd fallen from the path with Darius. His ribs were wrapped and his arm immobilized. She could see the pain he was in. He'd absorbed the brunt of impact to save her son. She caught his eye.

"Thank you. *Mersi.* There are no more heartfelt words I can say to you. I'm forever indebted to you."

He nodded.

Soraya found the small bag of almonds still hidden in her waistband and slipped it to her son. "Eat slowly."

She'd intended to give half to him, and eat the other half herself, but a burgeoning maternal instinct stopped her.

Let her stomach complain. The two sat quietly inside the cave the entire day. Merely breathing the same air, with their fingers entwined, was healing.

Outside the cave, the smugglers were in discussion. There was no food and little water left. The thin leader gave instructions to the youngest smuggler, who spat in disagreement. The leader sprang like a cobra, shoving him up against a rock. Repeating whatever he'd said, he pushed the young man down the path toward the desert floor, following close behind him. If anyone harbored thoughts about disagreeing with the leader, they didn't any more. There would be no questioning this man. In an odd way, it made the group believe that he knew what he was doing.

They were right. He was certain the Dasht River had a seasonal tributary nearby. There they could refill the water bottles and then, hopefully, he'd track a tribe of peaceful nomads. Then he could cajole, threaten or bribe the tribe into believing that they wanted to host temporary guests.

Chapter 34

Nomads

THE TRAVELERS were beyond hungry and even more tired. Soraya had shared crackers with the group, but she kept the apple hidden, just in case. She and Darius finally ventured out of the cave mid-morning, moving gingerly. Darius pointed.

"Look, Mama, look! Nomads!"

Off in the distance, a pencil-thin line was snaking its way toward them across the vast sand.

"You're right, son, it's a caravan, and they're coming for us," said Asad, who like everyone else, was buoyed by the prospect of food.

When they got close enough, Soraya saw that these were not like the desperately poor nomads on the roadside near Birjand. These men rode gaily-festooned camels that bore large baskets. The men were part of a Baloch tribe that was wintering with their livestock nearby.

The Balochs were pastoral, semi-sedentary nomads, who

moved seasonally, following food sources for their goats, sheep, and camels; bartering animal products for grains and vegetables in small towns they passed along the way.

The men opened up their baskets for the ragged refugees, who first drank the water poured from sheep wineskins. It helped them swallow the dust coating their throats. Then they ate only enough to feel satisfied before they were mounted on the animals, both camels and donkeys, for the trip back to the tribal community.

Darius was placed on a donkey since the smaller mount was gentler to his injuries, although his growing anticipation of staying with nomads nearly made him forget about his scrapes and bruises. He was eager to ask the children how they moved their toys from place to place.

He caught his mother's look of revulsion as she climbed onto a kneeling camel, and he couldn't resist teasing her.

"Mama, tell me which smells worse, your camel or the bus we rode when we left home?"

"Prayers to Allah that I never ride on either one again," she said emphatically, "but I fear I reek so badly that I can't tell which of us smells worse. However, my foot tells me that riding anything is better than walking for now."

Nearing the nomads' camp, Soraya's anxieties rose. She'd been taught that nomads were an untrustworthy, rootless and uneducated group. She only hoped this was an over night stop.

Children streamed out of large tents to welcome the guests. Excited and curious about the strangers, they ran alongside the caravan, cheering and waving. Darius grinned and waved back. This was going to be fun.

"Mama, do you see their pretty clothes?" he shouted, pointing at the children, who were clad in riotous colors.

Soraya nodded absently, focused on her camel, which spit his disdain of her as they entered the camp.

"Nasty brute," she muttered, sliding off.

Asad carried Darius, encouraging Soraya to lean on him as she hobbled along. The traffickers and the Baloch tribal leaders were assembled just out of earshot. After much gesticulation and many head nods, a deal must have been struck because the lead smuggler plunked a stack of bills into the chief's hands and everyone nodded again. The chief gestured for the travelers to follow him. These nomads only spoke Balochi, so everyone would be gesturing a lot.

But first, the lead smuggler had final instructions for the group. "You will be staying here for awhile. We are leaving you. You will be picked up once I've secured your forged passports allowing you to legally enter and exit Pakistan, which then allows you to fly on to Europe."

"We're staying here for awhile?" the toddler's father asked. "Define 'awhile,' please. I don't understand at all."

Grandmama had had enough. "When will we have hotel accommodations? How much longer will we spend in this god-forsaken desert? I'm too old for this."

The smuggler's eyes narrowed. "You're too old and your old mind is failing, Grandmama. The desert is not your problem. Your problem is the same as ours: Getting safely out of this desert. It's not about getting out of it quickly. It takes as long as it takes."

Soraya's heart sank. Her delusion of that "Cadillac" escape consisting of a few days' drive and a flight to America was gone. This was a marathon, and one with an uncertain outcome.

"How many more days do you estimate to our final destination?" she asked as politely as she could manage.

He smirked.

The teenager tried a different approach.

"How many days before you come back for us?"

"The day you see someone drive back into camp is the day you can stop wondering."

With that, he wheeled around and joined the other smugglers. As they drove away, the refugees forlornly watched them disappear into the distance. Now they were on their own, at the mercy of these nomads who spoke an unintelligible language.

The chief again motioned his guests into the central

tent. Its colorful interior was a welcome sight. Dim but comfortable, Soraya noticed first the beautifully woven Persian rugs covering the floor. Filigreed brass kerosene lamps hung from the inside tent poles. Huge pillows lay scattered on the rugs and their hosts gestured for the group to recline on them. Soraya elected to sit on a nearby chest instead, but before her posterior touched the lid, the tribal chief leapt up, yelling at her. She quickly stood back up, bewildered. Asad had caught enough words to guess what was wrong.

"I believe you were about to sit on a chest containing the Holy Qur'an."

"Oh, my, I'm so sorry," said Soraya, bowing and clasping her hands in apology as she stepped away from the chest.

How distressing. She'd already seen the firearms lying about, within reach of each man and so she'd no desire to anger them. Humbly kneeling on a large pillow even as their disapproving stares stung her, she waited meekly as sweet lumps were passed around for the guests to hold in their mouths before drinking the nomads' bitter tea.

While the refugees pretended to enjoy the drink, three gamey-smelling goats wandered into the tent. Soraya waited for the nomads to chase them out. Apparently though, livestock was free to roam the camp. It wasn't a pleasant realization, but one that was exceeded when the Billy Goat defecated near her. Soraya swallowed her disgust, lest she further insult the *tarof* they were being shown, but she was happy when the group's females were taken to a tent of mothers and their children. A boy about the same age as Darius motioned for him to come out and play.

"Can I, Mama? Can I play with the nomads? Please?"

Dirty nomad boy, she thought. What happened to the Bee Gees? She unconsciously wrinkled her nose, but she wouldn't stop Darius from having fun.

"If you're not in too much pain." His injuries looked ugly, but he seemed enthusiastic. "Stay away from the camels. They spit!"

"Okay," said Darius, "but did you see those red tassels they wear and how they look like they're always smiling?"

"They're smiling because they're preparing to spit on you, so please avoid both them and the animal messes."

"Okay, Mama!" he promised, hobbling after the boy.

Soraya had never been this dirty in her life. How many days had she been wearing the layers of clothing, and how long since she'd seen soap? Five days? Six? She'd lost count, but it was forever ago. She smiled ingratiatingly at a young woman, pointing at her own clothes and making a washing-like motion. At least she hoped it looked like washing. She'd personally never washed anything, nor had she any idea how the Baloch women washed their clothes in this desolate and dry land.

Interestingly though, apart from their leathery, sun-damaged skin, Soraya found these women peculiarly lovely, with exotic features and eyebrows so black they stood out even against the women's mahogany-brown complexions. Their dark skin tones set off their exquisite jewelry: Gold necklaces and heavy bracelets that seemed to shine exceptionally brightly. The intricate earrings they wore, called *dorr*, were so heavy that the women attached them with gold chains to their heads, helping to take most of the weight off of their earlobes. Soraya found it lovely.

Then there were their dresses: Explosions of turquoise, midnight blue, sunset red and throbbing purple fabric, joyously accented with contrasting embroidery. Even the little girls were dressed in brightly detailed smocks. The camp was a rainbow of colors in the middle of the desert's monochromatic palette.

Luckily, the woman understood Soraya's washing pantomime, although Soraya suspected the grime on her clothes made it obvious. She peeled off the layers, handing over a ratty sweater, several blouses, and skirts. When she finally uncovered her own nice clothes beneath the rags, she reverently placed them in a separate pile. The woman nodded, handing her a traditional Baloch outfit in exchange. Soraya was curious to wear the loose dress over the pair of pants. Slipping into the mustard yellow garment with black and red embroidery, Soraya wished she had a full-length mirror. The outfit felt beautiful. She'd have to find a good seamstress in the United States, and incorporate elements of the Baloch's style into her wardrobe.

It also occurred to Soraya that she'd best keep an eye on her own clothing. She didn't trust the women not to steal it. But when she found them, she was amazed to discover her clothes were being gently washed with sand. Fascinating. She didn't dare insult the women by pantomiming questions since they were handling her things so carefully.

Back at the tent, she found some clean wrappings for her foot set out for her, along with a large bowl of warm water and a cloth. Plunging the cloth into the water, she baptized her body into relative cleanliness.

If this harrowing journey had changed her in any way, Soraya decided, it had mellowed her preoccupation with precision and orderliness. She'd faced the messy side of life and survived. It had also shown her how fine was the line between black and white, good and bad. Hadn't she easily been reduced to rifling through cupboards and stealing food from SattAr's sister's house? She hadn't shared much of it, either. She pondered how quickly hunger, stress and fear had made her devolve.

But Soraya the Sage vanished at dinner, the moment she bit into goat meat as chewy as rubber bands. She choked down a bite or two of the gamey dish and gave up. Darius was very upset to learn that his dinner was one of those adorable goats. He refused to take even a bite, so the two of them filled up on *taak*, a hard stone-textured bread, and the dessert dates. Afterwards, they privately shared the apple Soraya had kept hidden all this time.

Sleeping in a tent that night with the unmarried sisters of the chief, on bedrolls tossed over rugs, was pure luxury compared to the conditions they had suffered thus far. Darius snuggled close to his mother, tired from playing with the children, but happy. His injuries were healing.

As they drifted off to sleep, the sweet hollow notes of a *ney* floated in from the camp's edge, played by the shepherds who would spend the night guarding the flocks. The double flute played a lullaby for the animals and people alike.

Darius whispered, "The goats are very funny, Mama."

"So are you. I'm glad you're having such a good time."

At sunrise, the women rolled up the mats and began chores. The aroma of baking *kaat* soon filled the air. After breakfast, Darius played with the children herding sheep. He was surprised to see the animals trot briskly toward a nearby sand dune. Darius climbed the dune with the children. At the top he turned and triumphantly shouted back to his mother. "Mama, guess what? There's a river."

Soraya was incredulous.

"What? You're teasing me!"

Daintily picking her way through the piles of animal excrement, she labored up the dune. The sight on the other side took her breath away: A glistening river, as alluring as a mirage, its banks adorned with scrub brush for the animals to eat. This was a tributary of the Dasht River. What a perfect wintering place, she thought. These nomads were superb survivors.

After four days in camp, Soraya was beginning to acclimate to nomadic life when she heard lambs bleating. Horrid memories of the lamb slaughtered at her wedding reception replayed in her mind. Minutes later, men walked by carrying freshly killed, gutted lambs that would be stuffed with rice and cooked whole. Oh well, she thought, I suppose, the nomads have to eat. She pinched her arm. When had she become so blasé? By noon it was obvious that something special was happening.

Excitement permeated the camp. Soraya gleaned that it was the chief's birthday. The scent of roasting lamb wafted through the air. Soraya heard the strumming and bowing of musical instruments emanating from tents.

Right after sunset, the feasting commenced. Soraya, Asad, Grandmama and all the refugees finally had the chance to socialize. Names were exchanged at long last, although now the information seemed superfluous. This group had bonded on a deeper level.

The tribe feasted while the musicians assembled. The assortment of strange instruments intrigued Soraya, although she did recognize the *suroz*, a stringed instrument that looked like a vertically played violin, and the *dohol*, a large drum with two skin heads that could make a listener's bones throb to its rhythm.

With one nod from the chief, music streamed into the night air. Men and women jumped up to sing and dance, as though possessed by the ancient melodies. The entire community joined in, swaying and clapping.

Darius was with a group of Baloch children. Soraya sat on a blanket with Asad on her right and the teenager, whose name she now knew was Esmat, on her left.

Asad looked Soraya and smiled.

"You're enjoying yourself, aren't you? I've not seen that look on your face before tonight. It's positively rapturous."

"Really? Well, I'd imagine that's because this is the first rapture-inducing event I've attended in several weeks."

Shattered Peacock

"Could you ever have imagined you'd be happy sitting on a blanket in the middle of the desert, not knowing when or if you'll ever get to leave?"

"Please, Asad. Don't say that! I'd rather die than stay here a day longer than necessary."

He listened to the music, contemplating something.

"Would you like to get away from these smoky fires? We could walk around the perimeter and pretend we're going somewhere."

She laughed. Putting an arm around Esmat, she asked, "Are you comfortable by yourself? I can show you where others from our group are sitting if you like."

"I'm fine," said Esmat. "My parents are at the back. I can find them if I want to."

Asad and Soraya strolled to the edge of camp, until the music faded into the background.

"Middle Eastern music is so different from European music," said Soraya. "And I say that as a Mozart aficionado. But our music is so deeply primal, somehow more raw and passionate. It speaks to a different kind of soul, don't you think?"

"I think you're right. One could say our music is as wedded to our identity as the bagpipes are to the Scottish."

"How far would you guess sound waves from the music they're playing right now travel through the desert?"

341

"I'd say, where the topography is flat, for a while. But heat pretty much kills the vibrations that carry sound."

Soraya looked up. "What about up into the sky?"

"Who knows? Without air, the waves aren't going to be audible anyway."

"Well, in my world the music keeps going and outer space sounds like an eternal symphony."

"Only in your world, Soraya."

She shook her head. "Except, I don't remember my world anymore. It's already a hazy memory. Whatever lies ahead won't be the same."

"Might be better."

"Better than home?"

"Define home. Our Tehran is no more. Home's not a place. We only think that it is."

"That reminds me of 'The Little Prince.'"

"I know the book. Very sweet, and the author is quite philosophic. Or did you mean Machiavelli's 'The Prince?' Now there's a book to interest every soldier."

"I don't even know what a Machiavelli is. I meant Saint-Exupéry's book. I can't quote it precisely, but the pilot who's crashed into the Sahara Desert, calls the desert 'beautiful' because hidden somewhere in the desert is a well of water, like a hidden treasure."

"I believe he goes on to say that what makes home

beautiful is invisible. He takes life to a metaphysical dimension, where we sense the eye of God watching us."

She looked at him with mock disgust.

"Please don't tell me you're a Bahá'í."

"No. I'm a Muslim, but I lean toward the mystical."

"I had you pegged as military, not philosopher."

"I've been involved in many things during my life, of which the military is one. Perhaps I'm philosophical because of my many careers. How did you guess the military?"

"First of all, you have survival skills. You're strong and calm. And your ... physique ... well, you have an air of authority." It was best to stop there.

"You're very perceptive, my dear."

Asad flinched. Those last two words carried too intimate a connotation. He hadn't meant to say them, yet they'd slipped out from his mouth. Soraya had heard them; he could tell from the awkward silence that followed, but he couldn't read her reaction.

She regrouped, regaining her composure.

"Life taken to a metaphysical dimension, you say." She looked up at the stars. "The desert sky is unbelievably poetic, I'll give you that," she continued. "It's a shame. I never really considered the stars until we trekked through the desert. Really 'seeing' them is uplifting. Am I close to sounding metaphysical? I'd like to be philosophical, too."

Asad was already caught up in the stars' magnificence. Standing side by side, their upturned faces were bathed in tender starlight. They absorbed the grandeur.

A sudden wonderment swept over Soraya. The grains of sand seemed to vibrate beneath her shoes like fluttering butterflies. Her thoughts catapulted toward the skies even though she knew she stood on *terra firma*. She could see herself roaming through space, and wondered vaguely if the Little Prince were nearby. The wholeness of the universe soaked into her. It was all connected. With her thoughts soaring higher and higher, she even thought she heard the Universe playing the music of the spheres, an eternal symphony in outer space.

Chapter 35

A Dangerous Dance

Baloch Camp, Pakistan
December 18, 1979

MEANWHILE, ESMAT was moving to the more earthly music being played in camp. She danced so beautifully, so sensuously, that one of the tribe's women pulled her up front so everyone could watch her dance of utter abandon. The camp was thrilled to see a guest lose herself in their music and egged her on. Esmat danced until sweat ran between her breasts and droplets flew from her hair when she twirled. When the music ended, she curtsied to the chief, who applauded and motioned her over to his chair, dabbing her forehead with his robe before kissing her on the cheek.

Soraya and Asad were strolling back as families were walking back to their tents. Esmat, still flushed with excitement, ran up to Soraya.

"Did you see me?"

"See you what?"

"Darn, you missed it. I danced for the whole camp and

the chief personally thanked me."

"Esmat, that's so exciting. Did your parents and Grandmama get to see you dance?"

"No, they left early. Grandmama was tired and needed help getting to bed. I'm wide-awake. May I stay up with you for awhile?"

"I'd love your company, sweetheart. I'm not sleepy, either. It's been quite a night."

Asad left them to their privacy. Soraya made tea, and the two contented women settled outside the tent to unwind under the night's the maturing sky.

"I don't mind being here," said Esmat. "At least here I can do things on my own here without having my parents or grandmama standing guard over me. I can't wait until I'm out of school and on my own."

"Being here isn't as bad as I feared, but our fate is not here the desert, Esmat. You'll be independent soon enough, free to achieve, to fall in love and have a family. Don't rush things. Along with freedom comes the opportunity to make life-altering mistakes."

They chatted, learning about each other's life. One of the chief's assistants approached them. He bowed politely, pointing at Esmat and then to the chief's tent, which stood about six tents away. The women were confused. The man bowed again and left, quickly returning. And again he pointed to Esmat and then at the chief's tent, opening a box to reveal an elaborate gold brooch.

"That's a stunning piece of jewelry," said Soraya.

"Is that for me?" asked Esmat, extending her hands.

The man shook his head no, pointing again to the chief's tent and then to her.

"I think the chief wants to formally present it to you," said Soraya. "You must have made quite an impression."

"How exciting," said Esmat, rising. "Will you come with me to watch?"

"I'd love to," said Soraya, but as she stood up, the man gestured for her to stay behind.

"Sorry. I guess it's an invitation-only ceremony," said Esmat, grinning. "I'll come back and tell you about it."

"That's fine. I'll be right here."

Soraya sat and sipped her tea, looking at the stars and vibrating with joy. But after fifteen minutes, concern floated to the top of her mind. She looked toward the chief's tent. No, she thought, and pushed away the worry. The nomads had been very kind to them.

But ten more minutes went by, making Soraya's stomach churn. She'd assumed others were in the tent with the chief and Esmat. What if Esmat was alone with the chief? She fought to stay calm. Her intuition told her that Esmat needed her. But as a woman she was powerless against the chief. Furthermore, she doubted any tribal woman would want to cross him. What if she barged into the tent and everything was fine? She'd humiliate Esmat and herself.

Staring at the tent, she determined that she had to trust her instincts. There were certain lessons Esmat didn't need to learn. She ran quickly but quietly to Asad's tent, trying not to rouse the camp and create a scene.

"Asad!" She hissed. "I need you! Please come out!"

He threw open the tent flap.

"Soraya, what's wrong?"

She grabbed his hand.

"Esmat. The chief's tent. She's in trouble. I know it."

"How can you know? This will look very bad if you're mistaken."

"I can't explain … trust me. Asad, go before he …"

Asad ducked back into the tent and came out shoving something inside his waistband.

"Let's go."

As they quickly ran toward the tent, Asad whispered instructions to her.

"I'll go in first. Let me do the talking."

He didn't even break stride as he burst through the tent's opening. Soraya was not far behind. Inside was Esmat, on her knees, naked and crying. The chief towered over her, his pants around his ankles and his hands on her head, controlling her movements while he moaned with pleasure. Glancing only briefly at Asad, he returned his attention to Esmat.

Asad growled, in a tone that frightened even Soraya.

"Let her go."

The chief cleared his throat. He patted Esmat gently on the head, and then shoved her to the ground before spitting on her. Esmat grabbed her clothes and ran into Soraya's arms. Soraya rocked her like a child.

"It's all over. You're safe now. We'll get through this, sweetheart. I promise. I'll help you, darling. Let's get you dressed. Tonight you'll sleep in my tent, next to me. I'll explain the situation to your parents in the morning. Asad will let them know that you're staying with me."

But the pain and fear in Esmat's eyes made Soraya suddenly lose control. She ran at the chief, screaming furiously and pounding him on the chest.

"You son of a bitch! You filthy predator! What you've stolen from her she'll never have again. I hate you, I hate you. I hate both of you!"

The chief shrugged.

Asad pulled Soraya off the chief and held her for just a moment. He talked calmly, but intensely.

"Dearest Soraya, take Esmat to your tent and let her bathe. Stay with her until she goes to sleep, then you and I will talk. Don't worry if she doesn't fall asleep until dawn. I'll still be watching and waiting."

Soraya took a shaky breath and relaxed a bit. She reached up and brushed her fingers across Asad's cheek in gratitude. He swallowed hard.

"Go."

Soraya gently wrapped Esmat in her clothes. Then she guided the teenager out of the tent, walking her out into a changed world.

Asad hadn't moved. The chief turned to face him. Eyeing each other, the men weighed their options. The chief glanced around at his sumptuous surroundings. He was a powerful man. Asad had embarrassed him in front of Esmat and Soraya, but no one would believe their stories anyway. They were only women, plus they were strangers and they meant nothing to him. He decided that Asad wouldn't risk a chief's wrath by pressing the issue. Besides, Asad was a man, too, with a man's sexual appetite. It was a need they shared. He flashed a conciliatory smile, opening his palms in a let-bygones-be-bygones gesture.

Asad took a giant step toward him and threw a single punch, dropping the chief to the ground. Looming over him, Asad stared down with disdain.

"It's not as much fun when you're the one on your knees and helpless, is it? And you're not a young girl."

Slightly dazed, the chief struggled to his feet, fury in his eyes. He started to reach for the gun on a nearby table, but Asad was a well-trained soldier. He grabbed the chief's arm, and spinning him around, painfully twisted the arm behind him. A second later, he pulled the knife he'd hidden in his waistband, holding it to the chief's neck.

They were at a dangerous impasse. The chief knew Asad wasn't really going to slit his throat because the men of his tribe would instantly kill him. The knife was a message not to retaliate, and to forget about the incident. The chief also knew he could call out for help, but then he would look weak. He could tell that if this man were cornered right now, blood would be spilled and some of it would be his.

Asad felt the chief's body let go in surrender. He gradually released the chief, who moved deferentially away.

Their eyes locked in mutual hatred. Asad backed out of the tent, his knife at the ready. He checked over his shoulder repeatedly as he walked away.

Esmat washed herself with warm water from a bowl, her eyes downcast. Soraya prattled some nonsense, hoping to distract the girl. The other women in the tent avoided them. Soraya realized that the chief's abuse of girls must be rampant. The women were either desensitized to abuse or too afraid to say anything.

Darius was already asleep. Soraya laid down two mats near him, for herself and Esmat.

"You are still a virgin, Esmat. Remember that. This wasn't your fault. It's a nightmare, and it's over. Don't keep replaying it in your mind, because then the nightmare never ends, not for your whole life. We'll talk about this tomorrow, next week, next month, whenever you want and we'll do whatever it takes until you're better."

"I want to leave this place right now. I hate it. Please, take me away from here right now. I hate these people. I hate it here."

"Me, too, sweetheart."

Soraya massaged her shoulders. Once the girl got drowsy, Soraya began stroking the inside of her wrists. She let her touch become lighter and lighter until Esmat had drifted into a fitful sleep. Then she tiptoed outside to see if Asad was waiting for her. He stepped from out of the shadows, startling her.

"Let's get away from the tents," he said, puffing on a cigarette as they walked.

"I didn't know you smoked."

"I quit eight years ago, but tonight seemed like a good time to take it up again. I bummed these off my tent mate."

They wandered out into the darkness. He lit another cigarette.

"How is Esmat doing?"

"She's asleep. She's doing as well as you'd expect. What happened after we left?"

"Not much. A small scuffle, perhaps. Did I mention that I boxed while I was in the Imperial Guard?"

"No, you never mentioned you boxed, or about being in the Imperial Guard."

"Yes, well, I did and I was. I still have a good right hook. Ask the chief."

"Seriously? What did he do after you hit him?"

"He didn't say much. He's going to have a tough time explaining the black eye, though."

"Asad, are you in trouble? Will they come after you?"

"They may try something. It's possible. I'm going to lay low. You won't see much of me until we leave here. If you can get a blanket to me, I can survive a awhile on my own."

"This is terrible. Thank you, Asad, for risking so much to rescue Esmat. Who knows what might have happened if you hadn't?"

"The way you attacked the chief, you might have been able to rescue her on your own."

"Well, of course. Naturally. I had adrenaline. I was angry."

"You were more than angry. You were a wounded lion attacking its hunter. You took that molestation personally."

"Only in the sense that I'm a woman."

They walked on. Asad put out his cigarette as they sat down on a rock.

"Who abused you, Soraya?"

She snapped back at him.

"What? How dare you? What are you implying?"

"I'm implying nothing. I'm simply stating the apparent. A few hours ago, you said to the chief, 'I hate you *both*.' Some man gave you a heavy burden to carry."

Soraya's eyes were wide. Had she really said that in the heat of the moment? Well, it was none of his business.

"You're presumptuous," she said.

"True." He lit up again. "Nonetheless, I'm here if you choose to share anything."

Soraya set her jaw. She owed him nothing. Who did he think he was?

"You don't have to share." Asad said. "It's okay."

He looked away, allowing space to fall between them. Soraya stared at her lap, her emotions waging war. On one side was denial. On the other side was a shattered seven-year-old Soraya, doing her best to be brave.

"I have nothing to share," she said, "and certainly nothing to say," even while wiping away an errant tear.

"Good. Let's talk about something else."

"Good? What about your rude assumption?"

But another tear slid from her eye before she could blink it back. The dam broke. Asad laid his handkerchief in her lap. He smoked while she cried it out.

Those years unspooled before her eyes, every single horrible, painful, lonely day. She'd repressed those memories for so long that she'd forgotten about the sick feeling in her stomach, the dread, the confusion, and the betrayal. Her pain washed out in tonight's tears. Adult Soraya finally mourned for the young, innocent Soraya.

"The bastard. My Grandpapa, General Zhuban Cyrus. He was a hero in World War I. He always looked so sad. Grandmama explained about the war and said we had to do everything we could to make him happy, so I tried. He liked for me to sit on his lap. But it scared me when I felt his lap get hard ..."

She inhaled sharply. She wanted to share everything, but there were times when truth had no words.

"One day, he reached underneath my skirt."

There were details she'd never be able to articulate.

"Things progressed. He always seemed happier afterwards, so I thought I'd done the right thing even though I hated it. He was strict about our special secret, so I told no one. After three years of it – I was ten years old and braver – I tried telling Grandmama that his way of being happy made me unhappy. She called me a liar. So I didn't tell anyone else."

Soraya had already emptied her pain into the void. She was dry-eyed now.

Asad, on the other hand, had to wipe away a tear.

"I wish I could change the past."

"Maybe you're changing the future. You're the only person I've ever told."

"That's a lot of years to hide such a deep wound."

"I became diligent about keeping my world beautiful. I'm living proof that you can sweep a lot of hurt under a 17th-century Savonnerie rug."

"You're a survivor, Soraya. You've carved out a good life despite your grandfather."

Tonight the memories had been unleashed from the dark corners of her mind. She could start facing them now.

"Thank you, Asad. You're very good to me."

"I'm honored that you trust me."

For just a moment, the two were one. A firefly of intimacy flew between them, a spark of unspoken affection, bonding and sealing their souls together in the stars above.

Chapter 36

Snake

TWO DAYS LATER, on day eight at the camp, the morning began routinely. Breakfast had ended and Darius was playing with the group's toddler.

"Tika," Darius spoke to her sweetly. "Look what I've made just for you."

He held up a doll. One of the women had shown him how to bind sticks with leather strips to form a body and wrap it in soft sheepskin clothing. The doll had twig legs and arms, and wore a tiny dress. Her head was a leather-covered ball of wool sewn directly to the neckline of the dress, with the long curly hair shorn from a black sheep held in place by delicately sewn threads.

Tika kissed it.

"She likes it, Mama!"

"Wonderful, *Aziz Talah,* my dearest golden child. "

Darius couldn't stop grinning.

One of his nomad friends ran up, very excited.

"What?"

The boy pointed. Darius followed his finger, squinting into the distance. He let out a whoop.

"Cars are coming! Mama, they're here, they're here!"

Darius and his friend grabbed two beat-up bicycles and rode through the dust to escort the vehicles into camp.

Twenty minutes passed before the two shiny, new, black SUVs arrived. They were so beautiful they looked like a mirage, Soraya thought jubilantly. At last, she would travel in comfort.

She wondered if Asad had seen the vehicles coming. Sure enough, he appeared as they pulled into camp. She noticed he immediately stood near the armed drivers. He was taking no chances.

There were only two men, just the drivers, and they wore no masks, but they were carrying firearms. Neither of these men was from the original team of smugglers. In fact, these men actually had manners. They didn't offer their names, but the gray bearded man held a bundle of passports. He called out names. Soraya quickly flipped open her passport. A fake Pakistani passport, it looked very authentic and bore the same photo as her Iranian passport. She was curious about where they'd been made, but she didn't really care. Now no one could accuse them of escaping from Iran. They were now officially Pakistanis.

Soraya thought back to that phone call with Zamian. He'd mentioned Karachi. That's where they were going! Anticipating the storied city was heady. To think of real hotels with bathtubs – surely they'd be flying from Karachi to Portugal! From there: On to America. The trek was nearly over.

Gray Beard instructed them to gather their things, but to leave behind the shabby outer layers. They'd soon need to look like tourists. Soraya and Darius hurried to don their layers of clothing from home, giving Soraya an idea.

"Darius, we can buy new things when we see Papa. Let's leave some of our nice clothes for the nomads. Wouldn't they like that?"

Darius was enthusiastic.

"I'm going to give my red sweater to my friend. His sweater has so many holes in it."

Soraya smiled at her son. "Just please keep enough layers for a few more nights in the desert."

Gesturing to the women of her tent, she gave them two blouses, two skirts and some of her silk underwear, knowing each piece of clothing would be treasured. The women conversed animatedly. Agreeing on something, one woman covered Soraya's eyes. Another took her hand and began filling her palm. When Soraya opened her eyes she'd been gifted with two pair of gold earrings, a bracelet set with gems, and a large gold brooch. She was touched.

Darius reappeared, flushed with the joy of giving.

"My friend was so happy to get the sweater, Mama!"

After spending more than a week here, it was finally time to leave. Stepping over piles of camel excrement, a skill at which the travelers had become adept, they hurried to the vehicles, shouting goodbyes to their hosts.

Soraya, Darius and little Tika, who wanted to sit next to Darius, along with her parents, climbed into the first car. The other four travelers: Esmat, her feisty grandmama, as well as her mother and father buckled themselves into the second vehicle. Asad joined them.

Everyone except the chief assembled to see them off. The children ran alongside the cars for a quarter of a mile before peeling away. They waved for a long time as they watched the cars grow smaller and smaller.

Gray Beard drove Soraya and Darius' car. He was a chatty fellow, a natural travel guide.

"As we drive into the Thar Desert you'll see more nomads and a lot more wildlife. All kinds of reptiles, blackbucks and chinkara gazelles live here. We'll sleep in the desert tonight but late tomorrow we'll arrive in Karachi."

A cheer went up.

Darius stayed on the lookout for wildlife, pointing out to everything he saw to the others with wild enthusiasm.

"Look at the herd with those long, fancy horns! Are those the blackbucks?" He didn't wait for an answer. "Yes, they must be. You know if they had only one horn they'd look like unicorns!"

Twenty minutes later, he pointed and shouted, "Look at the gigantic lizard!"

Gray Beard was as surprised as Darius.

"My goodness. That's a Desert Monitor, living rather outside his normal territory. How unusual to see him out in the daylight. Let's be glad he's out there and we're in here."

After a long but comfortable day, the caravan rolled to a stop. The drivers pulled four tents from the SUV. Tonight they'd sleep in decent conditions.

Gray Beard put a dent in their enthusiasm.

"The desert contains much wildlife. We've seen some of it today. These tents should keep curious nocturnal animals from getting up close and personal. However, regardless of whatever noises you hear tonight, stay inside your tents unless we instruct you otherwise. Okay, I need the men to help get the tents up before dark."

Darius was nervous about the Desert Monitors, but Soraya brushed aside his fears.

"We'll be fine. After all we've been through? But as they say, let's bake while the oven is hot. Let's find some bushes for privacy. We should go to the bathroom for the night."

Little Tika trailed right behind Darius. She'd attached herself to him. He took her hand, saying, "Come, little girl. Come with us."

A blazing sunset was fading from the sky and turning it steel gray. Soraya headed for a thick clump of bushes not far from where the tents were going up.

"No one can see us from behind here. Darius, please watch Tika. I'll go first and then help her."

Once she'd emptied her bladder, Soraya lifted Tika's dress to pull down her panties. The little girl squatted.

Darius spoke in a frightened whisper, so softly that Soraya could hardly make out the words.

"Don't move, Mama. Do you see? There's a snake between Tika and me. He's staring at her."

Soraya froze. Trying to look around without moving her head, she searched the sand between the children. It was difficult to make out the snake in the rapidly dimming light, but she glimpsed a flash of its golden stripe, noting how overtly annoyed it looked.

Soraya's first thought was that she hadn't survived this journey for a tragic ending. If I'm fast enough, she thought, I can distract the snake. But I have to be fast enough. She looked about for some way to create a smoke screen. There were small pebbles within kicking distance.

Little Tika was almost finished peeing and would stand

up in a few seconds.

"Sweet Tika," Soraya sang in a low voice, "darling, can you pretend you're the doll Darius made for you and not move? Good girl. Stay very still, little doll."

To Darius she whispered, "When I say 'Go,' run as fast as you can back to the camp, yelling 'Snake.' Don't look back to see if it's following you. It won't. Get help. I'll take care of Tika. Do you understand?"

"Yes," Darius whispered back.

"I'm going to count to three and then say 'Go.'"

"Okay."

"One ... two ... three ... go."

Darius ran as fast as he could, yelling. The snake whipped around, tracking Darius' sudden movement. In that instant, Soraya scooped up Tika with one arm and kicked the pebbles as hard as she could before starting to run. The snake swung around to lunge at her. She clung to Tika and kept running.

Gray Beard was already on his way, a flashlight in one hand and his pistol in the other.

"Where?" he shouted.

She pointed back at the bushes.

Three loud bangs split the air.

Gray Beard bent over to examine the dead reptile and motioned for Soraya to come back and take a look.

"No, I don't want to see it," she said. "I won't."

"You must," he insisted. Gray Beard shone his flashlight over the shreds of snake. "This is a common Krait. He's nocturnal, so his day was just beginning. They're slow during the day but very fast at night. You caught him in-between, not overly fast but certainly not slow."

"So we would have been okay?"

"My dear," he said, "you most likely saved the little girl's life. This snake has a deadly bite."

Soraya's knees knocked together. Gray Beard patted her shoulder. "No need to frighten the others. We'll say it was a harmless snake that you assumed was venomous, because how would you know?"

"All right."

"You are Mrs. Sultan, aren't you?"

"Yes."

"Mrs. Sultan, you are a brave woman."

"No one has ever said so. I don't feel brave."

"Perhaps you haven't recognized your courage."

She stared at the snake. Gray Beard looked at her.

"The others will never know you were a hero tonight. But I will. I hope that's enough for you."

She was about to collapse. That night her dreams were filled with slithering snakes and huge lizards.

Chapter 37

Civilization

Karachi, Pakistan
December 21, 1979

THEY BROKE CAMP and departed for Karachi early the next morning. Munching on snacks and sipping water, the travelers watched the desert through the windows of the SUV. They enjoyed paved roads part of the way, but Gray Beard drove as the crow flies, so more often than not, the 200 miles to Karachi plowed through sand, went over hills on gravel, and bumped through rocky patches.

They reached the outskirts of Karachi, near the southern tip of Pakistan, late in the afternoon. An excited Darius bounced in his seat.

"Let's call Papa as soon as we get to the hotel. Can we eat at a restaurant tonight?"

"Yes and yes, but not until after I take a long bath!"

Soraya was ecstatic. Now Mehdi could book their flights to America. They had left Tehran with Arash the morning of November 26th and been out of communication since December 8th. That was thirteen days ago. Did he think they were dead?

Before entering downtown Karachi, Gray Beard explained the evening's ruse. "This is extremely important. You are not Iranians. You are Pakistani tourists and this is the highlight of your trip. Avoid speaking Persian in front of others. It will give you away. Remember, your passports say you are Pakistani. If someone hears you speak Persian, and asks, say you have dual citizenship, or that your relatives live in Iran, whatever. Talk about the sights you want to see, how this is the loveliest place you've stayed thus far on the "tour," etc. Above all else, do not talk about flying to Lisbon because they'll immediately know you're Iranian refugees. All illegals fly from here to Lisbon because Portugal doesn't require a visa. Tomorrow afternoon you will be driven to the airport. Is any part of what I explained not clear? Ask now, because I can't help you if your real identity is uncovered."

There were no questions.

"Good. Tonight's dinner is in a private dining room where you'll be able to speak freely."

Their anticipation was rising. Gray Beard derived satisfaction from delivering people to safety. It was worth the danger he faced. Karachi's roads were jammed with afternoon commuters. The vans wound through the city center at a snail's pace. Although they were only two blocks from the hotel, Gray Beard stayed mum. The turn he was about to make would reveal a spectacular sight.

There came a collective gasp. "The Arabian Sea!"

The van erupted in hoorays and laughter.

Gray Beard added, "And on your right is your hotel."

"Oh, Darius," said Soraya, "maybe we'll have an ocean view. Think of it. After living for so many days in an ocean of sand, we'll wake up to water!"

People were eager to get to their rooms but Gray Beard and the other driver made them wait. Donning caps embroidered with the logo, "Arabian Tours," the two strolled casually into the lobby and up to the front desk, returning ten minutes later with room keys.

"You're all on the same floor. Go to your rooms and relax. We've brought empty suitcases, which we'll bring to your rooms. Use them to pack any extra clothing or gifts you may buy at the hotel. Dinner will be in the smaller private dining room downstairs. You have two hours to rest. Remember to act like tourists."

Darius couldn't control his glee and for once, Soraya was equally gleeful. Her hands trembled so much from excitement that it took her three tries to fit the room key into the lock. She threw open the door to reveal two beds, a desk, a sofa and a dramatic view of the Arabian Ocean.

Darius leaped onto the nearest bed and bounced.

"We did it!" he shouted. "We did it! Oh, I wish Nanny was here to see this! Let's call her!"

"We will, *Naz Nazy*, although probably not today. Let's call your father right now and let him know we're safe."

Soraya dialed the hotel operator, requesting an international, person-to-person call to Washington, D.C.

"Darius, come here. You talk to Papa first."

Darius grabbed the phone.

His father's voice answered.

"Hello?"

Before Darius could speak, the operator broke in.

"I have a person-to-person call from Soraya Sultan. Will you accept the charges?"

Darius heard his father say, "Oh, dear God, finally. Yes, of course."

"Go ahead," said the operator.

"Papa!" Darius yelled over the operator's voice. "It's us! We're in Karachi!"

"My son!" Mehdi broke down in tears. "This is the happiest day of my life. Are you all right?"

Darius exploded into a monologue.

"Yes, and we have so many stories to tell you. Guess what? I fell off a cliff. Mama and I killed a snake, well, maybe we didn't exactly kill it, but almost, and it might have been very dangerous, and before that, we lived with nomads and before that, we had to sleep in the desert and before that we were locked in a basement, at least I think the door was locked, and tomorrow …"

Mehdi was desperate to speak to his wife.

"Darius, I want to hear about every moment of your journey, but first, let me speak to Mama."

Soraya took the phone, too emotional to form words, but Mehdi could hear her breathing.

"*Jeegareto bokhoram*, I love you more than anything."

"*Eshgam*, my love. Mehdi, I miss you so much."

"I've been frantic. I was afraid something horrible had happened and here I sat, completely useless."

"I think the traffickers wanted you to think it was a brief, luxurious escape, but it wasn't. I've lost count of the deserts we went through."

"You must be exhausted. Are you all right?"

"We're tired, but I'm so happy to be in a hotel, I think may go dancing tonight at one of Karachi's night clubs!"

Mehdi's familiar laugh brought tears to Soraya's eyes.

"Wait until I can go with you!" he said. "We'll stay out every night, if you like. I'm so happy to hear your sweet voice. The arrangements I made with the smugglers end when you disembark in Lisbon. It's my job to fly you to Washington. When are you leaving Pakistan for Portugal?"

"We fly out tomorrow afternoon."

Mehdi sighed. "Karachi to Lisbon is about seventeen hours. I'm sorry it's such a long flight."

Soraya burst out laughing.

"Seventeen hours on a cushioned seat with a foot rest, and with people bringing food, in a plane carrying us to you? That's heaven!"

I'm the luckiest man in the world to have you as my wife because you still love me despite what I've put you through. I'll find a flight for you right now. I love you, Soraya."

She teased him with newfound confidence.

"Well, of course you love me. How could you not? Not only do I have a finishing school degree, but I've also earned a higher degree in survival."

"I don't want to hear about the horrors I perpetrated on you until you're safe in my arms. I admire you so much, my warrior wife."

"All right, but the longer you wait, the more heroic I become in my stories."

"By the way, Christmas is only a few days away. Knowing you and Darius are safe was the only present I wanted. I have a view of the National Christmas tree out my window, and today it finally looks beautiful."

Once they'd said goodbye, Soraya turned to her son.

"Darius, watch whatever you want on TV. I'm taking the world's longest shower, and if enough drops of hot water remain when I'm finished, you can remove your top three layers of grime so I can recognize you. I suspect you're really a nomad boy who has switched places with my son. The real Darius is probably herding goats right now."

"It's true, Mama. I mean, Mrs. Sultan. But you'll like me much better than him! I'm smarter and funnier than Darius ever was."

"In that case, I got the better end of the deal."

She flipped on the television for him and headed to the bathroom. Opening the door, she stopped and stared as though she'd never seen a modern bathroom. The pristine white porcelain gleamed like snow. Slowly, reverently, she sat on the cool toilet seat, acutely aware of its smooth magnificence. She gently unrolled the toilet paper like a bolt of finest silk, and then, astonished by such convenience, she pushed a handle to make water gush and swirl the human waste away. Remarkable. Ingenious. How had she ever taken all this for granted? She saw her face in a mirror for the first time since Zabol. The woman looking back at her was unrecognizable. Her professionally waxed and shaped eyebrows had regrown into a unibrow. She'd fix that before dinner. Her skin was rough and brown. But right now, all she wanted was a shower. Planting herself under the hot water she let it flood her hair and spill over her body. Filling her hand with shampoo, she scrubbed her scalp until the suds were as thick and white as lamb's fleece.

The two hours before dinner flew by. Clean and dressed, the travelers barely recognized one other.

Soraya hugged Esmat. "Look how beautiful you are," she said. She handed the girl some of the money she'd carried from home. "Buy a new outfit for your new life."

"I can't take this. You've already helped me so much, Mrs. Sultan. I couldn't have survived that nightmare if you hadn't been there for me."

"I'm here whenever you need me." She folded Esmat's hand over the money. "Think of me whenever you wear the dress. Here's my husband's phone number in D.C. You'll call, yes? You'll need to talk some more."

"I promise you. And thank you for sharing your story with me. It means so much that you truly understand."

"I do. You and I are survivors. The past will not break us. We're stronger than we know. And Esmat, please be kind to yourself."

The dinner was filled with loud, happy conversation. Jokes abounded; the hazardous trip was recounted and future plans discussed. Asad and Soraya sat together.

"Where will you meet your husband?" he asked.

"Washington, D.C.," she said. "What are your plans?"

"I'm headed to Paris for a few months to check out opportunities. I have relatives there. I want to give all new avenues their due consideration."

Darius ran up and tugged on her sleeve.

"Mama, I mean, Mrs. Sultan, they've put out dessert. May I have one of everything?"

"Of course, Nomad Boy. Go. Enjoy."

Soraya and Asad's conversation took an awkward turn. After tomorrow they wouldn't see each other again. What could be said that didn't sound like regret?

"Meeting you has been a pleasure, Asad."

He hesitated. "Actually," he said, "we met years ago."

"What do you mean?"

"I attended your wedding."

"How is that possible? I don't remember you, and I'm sure I would. I'm terribly embarrassed. I didn't personally know all of the guests, you understand.

"Don't feel embarrassed. You were drowning in a sea of people. I was one of many guests and you were the only bride. I do remember thinking that your husband was one lucky son of a bitch and I wondered how he won you."

Now Asad was embarrassed. "Please, I meant no disrespect to you or your husband."

"Of course, I understand," she reassured him. She was furiously blushing. "You've given us a kind compliment."

Riding the elevator upstairs after dinner, it was obvious that Asad wanted to say something else, but it wasn't until they'd said goodnight and headed opposite ways down the hall to their rooms that he turned back and finally spoke.

"Pahlavi."

"Excuse me?"

"That's my bloodline, my last name. It's Pahlavi. I'm his cousin. It's why I was at your wedding. I was standing in for the Shah."

In an instant, everything about Asad made sense: His masculinity, his intelligence, his depth, his athleticism, and his elegant bearing. She wondered what might have been if she'd met him before Mehdi, immediately erasing the thought and burying it forever, she hoped.

"The best of luck to you, Asad Pahlavi."

"And to you. If I never see you again, know that you are much appreciated."

"Thank you, Asad."

He nodded and walked away, a gentle man to the core.

Chapter 38

Portugal

Lisbon, December 23, 1979

SORAYA TOOK ADVANTAGE of their morning stay in Lisbon to show Darius around. They shopped with her hidden cash for new clothes on the *Baixa's Rua Augusta.* Soraya was in heaven. She found a lacy, figure-flattering burnt-orange dress she knew would stoke Mehdi's libido. Darius had trouble making up his mind.

"I want Papa to see how much older I am now."

"No matter what you wear, you'll look more mature than when we left Tehran," said Soraya. "Which is why I still have my suspicions about you, Nomad Boy."

Darius giggled. She'd be sad when he outgrew that giggle. He made her think of a Hafiz poem:

You carry all the ingredients

To turn your existence into joy,

Mix them.

Mix them!

Her son "mixed" those ingredients well.

Tired but happy, they returned to the hotel to eat some

lunch, then went to the room to pack up their new things. Soraya pulled her chador from the closet and began ripping it apart. Darius came out of the bathroom in his new outfit.

"Mama, whatever are you doing?

There was a mischievous glint in her eyes.

"Wait and see," she said, ripping open another seam.

Darius curled up on the bed to watch. Soraya ran her fingers along the hem, yanked some threads and retrieved her great-grandmother's emerald ring.

"Mama! Aren't you clever! You brought it all the way from home?"

"I'm not finished yet."

She ripped the garment to shreds. By the time she tossed its remnants into the wastebasket, a pile of jewelry and money laid spread out on the duvet. Soraya and Darius stared. The reminders of their old life seemed unfamiliar, even incongruous, after all they'd been through. They stirred fond memories and Soraya was glad to have them, but she'd detached from their importance somewhere along the journey. How odd.

While Darius watched TV, Soraya gazed out the window at the line of cars snaking along the shoreline. She caught sight of her reflection in the glass. Her face had a new patina, earned through adversity, which had softened its beauty. This face was animated by a new light emanating from somewhere inside of her.

She was different, perhaps because she'd learned to take life as it came. She was powerless to control it, but she could survive it with a strength that ran too deep to be shaken by circumstances.

"Darius, do you remember when I read "The Little Prince" to you and the other children?"

"Uh-huh. At least, I remember it sounded prettier in French, but I didn't understand much of it in either language."

Soraya said, "A line from the book keeps popping into my head: 'What I'm looking at is only a shell. What's most important is invisible …'"

"I don't get it," said Darius, shaking his head.

"That's okay. I'm only beginning to understand it. Finish up packing, Darius. Once we're on the plane we'll be about thirteen hours away from Papa. And we'll arrive in time for our first Christmas."

"Do you think my present will be the Bee Gees welcoming me to America?"

"Ah ha. The Bee Gees live again. Now I'm thinking that you are not Nomad Boy; however, no, I don't think the Bee Gees will be welcoming you at the airport."

Darius had many stories to tell his father. But then he

realized he had no one else to tell. He wouldn't know any of the children where they were going. He'd have to make all new friends. But that didn't sound so hard.

"We did it, Mama."

"Yes we did, my darling. Aren't we lucky."

As they closed their suitcases, Darius became pensive.

"Mama, you know I've always wondered how the nomad children carried their toys from place to place. I think I've figured out their secret."

"Yes?"

"Well, my friend only had one toy of his own - a ball that he shared with everyone. I think nomad children just play with each other, no matter what they're doing. And they make up games that they can play wherever they are, so they don't have to carry toys from place to place."

"I guess they've learned how to take their happiness with them. Well, today we're nomads, too, moving to a different place. Shall we be happy wherever we set up our tent?"

"Having some baby goats in the tent would make it easier to be happy."

"No goats, Nomad Boy, but what if Darius had a small dog in a nice house instead?"

"Really? My very own dog? Oh, Mama – forget about Nomad Boy. I'm Darius, and I love the Bee Gees."

Epilogue

Montrose, California
June 28, 1980

Dearest Fatima,

Greetings from Los Angeles, or to be more specific, greetings from Montrose, a cute little town. It's not near the beach, but at least we found an affordable home here.

Your wedding photos arrived today. Darius ripped opened up the package and spread the pictures across the kitchen table like a lovely mosaic. Fatima, you are radiant in your wedding dress. You exude elegance as beautifully as any Persian princess.

After living here for three months, I'm proud to say that Darius has adjusted splendidly. He has new friends and is speaking English like a native, at least to my ears. I've enclosed a Polaroid to show you how much he's grown.

I continue struggling with my English. Mehdi just shakes his head at me. I've promised him I'll take a night course somewhere. Oh, Fatima, let's be real: I don't have a chef, I don't have an assistant, I don't have a butler and I don't have a nanny here. I did inform Mehdi that I absolutely refuse to do the housework, so he's hired a cleaning company to come in weekly, and we have gardeners, but aside from that, I'm doing the work I used to pay other people to do! Actually, I do it all quite well. I even drive Darius to school. As long as I don't have to get on a freeway, I'm a decent driver.

You know, in Tehran I loved everything American. Now I ache for things Persian, even though I know that my Iran is no more. Still – it's hard to forget. I find myself listening to tapes of the Golha Radio programs.

But let's sound more positive! There are lots of things to do here and much culture to enjoy. Darius went to Disneyland last month. He loved it, of course.

Our adorable, 1930's hacienda-style house, (it's very Southern Californian) has two bedrooms and two baths. That's cozy compared to the Tehran compound, yes? But because we're splitting our time between here and the condo in D.C., "cozy" works well enough, although I'm hoping we'll move closer to the beach next year. My industrious husband is reorganizing the business. His hard work is beginning to pay off, even if we don't get to see much of him. But what else is new?

Mehdi's American friends have been instrumental in finding investors. In return, he tracks down Iran's former political and business leaders, those still alive, anyway, and then shares their information concerning Khomeini and his minions with the Americans.

Our mansion is being used as government offices? Do I congratulate the government on good taste, or weep, knowing the destruction they've wreaked on it? Distressing.

Darius loves the United States, but I remind him that he has 100 % Persian blood running through his veins.

My heart mourns the death of our beloved Shah. Some day we will visit Cairo to pay our respects. How Queen Farah must be grieving! I pray (yes, I pray - occasionally), that some day we'll return to an Iran governed by its rightful heir, young Prince Reza Pahlavi. Iranians will throw off the current oppression, I'm sure. The world certainly will be safer when they do.

I'm working to live each day in the present, more aware of life's joys. Oh goodness, don't I sound like a Southern Californian? Perhaps I've assimilated more than I realize.

The welcome mat is always out for you. I hope you and Jamal will come visit as soon as the government will allow.

Darius says to tell you:

"I love you up and down and all around;

Forever and for always."

I concur.

Fondly,

Soraya

Historical Biographies:

While the central characters in "Shattered Peacock" are fictional and created by the author, certain historical figures pertinent to the plot's events have been included. Below are bios of the real life personages featured in the book.

The Pahlavi Dynasty:

Mohammad Reza Shah Pahlavi
October 26, 1919 - July 27, 1980
Successor to his father, Reza Shah Pahlavi, Mohammad Reza Shah ruled Iran from 1941 – 1979. He was the first Muslim leader to recognize the state of Israel. When he was deposed by a revolution fueled by the Ayatollah Ruholla Khomeini and made possible when the United States and Great Britain withdrew their support, he went into exile, eventually dying of cancer in the United States. President Anwar El-Sadat of Egypt granted the Shah his final asylum. He is buried in Cairo.

Farah Diba – Born October 14, 1938
Farah Diba Pahlavi was elevated to the title of Empress, consort of Iran, or *Shahbanu*, in 1967. Born into an upper-class family, she was an athlete and studied architecture. The Shah met Farah at the École Spéciale d'Architecture in Paris during a royal visit to meet with the school's Persian students. Their marriage produced four children: Crown Prince Reza Pahlavi, Princess Farahnaz, Prince Alireza Pahlavi, and Princess Leila Pahlavi. In 2001, Princess Leila died of a drug overdose. Prince Alireza committed suicide in 2011. Today Empress Farah Diba Pahlavi

divides her time between Washington, D.C. and Paris.

Crown Prince Reza Pahlavi – Born July 27, 1960

Eldest son of Shah Pahlavi and Empress Farah, the crown prince and heir to his father's throne has written several books about Iran. He remains a popular Persian figure, and is known for championing human rights and democracy for Iranians.

The Iranian Revolution:

Shapour Bakhtiar – June 26, 1914 - August 6, 1991

Dr. Bakhtiar was born into a family of tribal nobility. Bakhtiar's mother died when he was a child, while Reza Shah executed his father when Dr. Bakhtiar was 20 years old.

An outspoken critic of the Pahlavi dynasty's totalitarianism, he spent nearly six years in prison under Mohammad Reza Shah. Paradoxically, when the last Shah began losing power in 1978, he appointed Bakhtiar as prime minister in an attempt to appease dissidents. Although Bakhtiar quickly freed political prisoners and dissolved SAVAK, he held power for 36 days.

The Islamic Republic included him in a general death sentence, which automatically convicted anyone connected with the Pahlavi government. After one failed attempt, five assassins murdered Bakhtiar in his Paris home using kitchen knives.

Ayatollah Ruholla Khomeini
December 14, 1902 - June 3, 1989

Arrested by the Shah in November of 1964 and forced from Iran for his opposition to the monarchy, Ayatollah Ruholla

Khomeini lived in exile for thirteen years in Iraq and another
two years in France. He returned triumphantly to Iran in in the
midst of the 1979 Iranian Revolution to found the Republic of
Iran. As its Supreme Leader, he wielded complete political and
religious control. Khomeini once said, "Don't listen to those
who speak of democracy. They all are against Islam. They want
to take the nation away from its mission. We will break all the
poison pens of those who speak of nationalism, democracy, and
such things."

When students overran the American Embassy on November 4,
1979, Khomeini initially ordered them to release the hostages,
but recanted after discovering how popular the hostage situation
was in the Middle East. He concluded that America *"...hich
ghalati nemitooneh bokoneh."* (America cannot do a damned thing.)

Sadegh Khalkhali – July 27, 1926 - November 26, 2003
Known as Iran's "Hanging Judge," Khalkhali was a hardline
jurist, handpicked by the Ayatollah Khomeini to head his Sharia
Revolutionary Courts. Speculations are that Khalkhali handed
out 8000 death sentences, some of which he personally carried
out. He was well known for his girlish, high-pitched giggle.
Following the United States' disastrous attempt to rescue the
American Embassy hostages on April 24, 1980, Khalkhali
ordered that the charred and dismembered limbs of eight dead
U.S. soldiers be televised. He was filmed spitting on the bodies.

General Mehdi Rahimi – 1921 - February 16, 1979
Rahimi was Deputy commander of the Imperial Guard, Police
Chief of Tehran and president of the Wrestling Federation of
Iran. He was arrested, interrogated on television for five hours,
and then was tortured, during which his right arm was severed.
Near midnight he and three other generals faced the firing squad

after being sentenced by Sadegh Khalkhali. Rahimi refused a blindfold and reportedly shouted, "Long live the Shah" just before being shot.

Nematollah Nassiri –1921 - February 16, 1979
Nassiri was best known as the director of SAVAK, the Shah's feared intelligence agency. Stories of torture sullied the secret organization's reputation and in 1978 the Shah removed Nassiri from his post, making him ambassador to Pakistan in an attempt to placate revolutionaries and the United States. After the Shah was deposed, Nassiri was executed in a schoolyard along with Martial Law Administrator and Police Chief of Tehran, Mehdi Rahimi; Martial Law Administrator of Esfahan, Reza Naji; and Air Force Commander Manuchehr Khosrodad. Photos of their corpses were widely published.

Iran Hostage Crisis: 444 Days in Captivity (11/04/79 – 01/25/81)
President Jimmy Carter – Born October 1, 1924
The 39th President of the United States, Carter was in office during the Iranian Revolution and the Iranian Hostage Crisis. His relationship with the Shah was complicated by the monarch's apparent violations of human rights versus his unwavering loyalty to the U.S., as well as the undeniable improvements he made in his country's infrastructure; the modernizing of its education system; and the rights he instituted for women.

Prior to the Iranian Revolution, President Carter often reiterated his support of the Shah. At a speech in May of 1975, Carter said, "The visit of your imperial majesties reflects the cordial personal and close governmental relations between the United States and Iran ... Ours is an old and tested friendship. It will continue to be so in the future." These assurances gave the Shah a false sense of security. He believed the Americans would forever support him. Astonishingly, the CIA didn't think he needed rescuing. A 1978 analysis from the CIA expressed the opinion that, "Iran is not in a revolutionary or even a pre-revolutionary situation." Regardless, Carter's administration watched the Shah's power crumble, ultimately announcing that keeping him in power was not the responsibility of the United States.

After university students took Tehran's American Embassy staff hostage, Carter isolated himself in the White House for 100 days, trying to resolve the situation. Finally, he ordered Operation Eagle Claw, an all-out strategy to free America's hostages. The rescue attempt, commencing on April 24, 1980, was an unmitigated disaster. Of the eight helicopters sent to the initial staging area, only five arrived in operational condition. Carter then tried to abort the mission, but one of the departing helicopters crashed into a transport plane, killing eight elite U.S. troops, whose bodies, recovered by the Iranians, were televised worldwide.

Iran exploited America's humiliation. In a final gesture of disrespect to the president, Iran refrained from releasing the hostages until after President Ronald Reagan was sworn in and his inaugural speech had been delivered.

Lowell Bruce Laingen – Born August 6, 1922
Laingen is best known as the senior American official held hostage during the Iran Hostage Crisis. He later received the State Department's Award for Valor.

Staff Sergeant Michael E. Moeller – Born 1949

Thirty-one-year-old Staff Sergeant Moeller headed the USMC Guard Unit at the American Embassy in Tehran when the post was overrun. He and eight other Marines valiantly attempted to defend the embassy. After his release, Moeller re-enlisted and was given a computer job in Quantico, Virginia.

Richard Queen – August 7, 1951 - August 14, 2002

Queen was serving as Vice Consul at the American Embassy in Tehran when he was taken hostage. He fell ill early on in captivity but was misdiagnosed by the Iranian doctors. His health deteriorated until he finally was released on July 11, 1980, after 250 days of captivity. Queen was diagnosed with multiple sclerosis and died from complications of the disease.

William H. Sullivan – October 12, 1922 - October 11, 2013

The last U.S. ambassador to Iran following the revolution, Sullivan earlier had helped negotiate the end of American involvement in Vietnam. The veteran diplomat served in World War II, and was part of both the Normandy Invasion and the invasion of Okinawa.

Ali Zahmatkesh (birth/death unknown)

The leader of the students who stormed the American embassy, he later became an engineer. Sources suggest he works or did work for the Tavanir Company in Tehran, an electrical power corporation owned by the Ministry of Power.

Selected Bibliography

Print:
Afkhani, Gholem Reza, *The Life and Times of the Shah,* Berkeley: University of California Press, 2009

Farmaian, Sattareh Farman, with Dona Munker, *Daughter of Persia,* New York: Three Rivers Press, 1992

Keddie, Nikki R., *Modern Iran, Roots and Results of Revolution, Updated Edition,* New Haven & London: Yale University Press, 2006

Pahlavi, Diba, *An Enduring Love: My Life with the Shah,* New York: Miramax, 2004

Pahlavi, Mohammad Reza, Shah of Iran, *Answer to History,* New York: Stein and Day, 1980

Saint-Exupéry, Antoine de, *The Little Prince,* New York, Boston: Houghton, Mifflin, Harcourt, 1943

Saint-Exupéry, Antoine de, *Le Petit Prince,* New York, London: Houghton, Mifflin, Harcourt, 1943

Film Documentaries:
Declassified: Ayatollah Khomeini, The History Channel, 2006

The Queen and I, Director: Nahid Persson Sarvestani, 2008

Broadcast News Interviews and Internet Clips:
ABC News' 20/20: David Frost interviews the Shah of Iran, Host Hugh Downs, Contadora, Panama, February, 1980

ABC News: World News Tonight. Barrie Dunsmore reporting,

January 9, 1979. Uploaded to Youtube, May 8, 2009, by Mazdak Caspian.

Amnesty International Amasses Reports of Torture in Iran, Over 4000 Executed Since Revolution and Victims and Witnesses.

Iranrights.org. Human Rights & Democracy for Iran, a project of the Abdorrahman Boroumand Foundation.

Ayatullah Ruhullah Khomeini Returns Triumphant to Iran - February 1, 1979, YouTube, uploaded by Halomaster7, 2009

Iran Before 1979, YouTube, uploaded by Josh Peace, 2011

Shah of Iran: The Fall of the Great Civilisation, YouTube, uploaded by Imperialpsalm, 2010

Online Essays and Articles:
1979 – Four Generals of the Shah. ExecutedToday.com, 2010
.
Arrival Statement for Shah of Iran. Fordlibrarymuseum.gov/library, May 15, 1975.

Clark, Richard. Women and the Death Penalty in Modern Iran. Capitalpunishmentuk.org/iranfem.html. Updated 2016.

Global Nonviolent Action Database. Iranians overthrow the Shah, 1977-1979. http://nvdatabase.swarthmore.edu/content/iranians-overthrow-shah-1977-79.

Fallaci, Oriana. The Shah of Iran: An Interview with Mohammad Reza Pahlavi. NewRepublic.com, 1973.

Hakimzadeh, Shirin. Iran: A Vast Diaspora Abroad and Millions of Refugees at Home. Migration Policy.org.

The Hostages and the Casualties.
Jimmycarterlibrary.gov/documents/

Matini, Jalal. Democracy? I Meant Theocracy: The most truthful individual in recent history.
Iranian.com/opinion/2003/August/Khomeini, 2003.

Rosen, Armin. How One Man's Illness May Have Changed the Course of Middle Eastern History.
http://www.businessinsider.com/how-the-shahs-cancer-may-have-changed-history-2014-10. October, 2014.

Sahimi, Muhammad. The Hostage Crisis, 30 Years On. PBS.org, Frontline, Tehran Bureau, November 3, 2009.

Smitha, Frank. The Pahlavi Monarchy Falls, and Power to the Clerics. Macro History and World Timeline, Fsmitha.com.

Schlussel, Debbie. Kevin Hermening: Youngest U.S. Hostage, Marine Guard at Iranian Embassy Remembers.
www.debbieschlussel.com/55288/kevin-hermening-youngest-u-s-hostage-marine-guard-iranian-embassy-remembers/ October 14, 2012.

Swenson, Elmer. What Happens When Islamists Take Power? The Case of Iran.
Gemsofislamism.tripod.com/Khomeini_promises_kept

49373952R00224

Made in the USA
San Bernardino, CA
22 May 2017